A MAGICAL
NEW YORK
CHRISTMAS

Also by Anita Hughes

A MAGICAL NEW YORK CHRISTMAS

ANITA HUGHES

ST. MARTIN'S
GRIFFIN
NEW YORK

First published in the United States by St. Martin's Griffin, an imprint of St. Martin's Publishing Group

A MAGICAL NEW YORK CHRISTMAS. Copyright © 2021 by Anita Hughes. All rights reserved. Printed in the United States of America. For information, address St. Martin's Publishing Group, 120 Broadway, New York, NY 10271.

www.stmartins.com

Library of Congress Cataloging-in-Publication Data

Names: Hughes, Anita, author.
Title: A magical New York Christmas / Anita Hughes.
Description: First edition. | New York, NY : St. Martin's Griffin, 2021.
Identifiers: LCCN 2021015694 | ISBN 9781250774521 (trade paperback) |
    ISBN 9781250774538 (ebook)
Subjects: LCSH: Christmas stories. | GSAFD: Love stories.
Classification: LCC PS3608.U356755 M35 2021 | DDC 813/.6—dc23
LC record available at https://lccn.loc.gov/2021015694

Our books may be purchased in bulk for promotional, educational, or business use. Please contact your local bookseller or the Macmillan Corporate and Premium Sales Department at 1-800-221-7945, extension 5442, or by email at MacmillanSpecialMarkets@macmillan.com.

First Edition: 2021

10 9 8 7 6 5 4 3 2 1

To my mother

A MAGICAL
NEW YORK
CHRISTMAS

One

There really was nothing like the Plaza Hotel in New York at Christmas. The Pulitzer Fountain on Fifth Avenue was strung with silver lights, and the valets resembled chocolate soldiers in their red velvet coats and gold caps. But it was the lobby itself—white and gold columns wrapped in satin bows and glass tables scattered with presents—that took Sabrina's breath away.

She reminded herself she wasn't a tourist about to go ice-skating in Rockefeller Center or see a show at Radio City Music Hall. She was here to work. But her heels clicked faster on the marble and when she saw the Christmas tree, yards and yards of lights and ornaments reaching to the ceiling, she couldn't squelch her excitement.

"Hi, I'm here to see Mr. Prescott," she said as she approached the concierge desk.

"We're happy to have Mr. Prescott back at the Plaza." The man tapped on his computer. He glanced up at Sabrina. "You must be Miss Post. A butler will show you up to his suite."

"Oh, that's not necessary." Sabrina shifted and wondered what the concierge thought of her outfit. The skirt was a designer knockoff that she'd had since her first postcollege job but the blouse was a recent purchase. The salesgirl had said it could be worn anywhere from the office to a holiday party, but that probably didn't include the Plaza Hotel, where other guests wore cashmere sweaters and the softest Burberry slacks.

"What's not necessary elsewhere is standard at the Plaza." The concierge snapped his fingers and a butler appeared as if by magic.

Sabrina tried to think of something to say to the butler in the elevator but she was too nervous. There were six hundred dollars in her bank account and if she didn't get this job, she'd be eating beans the whole week between Christmas and New Year's. Not to mention the rent on her apartment in Queens. Her parents would be happy to send the rent check as a Christmas present. But it had been four years since Sabrina received her journalism degree, and it was time she was financially independent. Then she thought of one of her favorite books, Dickens's *A Christmas Carol,* which she had been reading on the subway. There was a reason Dickens wrote about poverty in his books: writers were usually on the verge of being broke.

"Mr. Prescott is in the Vanderbilt Suite," the butler said when the elevator doors opened. "Would you like me to announce your arrival?"

"No, thank you," Sabrina commented. If he escorted her any farther he would expect a tip, and he probably wouldn't accept the laundromat token in her purse.

The hallway was decorated in grays and yellows with thick beige carpeting and gold-framed paintings on the walls.

"Miss Post," Grayson Prescott said when she rang the doorbell. "Please come in."

Sabrina had googled him, of course. Grayson Prescott had

sold more than a billion dollars' worth of paintings during his career as a private art dealer and he was credited with sparking Beyoncé and Jay-Z's interest in the work of Damien Hirst. His clients ranged from Bill Gates to Mary-Kate Olsen and there wasn't a private collection from the Hamptons to Beverly Hills that Grayson hadn't been involved with.

"Can I get you something to drink? The orange juice is delicious." He waved at the minibar and Sabrina thought he looked younger than his eighty years. He had a full head of white hair and his eyes were clear and blue. He was over six feet tall and Sabrina could imagine him in one of those faded newspaper photos of college quarterbacks in the 1950s—all square shoulders and thick chests.

"I'm fine, thank you." Sabrina shook her head.

"Please, I won't feel as guilty if you join me." He poured her a glass. "The prices at the Plaza always make me feel that way. The last time I had the Wagyu beef at the Palm Court, I had such a guilty conscience I wrote a check for the same amount to the Red Cross."

Sabrina accepted the orange juice and took a small sip.

"You came highly recommended by an old friend, Chester White. I gather you're his goddaughter."

"Our families have known each other for years," Sabrina said with a nod. "I grew up in New Jersey and my parents are both professors."

"Anyone Chester recommends is good enough for me." Grayson leaned back in his chair. "I hadn't heard of ghostwriters before, let alone thought I needed one. When I signed with my publisher, I imagined writing a memoir would be fun. Who doesn't want to believe his life might be interesting to others? But then Leo's emails changed from rants about the Giants game with a polite sentence asking how the book was coming to pointed letters saying he needs the first draft by January."

"I'm sure I can do a good job." Sabrina was earnest. "I spent the last week researching your career. I was impressed with your early appreciation of Kenneth Noland. You sold one of his pieces to Robert De Niro when the only place they had been displayed was in Noland's guest bathroom."

"It was a clever place to hang it. Most dinner party guests are bound to use the powder room and notice it." Grayson's eyes twinkled. "I had a client in the south of France who kept a seventy-five-million-dollar Van Gogh above her bathtub. The insurance company didn't want to allow it, they were afraid it would warp. My client said if she paid that much for a painting, she wanted to hang it where she spent the most time." He looked at Sabrina thoughtfully. "Leo is expecting a tell-all, but that's not what I want to write. There will be some of that; I won't disappoint him. But isn't a memoir the only chance one has to teach something important?" He leaned forward. "I want to write about my own Christmas miracle."

"A Christmas miracle?" Sabrina repeated.

"Life is about three things: there's hard work. You can't be happy if you aren't passionate about what you do. But there's also luck. Luck can make the difference between leading a pleasant existence and having a life where every day is exciting and you can't wait to get out of bed."

"And the third thing?" Sabrina asked.

"That's the part a lot of people get wrong," he answered and a small cloud passed over his face. "Recognizing the luck when it arrives."

"It sounds interesting," Sabrina said doubtfully. She had to fill three hundred pages and it was easier to write about concrete names and places than nebulous ideas. But Grayson was paying her and she had to do what he said.

"It better be," Grayson chuckled. "Or people at the airport bookstore will pass over the book and buy the autobiography of that fellow who flips houses." He smiled at Sabrina and his face was almost boyish. "I believe my assistant discussed pay and accommodations. She booked you the Fitzgerald Suite, it's on the next floor."

"I don't need a suite!" Sabrina insisted.

"That's all that was available. And you can charge any food or drink at the hotel. You will be working over the holiday week and I don't want to seem like some kind of Scrooge."

Sabrina pictured eggs benedict and Belgian waffles for breakfast and lunches of French onion soup and the Plaza's famous burger and had to stop herself from blurting out that she'd work for free.

"That sounds fine," she said instead. "I brought a suitcase with a few clothes. I left them with the valet."

Thank God her best friend, Chloe, worked in fashion and regularly trolled the sample sales. Sabrina had begged to borrow Chloe's Vince sweater and Theory pantsuit.

"Excellent," he said, beaming. "And I promise we won't work all the time, if you might be meeting anyone."

Sabrina tried to remember the last time she'd had a date. It had been in August when a magazine writer had asked her to attend Shakespeare in the Park. Patrick had been as broke as she was, and even after pooling their resources, they could barely afford two hot dogs. He said he'd call after he got his next check but he never did.

"I don't have anyone to meet." Sabrina shook her head.

Grayson looked at Sabrina kindly and held out his hand. "Do we have a deal?"

For the first time since she'd entered, she allowed herself to glance around. The floors were parquet and there were gold upholstered armchairs and gray velvet sofas. The sideboard was set with blue-and-white china and there was a coffee table with a glass chess set. How could she pass up six nights at the Plaza and a paycheck that would allow her to pay the heating bill and get her hair cut in the same month?

Sabrina shook Grayson's hand and felt the same anticipation she experienced when she entered the Plaza's lobby: for a short time, her life could include paper-thin cucumber sandwiches at the Palm Court and holiday cocktails served in tinted glasses and topped with whipped cream.

"We have a deal."

They worked for an hour and then Grayson apologized that the combination of jet lag and old age was making him tired and he needed to lie down.

Sabrina took the elevator to the fifteenth floor and slipped the key into the door. There was a small salon with one wall of mirrors. An art deco desk stood by the window and stockings hung from a marble fireplace. The bookshelf held leather-bound books and a Christmas tree was decorated with glass ornaments.

In the bedroom, Sabrina discovered a four-poster bed and a bedside table with a Tiffany lamp. The welcome card detailed the 24-karat gold fixtures in the bathroom and the soaking tub that could be filled with a selection of bath salts. White-glove butler service was available twenty-four hours a day, and anything she needed was on the other end of the phone. But it was the bed itself—king-size with a padded headboard and white comforter as soft as fresh snow—that was the most inviting.

When was the last time she'd had a full night's sleep? She'd spent the last two weeks working twelve-hour days with an aging rock star until he decided he needed spiritual awakening before he could finish his memoir. The next day he'd flown off to Joshua Tree without paying her fee.

She peeled back the bedspread and rested her head on the pillow. She'd close her eyes for a few minutes and then she'd transcribe her notes.

When she woke up, the time on the bedside clock said 12:30 A.M. and for a moment she didn't remember where she was. She drew back the curtains and was stunned by the beauty of the night skyline. Fifth Avenue was a patchwork of colors far below. The Empire State Building was festooned with shiny green and red Christmas lights, and Central Park shimmered as brightly as an airport runway.

Then she sank back on the bed and realized she was starving. The only thing she had eaten all day was a turkey sandwich that she had fished out of the bottom of her purse when she got off the subway. When she'd taken it out from under her laptop it was completely flat and the mayonnaise had leaked into the plastic bag. She'd taken two bites and tossed it in the garbage.

Grayson had said she could sign for whatever she liked, but she didn't feel like ordering room service. She changed into the Vince sweater and a pair of slacks and stepped into the hallway. The sleeves were a bit long but Sabrina was glad she'd brought it. At least if anyone saw her, they wouldn't think she'd snuck into the Plaza for the free hot chocolate.

The Palm Court was dark except for the light of a vacuum

cleaner being pushed across the floral rugs. The Champagne Bar had closed at midnight and there were only a few Christmas cookies left on the complimentary display in the lobby. Sabrina took the stairs down to the Rose Club, but the sleek walnut bar was empty. She was about to go back to her room when she noticed a man asleep on the sofa. He wore an expensive-looking gray suit and there was a silver tray and an empty glass on the coffee table.

The man stirred and sat up.

"I'm sorry, I didn't mean to wake you."

"What time is it?" He rubbed his eyes. He had dark wavy hair and spoke with a British accent.

"Almost one a.m.," Sabrina said after glancing at her phone.

"That's six a.m. London time," the man groaned. "I don't usually fall asleep in public places, but I've been awake for almost twenty-four hours. I'm surprised someone didn't wake me before." He glanced around for a bartender but there was no one there. He grinned at Sabrina. "For all I know, a housekeeper was here to vacuum but didn't want to disturb me. I'll have to apologize to the front desk."

"Did you just arrive?" she asked.

"Last night." He waved his hand and Sabrina noticed his gold cuff links. "It's all a bit of a blur. My stomach wanted breakfast but the clock said it was time for dinner."

"That's why I came downstairs," Sabrina said. "I took a nap and woke up starving. But everything is closed."

He pointed to the tray.

"You're welcome to share some of mine."

"I couldn't do that." Sabrina shook her head.

The man sat up straighter and ran his hands through his hair.

"Please. This caviar is four hundred dollars an ounce; it would be a shame for it to go to waste. And the lobster rolls are delicious, I can't imagine where the Plaza gets fresh lobster at Christmas."

"They partner with a lobster farm in Maine," Sabrina answered. "The lobster is put on a train every morning and delivered directly from Grand Central Station to the Plaza."

"How did you know that?" he asked.

Sabrina blushed and shrugged her shoulders. "It's the kind of thing some New Yorkers know."

"So you live in New York and are staying at the Plaza?"

Sabrina was quiet. One of the rules of being a ghostwriter was to never disclose anything about her work or the client.

"I'm staying here for a project," she said offhandedly. "It's too distracting to work from home."

"Then you must join me," he insisted. "This is only my second time in New York and you can give me some tips. You know, like when tourists come to London and they're disappointed because Prince William and Kate aren't at any of the nightclubs and no matter how many times they walk past Buckingham Palace, they never see the Queen coming out."

Sabrina laughed and glanced longingly at the tray: caviar in silver bowls and pink lobster on pumpernickel. Wedges of cheese that looked as soft and buttery as whole cream.

"If you're sure." She could barely pull her eyes away. "I'm Sabrina."

"Ian." He piled a plate with caviar and melba toast and handed it to her. "I thought only Californians were friendly," he said, when he had poured two glasses of sparkling water from the bottle on the table. "But I couldn't walk through the lobby without being asked what temperature I liked my suite and whether I preferred a silk robe or cashmere pajamas. I've never discussed how I sleep with another man before." He grinned and she noticed how his eyes crinkled at the corners. "He would be disappointed that I wear a T-shirt and flannel pajama pants."

"That's only at the Plaza." Sabrina smiled. "If you want to meet grouchy New Yorkers, you only have to walk down Fifth Avenue at Christmastime. You can't enter Macy's because of the tourists standing in front of the window displays, and there are so many people sledding in Central Park, it's as dangerous as schussing in the Alps."

"Londoners are the same. We insist that everyone who comes to London must see the Christmas lights in Piccadilly Circus, and then we're cross that there aren't any taxis."

"New York at Christmas is magical," Sabrina sighed, biting into melba toast. She'd never had caviar before and at first it tasted foreign. But she took a second bite and the crunchy toast and salty fish eggs were a perfect combination. "My parents brought me to New York when I was eight. They wanted to show me the Natural History Museum and the children's floor at Saks but all I wanted was to come to the Plaza Hotel and meet Eloise."

"Eloise?" Ian repeated.

"I guess you've never been an eight-year-old girl," Sabrina laughed. "Eloise was the most beloved guest of the Plaza Hotel. She was six years old and lived in a suite with her nanny and her dog, Weenie, and her turtle, Skipperdee. She got into all sorts of trouble but she always managed to make things right. I looked for her everywhere: at the Palm Court and in the Persian Room. I even cajoled a butler into opening the Royal Suite to see if she was there."

"You must have been irresistible if someone showed you the Royal Suite. That's reserved for kings and heads of state."

She suddenly felt embarrassed. She had never talked about

Eloise with a guy before. It was like admitting she liked rom-coms or preferred a Snickers bar to imported chocolate.

"I didn't find her because she lived in a book," Sabrina finished awkwardly.

"I've discovered some of my best friends in books," Ian rejoined. "Harry Potter of course, but also Pip in *Great Expectations*. I wanted to be like Pip: street smart but with a heart of gold."

"You read Dickens?"

"He was one of my favorite authors growing up, along with John le Carré and Ian Fleming," he admitted. "After I outgrew Pip, I spent a few years wishing I was James Bond."

Sabrina was about to say she had a copy of Dickens's *A Christmas Carol* in her room and stopped. She was at the Plaza to work, not to flirt with strangers. Besides, any man who could afford to stay at the Plaza probably dated corporate CEOs or high-powered attorneys.

The screen on her phone blinked 1:30 A.M. She had to get some sleep or she wouldn't be alert in the morning.

"I really should go." She stood up. "Thank you for the caviar."

"I'll go up with you," Ian suggested. "If I stay here I might fall asleep again and I'll be in pain for days. Eight hours twisted like a pretzel on the plane and then a sofa cushion for a neck pillow instead of the down pillows they have in the suite."

The lobby was deserted except for the concierge idling behind his desk. The Christmas tree glittered under white chandeliers, and Sabrina was reminded of the scene in *The Nutcracker* when everyone had gone to bed and the toys had woken up and become real.

"What floor are you on?" Ian asked when they stepped in the elevator.

"Fifteenth floor, please."

"It looks like we're neighbors," he said pleasantly.

Sabrina stood toward the back. The intimate mood in the Rose Club—the crushed velvet of the sofa under dimmed lighting, the novelty of eating melba toast and caviar—evaporated, and she felt self-conscious. What had she been thinking, sharing a meal with a stranger past midnight?

The elevator stopped and Ian took out his key. He turned to Sabrina and held out his hand. "It was nice meeting you, Sabrina."

"It was nice meeting you too," she answered. His hand was warm and smooth and she wondered if she would see him again. "I hope you enjoy your stay in New York."

Sabrina put the key in her door and it clicked open.

"Sabrina," Ian called from across the hall.

"Yes?"

"I think you're wrong about Eloise. I guarantee that you're the most delightful guest the Plaza has ever had."

Two

Ian entered the Pulitzer Suite and slumped against the gray-and-yellow-striped wallpaper. What was he doing, eating caviar with a strange girl at 1:00 A.M.? Even if she was pretty. He recalled her blue eyes and heart-shaped face. His job was to make sure Spencer didn't get into trouble. Spencer! He'd gone to ask the carolers to sing "God Rest Ye Merry Gentlemen" and never returned.

Ian strode to the master bedroom and saw Spencer, who was sprawled across the bed. His shirt was wrinkled and his John Lobb loafers were missing, but his breathing was even.

He'd warned Spencer not to drink so soon after they arrived. Spencer had already drained a bottle of champagne on the plane. But the cocktail waitress at the Rose Club had brought over a menu, and Spencer had said it would be impolite not to take a look. The next thing Ian knew, they were being served the Plaza's Christmas punch accompanied by Beluga Imperial caviar and lobster rolls.

Thank god the bill went straight to Spencer's accountant. Ian's shoulders knotted just thinking about it.

Spencer turned over and one eye opened. He pulled himself up and leaned against the silver headboard.

"One should never trust a cocktail that tastes like a candy cane." Spencer rubbed his brow. "Give me a gin and tonic any day. At least you know you're going to get drunk."

"Where did you go?" Ian sat on the armchair. "You were talking to the carolers and didn't come back."

"I told Tabitha I have an estate in Hampshire, and she wanted to know if I've been inside the castle where they filmed *Downton Abbey*," he said with a grimace. "As if all the country houses in England were lined up next to each other."

"Who is Tabitha? And please tell me you didn't mention you have a title," Ian asked in alarm.

"Tabitha is one of the carolers. Her bonnet covered some very pretty blond hair and she's getting a Ph.D. in history at Columbia," Spencer said, slightly irritated by Ian's question. "Don't worry, I didn't tell her anything about myself."

"That's a relief." Ian sank back in the chair.

The last time Spencer had told a strange girl that he was the Earl of Braxton and showed her a picture on his phone of the family seat with its seventeenth-century manor and acres of land, Ian had been forced to lie that Spencer was illegitimate so she would stop sending texts.

"We are in New York on business," Ian reminded him.

"You're my personal secretary—you take care of business." Spencer reached for the glass on the bedside table. "I'm here to experience the city that never sleeps at Christmas. Tabitha suggested we meet for drinks at the Aviary tomorrow night."

"The Aviary is on the thirty-fifth floor of the Mandarin Oriental Hotel and there are floor-to-ceiling windows." Ian was suddenly worried again. "You get dizzy when you've had too much to drink."

"I promise I'll stick to sparkling water." Spencer brought the glass to his lips. "If you let me finish this gin, I'd like to go back to sleep and dream about a certain attractive blonde."

"First tell me, where are your loafers?" Ian pointed to his feet.

Spencer scratched his head.

"Now I remember! Tabitha mentioned she hadn't bought her father a Christmas present and he was a big fan of John Lobb shoes. We're even the same size." He looked down at his socks. "She was very grateful. She's going to take me on a horse-and-buggy ride in Central Park."

Ian stood up to go into the living room. If he heard any more, he'd need a whole bottle of nighttime Tylenol.

A fire crackled in the fireplace and he breathed deeply. At moments like this, when Spencer behaved like a fractious teen-ager instead of a twenty-seven-year-old member of the British aristocracy, Ian tried to remember the satisfying parts of his job: the foundation that sponsored children's poetry workshops, the library where there were free language classes.

He recalled the day five years ago when Spencer's mother, Lady Violet, had ushered him into her study. Ian had sat across from Lady Violet at the Restoration desk and thought that no matter how much time he spent at Braxton Hall, he would still marvel at the John Sargent paintings on the walls and the marble statues scattered around the lawn.

Ian's parents had divorced when he was young, and his mother had moved away. He had been a fourteen-year-old scholarship student at Harrow when he met Spencer on the second day of school. Ian was slumped in the back of the dining commons, certain he'd never make a friend, when the most confident boy he'd ever seen sat beside him. Over kidney pie and cream of spinach soup, Spencer gave Ian advice on which teachers to avoid and how to sneak into the dorm past curfew. He noticed the patches on Ian's school blazer and offered to take him to Braxton Hall and get him some new clothes.

"I can't believe you and Spencer are about to graduate from university," Lady Violet began. "Do you know what you want to do?"

"I'd like to join a nonprofit," Ian replied. "Something to do with literacy in schools."

"Most nonprofits generate enough money to buy postage stamps," Violet said dismissively. "What about if you had access to real money—the kind that could build libraries and enhance school curriculums?"

"How would I do that?" he asked.

"Spencer has that kind of money from his trust." She fiddled with a letter opener. "You could manage it for him."

"You want me to run a foundation in Spencer's name?"

"That would be part of your responsibilities." Her fiddling increased. "You'd travel with him and take care of his social engagements."

"You want me to be Spencer's personal secretary?"

"You and Spencer have done everything together since you were fourteen." She set aside the letter opener. "He listens to you. You could do a lot of good together."

"Or I could stop him from getting into trouble with women."

"Spencer is honest and kind," Lady Violet said carefully. "When he was a little boy he spent his allowance on Christmas presents for the house staff. He made cards for his whole class on Valentine's Day, and every Easter he took his chocolate eggs to the retirement home. But he's always been a romantic," she sighed. "I blame myself. I made him believe that love can appear when you least expect it. No one thought his father and I would last, but we had twenty-five wonderful years."

Lady Violet came from a long line of British titles, but she had married one of Prince William's grooms. Spencer's father, Peter, had then become a successful horse breeder, until he died of a heart attack in Spencer's sophomore year at Oxford.

"Spencer has changed since he was nineteen," Ian said gently. "I'm sure he can take care of himself."

He knew the episode Violet was referring to, of course. During Ian and Spencer's second year at Oxford, Spencer had disappeared the week before winter holidays.

Ian had been cramming for exams when Spencer called and said he'd gotten engaged but his fiancée had run off with the ring. Ian fitted the story together: Spencer had followed a linguistics major named Marjorie to Gstaad and they had spent forty-eight hours skiing and eating fondue.

When Spencer woke the next morning, Marjorie was gone and so was Spencer's great-grandmother's ring. Ian asked what on earth Spencer was doing with an antique diamond and sapphire ring, and Spencer admitted he carried it around to impress his dates. Sometime between a moonlit sleigh ride and a midnight bottle of schnapps, Spencer had asked Marjorie to marry him.

Ian turned in his exam early and caught the next flight to Gstaad. He tracked Marjorie down at the chalet of an Arabian prince who had given her an even bigger diamond with a matching pendant. When Ian presented Spencer with the returned ring, Spencer sat on the bed and wept. Ian simply shrugged. They were best friends and that's what best friends did.

"Please consider it. You could accomplish great things," Lady Violet said, looking at Ian. "I am Spencer's mother. You can't fault a mother for wanting her son to be happy."

What was there to think about? If it hadn't been for Spencer, Ian wouldn't have had the courage to ask Evelyn Pike to the senior dance, and he would have gone through four years at Oxford without drinking apple cider at Turf Tavern.

Besides, his times at Braxton Hall were the happiest of his life. Every summer he was invited to fish, and during winter break there was a week of festivities. He got hungry just thinking about Christmas dinner: roast beef and pigs in a blanket and the best English treacle he'd ever tasted.

He could be Spencer's secretary for a couple of years and then start something of his own. By then Spencer would have learned to control his drinking around attractive women.

"I'd be honored to accept the position," Ian had said to Lady Violet.

That had been five years ago, and in that time he had rescued Spencer from an Italian countess with a palazzo that needed a new roof, and a French tour guide who he'd proposed to on top of the Eiffel Tower. Spencer claimed he'd dropped to his knee because he was dizzy. Not because he'd asked Marie to marry him.

Tomorrow Ian would meet with the assistant head of the Metropolitan Museum of Art to go over the museum's coming exhibit of the Braxton jewels. All Ian had to do was get Spencer through Christmas week without becoming engaged to some pretty American.

Ian's eyes roamed around the suite's living room: the plush velvet sofa and wool rug and minibar that had a better selection of snacks than his kitchen in London. There were worse ways to spend Christmas.

A good book would help put him to sleep. He scanned the John Grishams and Tom Clancys on the bookshelf. There was a large pink-and-white book and he took it out.

The cover read *Eloise: A Book for Precocious Grown Ups*. Inside was an illustration of a little girl wearing a black-and-white pinafore. Her face had an impish expression and she had straight, strawlike hair. There was a dog shaped like a hot dog and a turtle at the end of a leash.

This was the book Sabrina had mentioned, about the little girl who lived at the Plaza.

Ian told himself he was going to read it to learn more about the Plaza Hotel. But that wasn't quite true. Someday he'd lead his own life instead of chasing after Spencer. In the meantime, it wouldn't hurt to have something to talk about if he happened to run into Sabrina.

Three

When Sabrina woke the next morning she snuggled under the duvet and admired her surroundings. It was like something in a magazine: the gilded floral wallpaper and dove-colored drapes. The bathroom had mosaic floors and a bathtub almost the size of her studio apartment in Queens.

A soft snow was falling and the New York skyline looked so romantic. But she knew from experience that the snow would be followed by icy rain. By the evening rush hour, the streets would be slippery and everyone on the subway would be in a bad mood. She felt so lucky to be able to work all day without leaving the Plaza's central heating.

Her bedside clock said 9:00 A.M. and she sat upright in bed. She didn't want to keep Grayson waiting. She slipped on a blouse and slacks and ran a brush through her hair. Then she grabbed her laptop and took the elevator to the fourteenth floor.

"Good morning," Grayson said, answering the door. The suite smelled of fresh coffee and in the corner a Christmas tree twinkled with colored lights.

"I'm sorry if I overslept," Sabrina apologized.

"You didn't. Every year I wake up earlier, it's one of the curses of growing old." He motioned for her to sit across from him at the dining table. "I took the liberty of ordering breakfast. I hope there's something you like."

There was a selection of pastries and a platter of fresh fruit. Silver domes covered plates of scrambled eggs and an omelet that made Sabrina's mouth water.

"I usually just have toast and coffee for breakfast," Sabrina said.

She kept herself on a strict budget: Mondays and Wednesdays she grabbed a bagel and a salad for lunch but skipped breakfast altogether. Sunday was the only day she allowed herself three meals. Even then, she saved the leftovers and ate them the following night.

"We don't want to send any food back," Grayson said with a smile. "We'll hurt the butler's feelings."

Sabrina helped herself to coffee and a pastry and waited for Grayson to begin.

"I was a butler at the Plaza," he commented, eating a wedge of melon.

"You were a butler?" Sabrina said in surprise.

Grayson noticed her expression and laughed.

"I've managed to keep that out of the Google searches. I thought it might hurt my career. But I want to include it in my memoir—it taught me how to dream."

"I don't understand." Sabrina took a sip of coffee.

"Let me ask a question," he began. "What made you want to be a writer?"

"I studied journalism in college. My parents are both tenured professors; to them it sounded as risky as skydiving. I envisioned writing cutting-edge pieces for an influential website or having my own cubicle at a magazine. Someday I'd write a book that would help society." She stared into her cup. "That changed after graduation. The student loan bills piled up but the job leads didn't pan out. Now I take any writing assignment that will keep the heat on in my apartment."

Grayson bit into a Danish and looked at Sabrina thoughtfully.

"I'm glad you're ghostwriting or you wouldn't be here. But you can't give up on your dreams," he counseled.

"I'm quite happy. I only have one roommate and I haven't resorted to waitressing," she said, smiling. "I'm a terrible waitress. The only summer I waitressed, I spilled coffee on a customer. Luckily it had been sitting in the coffeepot for hours and was already cold."

"When I became a butler I thought I'd reached the top." Grayson put down the Danish. "I wore a gold uniform and met famous people. Elizabeth Taylor stayed here when she was married to Eddie Fisher. I'd been in love with her since I was a child and watched *Lassie*. And Andy Warhol took over a suite even though he lived a few blocks away. He hosted ice cream parties for his friends and the Plaza had fourteen different flavors. Kay made me see life differently."

"Kay?" Sabrina asked.

"Kay Thompson. She lived in a suite on the twelfth floor," he explained. "That's where she wrote the Eloise books."

"You were Kay Thompson's butler?" Sabrina's eyes widened.

"Kay was my favorite resident." He leaned back in the chair. "She was fifty when we met, but she had the energy of a teenager. And she had an excitement for life that was contagious," he chuckled. "If it weren't for Kay, I'd probably still be wearing those stiff white gloves and making sure that the suite of an Arabian prince was stocked with dates and figs." He smiled at the memory. "The first time we met, Kay asked the strangest question I'd ever heard."

Plaza Hotel, 1958

"What would you give a turtle for Christmas?"

Grayson stopped filling the minibar with Ryvita crackers and cottage cheese and turned to face the guest. She wore a pink suit and there was a ruby ring on her right hand.

"I'm sorry, Miss Thompson, I misheard you. Could you please repeat the question?"

"I'm writing *Eloise at Christmastime* and Eloise wants to give her pet turtle, Skipperdee, a Christmas present. It was easy to think of gifts for Nanny and Eloise's dog, Weenie. In *Eloise in Paris,* Nanny became fond of French cigarettes and every time Eloise took Weenie for his walk, he coveted a dog collar in the window at Bloomingdale's. But I have no idea what Eloise would give a turtle and I'm already behind deadline. I don't know how I get any writing done; Eloise has taken over my life. I have an assistant, of course. My assistant has an assistant! And I'm told that my publisher formed a whole division for Eloise merchandise.

"But there are some things I have to do myself. I have a photo shoot for *Look* magazine today." She waved at her suit.

"They wanted me to wear pink because everything in Eloise's world is pink. It's hideous on me; I resemble an aging flamingo. Did you know the Plaza has an Eloise suite? Little girls can pick up the phone and hear a greeting from Eloise. They offered to have an actress record the message, but I had to do it myself. I didn't want Eloise sounding like a throaty Hollywood ingenue."

"You look lovely in pink," Grayson said diplomatically.

Kay opened a pack of cigarettes and studied Grayson over her lighter.

"The only pink I like is this ruby." She waved her hand. "I bought it when Eloise sold the first hundred thousand copies. If I can't think of what Eloise gives Skipperdee for Christmas, there won't be a new Eloise book, and I may have to give the ruby back."

"The turtle might like a toy house. So he doesn't have to drag around his shell," Grayson offered.

Kay put down the lighter and scribbled on a notepad.

"Of course! Eloise goes to FAO Schwarz to buy a toy house and gets locked in overnight. She builds a bed out of Legos and holds a tea party for all the teddy bears. The next morning, Nanny is distraught, but she's had a wonderful time."

"I'm glad I could help, Miss Thompson." Grayson made a little bow. "Will there be anything else?"

"You must call me Kay. Miss Thompson sounds like a spinster librarian."

"I'm afraid that's not possible," Grayson said. "This is the Plaza."

"I've lived here for two years and the butler is supposed to do anything a guest asks," Kay reminded him.

"Yes, of course, Miss Thompson." Grayson was embarrassed. "But—"

"No buts. You'll call me Kay and I'll call you Grayson," she said, peering at his name tag. "Tell me about yourself."

"There's not much to tell." Grayson adjusted his gloves. "I grew up in the Bronx. There wasn't enough money for me to stay at school so I got a job at the Plaza when I was fourteen. I've worked in every department and now I'm a white glove butler."

"What do you want to do after this?" She lit her cigarette.

"Why would I do something else? Some butlers keep their positions for forty years. I meet all kinds of interesting and famous people, it's the best job in the world."

"Wouldn't you rather be rich and famous, instead of being around rich and famous people?"

"That's not likely." Grayson shrugged. "I don't have any talents."

"Talent is like potential: it will buy you a bagel at Katz delicatessen. Ambition will buy you the whole damn place. I wanted to be a star." She waved at her face. "Can you imagine? I look like a horse and I'm too tall for most leading men. When I filmed *Funny Face* with Fred Astaire two years ago, he had to stand on a box for our scenes. But I had more ambition than all those Rosalind Russell wannabees with their bras stuffed with tissue paper. My first break came in 1933 when I was on Bing Crosby's radio show. Then I signed with MGM and thought I was going to be huge. But they wanted me to teach actors how to sing, not to put me on the screen. I left Hollywood and started a nightclub act in Las Vegas." She snapped her fingers. "I made fifteen thousand dollars a week! We took the act all over the country and ended up at the Persian Room of the Plaza Hotel.

"One day Eloise popped into my head. A friend introduced me to Hilary Knight, my illustrator, and we took over a suite at the Plaza until Eloise's adventures were on paper," she laughed. "Luckily neither of us was married. Or some jealous spouse would have shown up with a shotgun to see what we were doing.

"Eloise made me so rich I can fly to Paris for the weekend or buy anything in the window at Tiffany's," she said, finishing her story. "Never be content with what you're doing. You'll miss the exciting thing waiting around the corner."

"I can't really think of anything," Grayson said.

"There must be something you desire," she prodded. "Something you'd walk over hot coals to get."

"I've always liked cars," he said thoughtfully. "A neighbor moved to Florida and became a real estate developer. One day he showed up driving a yellow convertible. The whole street crowded around it. He only parked long enough to pack up his mother and girlfriend but it was the sweetest thing I've ever seen."

"Why didn't you say so!" She jumped up. "Come on, let's go."

"Where are we going?" he asked.

"You'll see. You might want to take off those gloves, they'll spoil the experience."

Grayson scowled as if she'd asked him to strip naked.

"I can't take off my gloves! They're the mark of a white glove butler."

Kay grabbed her crocodile skin purse and tied a scarf around her head.

"You're never going to learn to be a butler unless you do exactly what a guest says."

The idea of walking through the lobby in his uniform but without his gloves gave him a sick feeling. But Kay was right. That was the number one commandment printed on the Plaza stationery he kept in his pocket.

Reluctantly, he peeled off his gloves and followed her into the elevator. They strode through the lobby and onto the sidewalk. A pink convertible was parked at the corner. The interior was creamy leather and there were bucket seats and a walnut steering wheel.

Kay opened the passenger door and motioned for Grayson to get in the driver's side.

"Whose car is this?" Grayson asked.

"It belongs to Ray Meadows Cadillac but it's parked here every day. Usually the driver is around but he must have gone for coffee."

"We can't steal a car!" Grayson protested.

"We're not stealing it." Kay checked her lipstick in the rearview mirror. "Ray offered me the car so he can advertise that Eloise drives in a Ray Meadows Cadillac. I keep saying no. I live at the Plaza and there's a chauffeur service. Why would I need a car?"

"I can't drive, I don't have a license," Grayson said.

Kay glanced at Grayson and shrugged.

"All right, change seats. I'll drive."

They sailed up Fifth Avenue. Kay took the Taconic State Parkway toward Westchester and zoomed along the Hudson. The radio played Frank Sinatra and the breeze whipped through the interior.

"That was exhilarating!" Kay said when they pulled up in front of the Plaza. "Perhaps I'll learn to drive after all."

"You don't have your license?" Grayson asked in horror. They had passed a motorcycle cop and Kay had even smiled and honked the horn.

"I'm like you, kiddo," she said and opened the door. "I live in New York. Why would I learn to drive?"

They took the elevator up to the suite and Grayson put on his gloves.

"Thank you for a pleasant afternoon." He bowed slightly. "Is there anything else?"

Kay took the key chain out of her purse and handed it to him. "This is for you."

"Please, Miss Thompson. I don't care what the Plaza's rules are." Grayson's cheeks turned red. "I can't accept a Cadillac."

Kay laughed and the sound was as loud and strong as a drum.

"I'm not giving you a car, you have to earn that yourself. I'm giving you a key chain so you want a car. Hang it somewhere you'll see it every day." She picked up her pen. "I wouldn't mind coffee with a splash of rum. I'm going to finish this book or every little girl in America will be upset that *Eloise at Christmastime* isn't under her Christmas tree."

Grayson put down his coffee cup and stared at the snow falling outside the window. His face had seemed so youthful while he was telling the story. Now Sabrina noticed the creases around his mouth and deep lines in his forehead.

"I used the key chain when I bought my first car," Grayson said. "A blue 1962 Ford Falcon."

"How did you afford the car?" Sabrina asked curiously.

Grayson glanced at his watch. "That will have to wait until this afternoon. I've got a Skype call with an Italian collector, and it's already evening in Milan. Why don't we take a break and meet after lunch?"

Sabrina spent an hour transcribing her notes and then took the elevator to the lobby. It was snowing harder outside but the lobby was warm and bright. Women wearing Elie Tahari wrap coats revived themselves from their morning shopping with glasses of champagne. Children sipped hot chocolate and glanced up in awe at the Christmas tree.

It was the perfect time to browse in the Plaza's shops. She'd walked past the entrances a dozen times but she'd never allowed herself to go inside.

She started with Assouline Books. The décor in the shop alone—antique tables and an oversized leather sofa—was enough to make Sabrina feel out of place. What would it be like to shop for gifts in a store that didn't have price tags? One had to take each item to the cash register to know the cost.

The minute she approached the shelves, she realized she could have stayed all afternoon. There was a gift set of Barbie books in a pink box and coffee table books on Chanel and Dior. Writing journals came in every shade of leather and there was a section devoted to travel.

Reluctantly she dragged herself away and entered the Krigler fragrance boutique. The plaque on the wall said it had been established in 1904 and there were sepia photos of men and women strolling down a promenade in the south of France. The salesgirl spritzed her wrists with Manhattan Rose and Sabrina agreed it smelled lovely. Then she saw the price sticker and gulped. If she dropped the bottle, it would take every penny in her bank account to pay for it.

She was about to cross the lobby when she noticed the glass case in Maurice Fine Jewelry. There was a brooch shaped like Santa's sleigh. Santa's outfit was made of rubies and there were gold presents.

"You should try it on." The salesgirl approached her. "The brooch is specially made for our store."

"I don't usually wear brooches." Sabrina hovered at the entrance.

"Try it on in front of the mirror," the woman encouraged her. "The rubies are lovely with your complexion."

Sabrina couldn't resist. She let the salesgirl fasten the brooch to her blouse. It made her look festive and sophisticated at the same time. Like the women who shopped at Bergdorf's so often they had to think of new things to buy.

"It's lovely but it's not my type of thing," Sabrina thanked her.

"Try the pendant." The salesgirl replaced the brooch with a diamond and emerald pendant. "The diamonds are in the shape of snowflakes and the emeralds resemble bows."

Sabrina gazed in the mirror and put her hand over her mouth.

"Oh, it's beautiful!" she gasped.

"I agree," a male voice said. "It's the perfect piece for Christmas."

Sabrina turned and Ian stood behind her. His overcoat was draped over his arm and he carried a shopping bag.

"Ian!" she said in surprise. "What are you doing?"

"The same as you. A little shopping." He held up the bag printed with the John Lobb logo. "It started snowing so I came back to the Plaza."

"Would you like me to put the pendant on hold for you?" the salesgirl interrupted gently.

"No!" Sabrina's hand flew to her neck. She had almost forgotten she was wearing the pendant.

"It's no trouble," the salesgirl prompted. "What suite are you staying in?"

"She's in the Fitzgerald Suite," Ian said to the salesgirl with a smile. "We're neighbors across the hall."

Sabrina handed the pendant to the salesgirl and pointed to Ian's bag.

"Aren't John Lobb shoes made in England?"

"How did you know that?" he asked. "You're right. The pair I brought on the plane seem to have disappeared."

"So you couldn't replace them with an American brand," she said teasingly.

"John Lobb's are special," Ian answered. "And it was a good excuse to explore Madison Avenue. I almost made it to Times Square before it started to snow."

"I'm not going outside today," Sabrina agreed.

"Why should you? Everything you need is here." He pointed to the glass cases. "The pendant suits you better than the brooch. Brooches remind me of visiting my aunt. Her brooch always pricked me when she embraced me. You can't hurt anyone wearing a pendant."

"Oh, I . . ." Sabrina was about to say she could never afford it but stopped. How could she explain that she was staying in the Fitzgerald Suite if she couldn't afford a piece of jewelry?

"If you give me your name, I'll hold it for twenty-four hours." The salesgirl waved the velvet case.

"It's Sabrina," Sabrina said quickly. She'd come back when she was alone and tell the salesgirl she'd changed her mind.

She turned to Ian and smiled. "I should go before she decides I need the matching earrings."

They strolled through the lobby and Sabrina felt oddly pleased that he was beside her.

"How is your first day in New York?" she asked.

"It started with room service," Ian said. "Apparently I simply wrote 'American breakfast' on the card so the butler picked the menu: scrambled eggs and hash browns and something called grits which they eat in the South. I went straight to the gym and I still don't think I'll be hungry for hours."

Sabrina thought of the omelet and pastries Grayson ordered and laughed.

"The Plaza isn't the place to go on a diet," she said.

"You'd never know it from the women in the lobby." Ian nodded at two women wearing almost identical cashmere slacks. They both had long legs and small waists cinched by belts.

"Some women in New York believe carbohydrates cause depression," Sabrina acknowledged.

"What about you?" He turned to Sabrina. "What makes you happy?"

Sabrina was caught off guard. How should she answer? The moment when she was working on an assignment and the words came faster than she could write, or walking through Central Park and having enough money in her purse for a warm pretzel and a hot chocolate. But if she said either of those things he might ask what she was doing staying at the Plaza.

They passed the Eloise store and the window was filled with pink-and-white sweaters and pink backpacks adorned with Eloise's picture.

"I've always felt like Eloise." She looked up at Ian. "Every day should be magical and you never know what's going to happen next. And Eloise loved meeting people. The best part of staying in a hotel is that a complete stranger can become a friend. . . ."

She stopped, suddenly embarrassed. Her journalism training taught her the easiest way to redirect a conversation was to ask questions of her own.

"What do you like?" she asked.

"Lots of things," Ian reflected. "The expression on a child's face when she opens a book. English toffees from Harrods at Christmas." He paused. "Meeting someone interesting and discovering she's more luminous when she talks than a diamond and emerald pendant." He looked at Sabrina. "I was wondering if—"

A buzzing sound came from Ian's pocket and he took out his phone.

"Excuse me," he said after glancing at the screen. "I have to take this."

Sabrina stood awkwardly while Ian talked into the receiver.

"Tabitha!" His voice was tight. "Yes, hold on. I'll be right there."

He pressed End and turned to Sabrina apologetically.

"I'm sorry, it's a bit of an emergency. I have to go."

"Of course." She forced herself to smile. "It was nice to run into you."

Sabrina ducked into the Eloise store. She'd wait until Ian was in the elevator and then she'd go and tell the woman at the jewelry store she wouldn't be buying the pendant.

What had Ian been about to ask her, and who was on the other end of the phone? She imagined some English girl named Tabitha who rode horses and wore floppy hats to Ascot.

"Aren't these Eloise socks cozy?" The salesgirl handed her a pair of pink socks. "They're the perfect stocking stuffer or present to yourself. I have a pair and they're so soft, I never want to take them off."

Sabrina was about to say she'd take them but then she glanced at the price. What was she thinking! A pair of Eloise socks cost more than her winter boots. She gave them back and mumbled that she was late for an appointment.

Ian was gone and the lobby was filled with the sounds of Christmas music and tinkling glasses. A woman strode by carrying a dog in a leather pouch. The dog had satin bows in its ears and wore a reindeer sweater.

Being at the Plaza at Christmas was living in a fantasy: The Christmas tree that was so tall it had to be delivered by a giant crane, the shops that sold first-edition books and jewelry worn by European royalty. The 24-karat gold fixtures in her bathroom and her own personal butler.

Next week she'd be back in her apartment in Queens. And what about Ian? He'd be on a plane to England where someone named Tabitha would be waiting for him with a box of Harrods caramel toffees.

She pressed the button and took the elevator to the fifteenth floor. A box stood by the door next to an envelope with her name printed in gold letters. She carried the box into her bedroom and untied the pink ribbon. Inside was a cashmere jacket that she guessed cost more than her entire wardrobe and a black cocktail dress.

She opened the card and read: "Just in case you meet a young man you want to spend time with—Regards, G."

Sabrina ran her hands over the jacket. It was the most beautiful thing she had ever owned. She'd have to thank Grayson in the morning.

She hung up the jacket and dress in the closet and caught her reflection in the mirror. Christmas week at the Plaza really was magical. There was nothing to do but enjoy it.

Four

Ian leaned against the floral wallpaper in the elevator and groaned. His phone had buzzed when he was about to ask Sabrina if she'd like to have a drink this evening at the Champagne Bar. He didn't know whether to be grateful that it had stopped him from making a mistake or to be frustrated that he'd missed his chance.

Ian gave up dating a few years ago when he and Spencer were in Greece for the opening of a new orphanage. Ian met a pretty woman named Phoebe and they were drinking Retsina—white wine flavored with resin—at a café overlooking the Adriatic Sea. Phoebe pointed to the sky and Ian noticed a line of skywriting that read, "ELENA WILL YOU MARRY ME? SPENCER."

Ian raced straight back to his hotel and confronted Spencer. Together they went to the port where Elena worked in her family's souvenir shop. Ian waited patiently while Spencer explained to Elena that he'd gotten carried away and it wasn't the right time to get engaged. Moving to Mykonos sounded like a dream but he couldn't ignore his responsibilities. And Elena wouldn't be happy in England. It rained all the time and Elena would miss her parents and four brothers and sisters.

After Spencer and Elena said goodbye, Ian went back to the café where he had left Phoebe but she was gone. He couldn't blame her. There were dozens of single men on the island. Why would she wait for a near stranger who had run off to help a friend?

But there was something about Sabrina that made him want to break his own rules. She was different from girls he knew in England who were stiff as cardboard and competed with each other for who could look the most bored. Sabrina was fresh and confident and had laughter in her eyes.

The elevator opened on the fifteenth floor and he didn't have time to think about Sabrina. Spencer said it was about Tabitha and it was an emergency.

"Where is she?" He opened the door.

Spencer stood in front of the stockings hanging from the mantel. A fire crackled in the fireplace and the coffee table was set with a silver tea set.

"Where's who?" Spencer turned around.

"Tabitha." Ian peered into the suite's bedroom. "Don't tell me she's taking a shower. It's too early in the day to see a naked woman walking out of the bathroom."

"I can't think of anything better." Spencer grinned. "But Tabitha hasn't been here."

"Did you come from her place?" Ian frowned. "Don't tell me a reporter saw you. The *Daily Mirror* will get hold of it and it will be all over London by evening."

"Hardly. Tabitha shares an apartment with three other gradu-ate students," Spencer said. "Anyway, I haven't seen her since last night."

"You said it was an emergency," Ian prodded.

"It is." Spencer moved to the dining table. "We're meeting for a horse-and-carriage ride and I bought her a present." He waved at a pile of tissue paper. "Should I give her the cashmere scarf or the sheepskin gloves? The scarf brings out the color of her eyes. But Tabitha spent a year on a sheep farm in Australia and she loves sheep."

"You already gave her the loafers for her father." Ian held up his shopping bag. "I had to walk through a blizzard to replace them."

"You're a lifesaver! I didn't realize how much I'd miss my John Lobb's." Spencer beamed and took his phone from his pocket. "And her father loves the shoes. She sent me a photo."

Ian studied the picture of an older man standing in front of the 9/11 Memorial wearing a reindeer sweater and suede loafers. At least Tabitha hadn't sold them on eBay.

"Give her the gloves, they'll keep her hands warm," he grunted and moved to the tea set.

"Good choice." Spencer folded the gloves in tissue paper. "You should have some fun. Why don't you go ice-skating in Central Park? It's an excellent way to meet women. You help them up when they fall and you're cast as some dashing Prince Charming."

"I'm having afternoon tea with the assistant head of the Met at the Palm Court." Ian poured tea into a Wedgewood cup. "She wants a written history of each piece of jewelry in the Braxton collection."

"I'm proud of the foundation's work. But seriously, Ian, we're in New York at Christmas," Spencer urged. "You can't spend all your time going over lists."

Ian recalled Sabrina's perfume and the way her face lit up when she talked about the Eloise books. He could send a message to her suite and ask if she'd like to share the Plaza's famous burger and a slice of New York cheesecake.

"There is a—" he began.

"I won't be back until much later," Spencer cut in. "After dinner, I arranged for a tour of the private salon at Tiffany's. That's where they keep the Tiffany Diamond. It has a fascinating history. It was discovered in a South African diamond mine one hundred and fifty years ago. In 1961, Tiffany's lent the diamond to Paramount for Audrey Hepburn to wear in publicity photos for *Breakfast at Tiffany's*. Can you imagine letting a movie star borrow your 128-carat diamond?"

Ian's eyebrows shot up and all thoughts of Sabrina disappeared.

"You can't take Tabitha to Tiffany's!" Ian declared.

"I'm not going to buy anything," Spencer assured him. "It will be after hours and the cash registers are closed. It's for the experience. The Tiffany's salon has a fully stocked wet bar and a dressing room where clientele can try on jewels in private."

Ian had read about it in a brochure: The salon's walls were painted robin's-egg blue and the carpet had special padding so clients weren't disturbed by the salesperson crossing the room to bring out the diamonds. French champagne was served in crystal flutes and there were plates of truffles.

"I'll go with you." Ian put down his teacup.

"No offense, but that sounds as romantic as when we double dated at Oxford after you had your wisdom teeth out."

Ian smiled at the memory. He had wanted to stay in their rooms with a hot compress and bottle of aspirin. But Spencer's date wouldn't go out unless her friend had a date too. Ian hadn't realized how bad he looked until he glanced in the mirror behind the bar and his cheeks were the size of golf balls.

"Then I'll sit in the waiting room," Ian conceded.

Spencer turned over his package reflectively. "If you insist. But one day you'll meet someone who makes you so happy, you'll want to shower her with presents. It's called love, Ian. It's more precious than the rarest diamond at Tiffany's."

Spencer left and Ian opened his laptop. Ian didn't need love; he had the foundation. For the last five years, he had been perfectly content. He had an office at Braxton Hall and his days were filled with running the foundation and being Spencer's personal secretary. Sometimes he regretted declining Lady Violet's offer of his own room at Braxton Hall. He worked such long hours he almost never reached his bedsit in the village until nighttime. When he did arrive home, he ended up eating cold leftovers because the electrical wiring didn't support using the hot plate and the heater at the same time and he didn't want to disturb his landlady in the kitchen.

None of that mattered when he saw the look on a child's face when they held a new book. He remembered the first year after graduation when getting the foundation off the ground seemed more unlikely than one of those giant Airbuses lifting its nose into the sky. His first few months of fundraising included being told no so many times over the phone that he flinched every time the secretary of Lady Rose Gilman or Lady Helen Taylor returned his call. One day just before Christmas all the rejection gave him a knot in his stomach and he went downstairs to Braxton Hall's vast kitchen for a cup of tea. He found a little girl named Holly curled up in the corner, reading a romance novel. They struck up a conversation and Ian learned that Holly's mother, Mary, was the new laundress. Holly's grandmother took care of Holly but she had bronchitis and Mary had to bring her to work. Holly didn't have anything to read except her grandmother's romance novels. The next day Ian returned with books appropriate for an eight-year-old girl: *Anne of Green Gables* and *The Secret Garden* and the Madeline books. Holly's mouth dropped open as if Ian were Santa Claus himself. The next day, Ian drove two hours through a snowstorm to see Lady Taylor and didn't leave until he had a check. Whenever he had any doubts over the last five years, he conjured up the image of Holly hugging her books and knew he was right where he belonged.

Ian closed his computer and walked to the window of the Pulitzer Suite. The snow had stopped and the trees were coated with thick powder. Taxis snaked down Fifth Avenue and the sidewalk teemed with people wearing long black coats.

The scarf on the dining table caught his eye and he picked it up. It was the same green as the emeralds in the diamond and emerald pendant Sabrina had tried on at the jewelry store.

Ian folded the scarf and put it back in the box. He should return it or Spencer would be tempted to give it to Tabitha.

He made a mental note and sank back on the sofa. First he had to prepare for his meeting with the assistant head of the Met. There was no time to see Sabrina even if he wanted to. He was at the Plaza to work.

Five

Sabrina wrapped herself in a towel and stepped out of the bathtub. She still couldn't get over the suite's bathroom: towels as soft as pillows and an enclosed shower stocked with vanilla-scented soaps.

The welcome card referred to the "soaking tub" and Sabrina thought that was silly. Weren't all bathtubs made for soaking? But when she lowered herself into the hot water she understood. The bath was so deep, her whole body was submerged and there was a shelf for her book. Glass jars held a selection of bath salts and a house phone connected you with room service so you didn't have to get out of the tub to order a club sandwich.

Sabrina could have happily sat there for hours, but Grayson would have finished his nap and she was eager to start their afternoon session. She patted herself dry and walked to the closet. Her two pairs of slacks and the Theory jumpsuit her friend Chloe had bought at a sample sale looked lost in the vast space. There were racks for shoes and shelves just waiting for cashmere sweaters.

What would it be like to be the kind of woman who could afford to stay at the Plaza? Someone who traveled with a steamer trunk because she couldn't decide which outfits to leave at home. A woman who thought nothing of ordering scallops in the middle of the night or buying a bracelet at the hotel gift shop because it looked pretty in the window.

But nothing excited her like writing: The empty computer screen that miraculously filled with her own thoughts. The chance to share her ideas on subjects that mattered.

Of course she wanted marriage and a family someday. But it could wait until she had accomplished something. She thought about Ian and felt a twinge, like when her phone was in her pocket and she received a text. That was silly—she barely knew him. It was just the magic of the Plaza at Christmas: the silver and gold lights on the Christmas tree and the scent of mistletoe blending with expensive cologne.

"Sabrina, come in," Grayson said when she rang the doorbell of his suite. "The butler was here asking what I'd like for lunch. I told him the breakfast dishes were just cleared away." He waved at the sideboard set with crustless sandwiches and a silver coffee-pot. "He left all this anyway. Please help yourself."

"I'd love a cup of coffee." Sabrina poured a cup and sat on the sofa. "I wanted to thank you for the jacket and dress. I shouldn't accept them."

"Of course you should. One thing I learned from Kay is never turn down a present," he said with a small smile. "You'll only hurt the gift giver's feelings. And you never know what will happen if you say yes. Especially at Christmas, it's part of the magic of the season."

"Then I accept." Sabrina nodded. "Though I don't know when I'll wear them."

"I hope I'm not boring you with stories about my youth," Grayson said, changing the subject. He sat opposite her.

"Of course not." Sabrina opened her laptop. "It's fascinating."

"I never considered what it takes to write a book," Grayson mused. "It's like a painting."

"What do you mean?"

"You put a dozen people in front of Botticelli's *Birth of Venus* and everyone will see something different: the myth of creation, a reimagining of Eve, or simply a naked woman who the artist should have draped in a sheet." He smiled. "Some people will read my book for the celebrity secrets and others will be intrigued by the art world's astronomical prices and there will be those who see nothing but a man who missed out on having a family because he buried himself in his career."

"Is that why you never got married and had children?" Sabrina leaned forward.

A cloud passed over Grayson's face and he opened his mouth to answer. Then he seemed to change his mind.

"Kay hated being interviewed about her career. She only did it to promote the Eloise books. I almost never saw her lose her composure except when she was watching herself on the suite's Panasonic black-and-white television."

"Grayson, I'm glad you're here." Kay looked up from where she sat in the suite's living room. The television was pulled into the middle of the room and a bottle of gin stood on the sideboard. "Could you please fix two gin fizzes and put out a bowl of peanuts?"

"Are you having company, Miss Thompson?" Grayson asked.

"Good heavens no," Kay answered.

Her hair was piled into a bun and she wore a tan suit and pumps.

"I wouldn't make anyone watch me on *The Tonight Show*. Once the program starts, I'm going to need the drinks faster than you can pour them, and the peanuts are to distract me from ripping out my fingernails."

"I'm sure you were fabulous." Grayson mixed gin with seltzer water. "Jack Paar was lucky to have you."

"I don't know why I agree to do these interviews." She accepted the glass from Grayson. "It's like getting the same tooth pulled twice. Appearing on the show and then watching it to see if I made a fool of myself. I told my publicist next time she better check who is sitting in the chair beside me. This couldn't have been worse if Paar paired Jack Kennedy with that Russian, Nikita Khrushchev."

"Who else was on the show?" Grayson asked, intrigued.

The television crackled and Jack Paar bounded onto the screen.

"Sit and watch," she said, motioning to Grayson. "You're about to find out."

Paar performed a skit about how, now that Kennedy had won the election, the American people had to learn to understand a Boston accent. Then he sat at his desk and turned to his guests.

"We're thrilled to have Kay Thompson, the author of the Eloise books, with us." Jack held up the pink-and-white book. "Kay, I saw your nightclub act at the Persian Room years ago. You don't seem the kind of woman to write a children's book."

Before Kay could answer, the woman next to her cut in. She was younger than Kay with a blond bouffant hairdo and fake eyelashes.

"I can address that for you, Jack," the woman said. "Actors crave an audience, much like Eloise."

"Thank you, Dr. Brothers." Jack Paar nodded at his guest. "For our viewers who don't know Dr. Joyce Brothers, she's the voice of modern psychology. She has a syndicated advice show and her own column in *Good Housekeeping*."

"That's very flattering, but I just say what I see." Dr. Brothers crossed her legs. "With Kay it's easy. She's had an incredible career starting with MGM and going on to her nightclub act. But the one thing she missed out on was marriage and children. What better way to soothe the emotional pain of not having a family than to create a little girl named Eloise?"

Kay turned to Dr. Brothers and her cheeks were the color of her scarlet twinset.

"Do you think I could take a stab at Jack's question?"

"Of course." Dr. Brothers was caught off guard. "With my professional background, I thought I'd offer—"

"Don't worry. I'm sure half the audience have been to shrinks who give their opinions on subjects without being asked: who serves the best noodle kugel in New York or whether Cassius

Clay is going to win his next fight," Kay said and the studio audience erupted into laughter. "You've got it wrong. I created Eloise because children know something about love that grown-ups forget."

"About love?" Dr. Brothers's forehead knotted.

"I'm sure you've heard of it. You do write an advice column," Kay said briskly and the audience twittered again. "Adults think they need to own other people. It starts when the guy slips a diamond ring on your finger. Then you stand in front of a priest and agree to each other's version of the Ten Commandments. From there you buy a house together and pop out children. Your lives become a trading post: honey, if you take the toaster to be repaired, I'll coach Johnny on the spelling bee.

"Eloise knows that's not love." Kay ignored Dr. Brothers who raised her hand like a child wanting her turn at the blackboard. "Love is how someone makes you feel about yourself. Eloise likes people who aren't boring because they make her feel bright and alive. And she makes everyone she meets—from Mr. Salomone, the Plaza's general manager, to the little old lady from Kansas who was a VIP in Topeka and is out of her depth in New York—feel the same."

"Forming relationships with strangers is fine, but it's no substitute for marriage and family," Dr. Brothers said haughtily.

"That's interesting coming from you." Kay folded her hands. "Don't you make a living offering advice to housewives who are so unhappy, they don't mind airing their dirty laundry on national television?"

"I can't watch anymore," Kay said and clicked off the television. "Jack sat there and let that woman attack me like a game hunter stalking a prize tiger."

"You were very good," Grayson assured her. "Everyone could tell that Dr. Brothers was out of her league."

"Do you think so?" Kay put down her cocktail. "Love isn't a game of poker, where you see who ends up with the best hand. It's about two people coming together and creating fireworks that only they can see. Eloise knows that, why is it hard for others to understand?"

"That's why they have you." Grayson walked to the bar and screwed caps on bottles. "You teach them through your books."

Kay popped a handful of peanuts in her mouth. "Jack didn't ask me a single question about *Eloise in Moscow*. Why did he think I came on the show in the first place?"

After two years of being Kay's butler, Grayson knew that often she didn't require him to answer.

"Can I get you anything else, Miss Thompson?" he said instead.

"You're young and you have your whole life ahead of you." She walked to the window. "Don't make the mistake of every other New Yorker who thinks love has to come with a house in Westchester. Sometimes love will leave you broke and you still feel like the richest person in the world." She stared at Fifth Avenue far below. "And if you reach a point in life that the only person you have to love is a six-year-old girl wearing a pinafore and the beret she bought in Paris, you still have something." She looked at Grayson and there was an uncharacteristic sadness in her expression. "Something is better than nothing."

Grayson stood in the corner of the Terrace Room and collected glasses on a tray. When he had downtime during his shift, he helped the banquet department clear the ballrooms.

The Grand Ballroom was his favorite. It could seat five hundred guests and it had hosted the most talked-about parties in New York, including Peter Lawford's wedding to Pat Kennedy. Grayson had seen the Grand Ballroom turned into a magical forest complete with actors dressed as unicorns for a child's birthday party, and into a winter wonderland for a Christmas party with fake snow and a ski jump constructed on the stage next to the orchestra.

There was a rustling sound and one of the tables moved.

"Damn it," a female voice said. "I don't see them anywhere."

The table jumped again and a young woman emerged from underneath. She wore a belted dress with a velvet collar.

"Can I help you?" he asked.

"Only if you're a magician." She dusted her skirt.

She was about Grayson's age with dark hair and large brown eyes.

"I was here for a Junior League committee meeting. We're planning the annual Christmas ball and I lost my car keys. They're brown with a Jaguar logo."

Grayson wondered what twenty-year-old drove a Jaguar but the girl was still talking.

"Technically the car keys belong to my father. So does the car," she continued. "But what's the point of owning a fancy sports car if it's going to sit in the garage all day while he's at work? A car has to be driven, don't you agree?"

"I suppose so," Grayson said doubtfully.

"Of course it does! Or the engine won't turn over and that creamy leather upholstery will get dusty. I was doing him a favor by borrowing the car. And I'm a good driver, I learned on my roommate's car last semester at Vassar." She sank onto a chair.

"My father won't see it that way. All he'll notice is that his precious Jag XK150 isn't in the garage. I'll be grounded until I'm so old, I'll be a spinster forever."

Grayson stifled a laugh. "Your father will understand. You didn't mean to lose the keys."

"You haven't met my father! He spent six months in a Japanese prison camp during World War Two and the prison guards were so afraid of him, they were almost glad when Japan surrendered." She looked at Grayson dolefully. "At least that's what he said. He might have been exaggerating so my brother would obey him."

"That does sound serious." Grayson put down his cleaning cloth. "Why don't I help you find them?" He held out his hand. "I'm Grayson Prescott."

"Veronica Fenton. My mother named me after her favorite actress, Veronica Lake." She rolled her eyes. "God knows why, my parents won't even let me go to the cinema. Except to a matinee, and nothing exciting happens at a matinee."

"It's nice to meet you, Veronica." He nodded. "Tell me what you did all morning."

"The usual committee meeting stuff," she said with a shrug. "Roll call and then we shared ideas for the Christmas ball. I suggested we turn the Terrace Room into a 1920s speakeasy. The girls would wear flapper dresses and we could even get Benny Goodman to perform, he's a friend of someone's uncle. The head of the committee thought it sounded too risqué. Junior League members are supposed to wear poufy ball gowns so their ankles don't show." She giggled. "I was going to ask if we should wear chastity belts under our dresses but I was afraid I'd get kicked off the committee. Then we broke for coffee and Danish."

"How do you drink your coffee?" Grayson asked.

Veronica wrinkled her brow and Grayson noticed the yellow flecks in her eyes. Her neck was long and graceful and her skin was the color of honey.

"Cream and two sugars. My mother said I should start watching my waistline." She put her hands on her hips. "But I'd rather have whipped cream with my desserts than have my ribs stick out like Suzy Parker's."

Veronica's waist was as small as a bird's but Grayson didn't have time to comment.

"I'll be right back." He strode through the doors to the kitchen.

Ten minutes later, he returned with the keys.

"Where did you find them?" she gasped.

"On the tray next to the coffeepot," Grayson said. "You need two hands to stir sugar into a cup of coffee."

Veronica jumped up and impulsively kissed Grayson on the cheek.

"I have to go." She grabbed her purse. "I have sixty-five minutes to get the Jaguar into the garage before my father arrives home." She looked at Grayson and her smile was wide. "You're a lifesaver, I don't know how to thank you."

Grayson took the white handkerchief from his pocket and wiped lipstick from his cheek. The lights of the chandelier glinted brightly and he remembered Kay saying that when two people fell in love they created fireworks only they could see. He picked up his cleaning cloth and wondered if Veronica had noticed the twinkling lights as well.

Grayson stood up and walked to the sideboard. A log glowed in the fireplace and the suite smelled of pine needles.

"I've been talking for hours." He refilled his coffee cup. "You must be starving."

Sabrina was surprised to see that it was midafternoon. She wasn't the least bit hungry. She wanted to hear more about Veronica.

"I'm fine, really." She shook her head. "Did you see Veronica again?"

Grayson sipped his coffee and glanced at his watch.

"We'll have to continue tomorrow. I'm meeting a collector shortly and then I'm having dinner with Sarah Jessica Parker and Matthew Broderick at the Four Seasons. You should treat yourself and eat dinner at the Palm Court. If I recall, they have a special holiday menu."

Sabrina blushed. She didn't want to dine at the Palm Court alone.

"I'm happy with a sandwich from room service."

"I insist," Grayson urged. "That cocktail dress won't do any good hanging in the closet."

"That's very kind, I'll think about it." She walked to the door.

Outside the window, the snow had started again and the lights twinkled on the Pulitzer Fountain.

"Kay taught me that if you just think about things, they never happen," Grayson counseled. "You're at the Plaza at Christmas. You should enjoy yourself."

Sabrina sat at a table in the Palm Court and consulted the afternoon tea menu. At dinnertime, the room would be filled with couples dressed in elegant evening wear. The waiter would look at her expectantly and ask if someone was joining her.

But afternoon tea was different. Half the tables were occupied by women sitting alone. They were surrounded by silver boxes from Saks and parcels wrapped in Bloomingdale's brown paper. Most of them were so busy tapping on their iPhones, they barely noticed the platters of watercress sandwiches placed in front of them.

Sabrina had purposely left her phone in her suite. She didn't want to miss a minute of the experience. The hostess led her to a table and she gasped at the padded banquette and silver bread cart. The restaurant was more magnificent than she had glimpsed from the lobby—it had a domed ceiling and ceramic pots festooned with festive bows. There was a mirrored bar and grand piano decorated with colored lights.

Sabrina sent the waiter away twice before she decided what to order. Should she have the savory selections: mushroom quichette and English cucumber on rye bread? Or should she try the pastries that had unfamiliar names but sounded delicious: Victoria sponge cake, chocolate sable cookies, and black currant and violet éclairs?

She finally settled on scones with Devonshire cream, and vanilla and strawberry shortcake. The waiter pointed out that the shortcake was from the children's menu but Sabrina asked if he could make an exception: it was one of Eloise's favorites and Sabrina had always longed to try it.

She nestled into the banquette and heard a familiar British accent.

"We feel so fortunate that the Met was interested in the Braxton jewels," the voice was saying.

It was Ian! Sabrina swiveled her head and saw Ian sitting on the banquette behind her. A middle-aged woman sat opposite him and the table was set with white china and sterling silverware.

Sabrina used her years of journalism training to sit perfectly still so she could hear what they were saying.

"The Met is lucky," the woman gushed. "To have the Braxton collection on loan for the month of January is a museum curator's dream. And it was so kind of you to personally bring the family jewels to New York."

"They're not the kind of thing that can be entrusted to FedEx," Ian joked.

"Is it true that the Braxton tiara was a gift from Henry the Eighth to Lady Margaret Braxton on her marriage?" The woman's voice dropped in awe.

"Henry had his eye on Lady Margaret as his seventh wife. But she had no desire to end up without a head, so she married the first man who came along. She told her parents he was an Austrian duke, but he was really the German gardener. By the time her parents learned the truth they were married and she was pregnant with twins!"

"That's a wonderful story," the woman sighed. "We expect record attendances. Ever since *Downton Abbey,* Americans can't get enough of the British aristocracy."

"We're very grateful to the Met for donating a percentage of the proceeds to the Braxton Foundation," Ian commented.

"Perhaps you can let me in on a little secret," the woman said confidentially. "I read in *Us* magazine that when Lady Violet was young, she pawned her mother's five-carat diamond earrings to buy a polo pony for her boyfriend. When her mother discovered that the earrings were missing, half of Scotland Yard was deployed to find them."

There was a pause and Sabrina waited for Ian to answer.

"I don't know how reliable *Us* magazine is," Ian replied. "But everyone makes errors when they're young. I'm sure an attractive woman like you got up to all sorts of mischief."

"I didn't read the whole article, only when I was in the supermarket checkout line," the woman said. "Lady Violet is still so beautiful and the photos of Braxton Hall . . . it looks right out of a Jane Austen novel. . . ."

The waiter brought their sandwiches and the table went silent.

Sabrina leaned against the banquette. No wonder Ian could afford a suite at the Plaza and a closet of John Lobb shoes. He was a member of the British aristocracy! She wished she had brought her phone so she could google Braxton Hall.

There were footsteps and she glanced up from her teacup. Ian stood in front of her. He wore a navy blazer and he looked even more handsome than she remembered.

"Sabrina!" His eyes twinkled and he seemed genuinely happy to see her. "This is a surprise."

Sabrina gulped and felt guilty for eavesdropping.

"One can't miss afternoon tea at the Palm Court." Her voice was bright. "It's the best part of staying at the Plaza."

"I agree. The deviled eggs are better than at Claridge's in London," he said pleasantly. "You're not wearing the pendant."

"The pendant?" she repeated.

"The diamond and emerald pendant at the jewelry store." His voice softened and he seemed to be studying her intently. "It looked lovely on you. It brought out the beauty of your complexion."

Her cheeks colored under his gaze.

"It's not the sort of thing you wear during the day," she blurted out before she could stop herself.

"Of course not," he agreed. He smiled as if he remembered something. "Would you like to have drinks this evening?"

"Tonight?" Sabrina hesitated. Why was she repeating what he said?

"I imagine we'll both be full for hours." He waved at the scones and pots of preserves arranged on the white tablecloth. "But we could go somewhere outside the hotel. You did say you'd tell me which are the hot spots in Manhattan."

Sabrina sipped her tea. Grayson was having dinner at the Four Seasons and he said she should enjoy herself. Why shouldn't she have a drink with Ian?

"I'd like that." She nodded.

"Excellent," Ian said, beaming. "Should we meet in the lobby at seven p.m.?"

Ian drifted off and Sabrina put down her teacup.

Carolers sang "Silent Night" and little girls wearing velvet dresses and patent leather shoes skipped across the marble floor. She took a bite of vanilla and strawberry shortcake and was tempted to pinch herself to make sure she wasn't dreaming. She was having afternoon tea at the Palm Court and a handsome young British lord had asked her out.

"Eloise was right," she said out loud. "The Plaza is the only place to be in New York."

Six

Ian stood in front of the mirror in the Pulitzer Suite and examined the Band-Aid on his chin. He was meeting Sabrina in the lobby in half an hour and he was so nervous, he'd cut himself shaving.

It wasn't that he was anxious about spending time with Sabrina. It was more that he had acted against his better judgment. But she had looked so charming sitting at the Palm Court. Her brown hair was smooth under the chandelier and when she noticed him, her cheeks glowed. It seemed the most natural thing to invite her for a drink.

Ian straightened his collar and told himself everything would work out. He would have plenty of time to get to Tiffany's before Spencer and Tabitha finished dinner. And he was in New York at Christmas. There was no harm in having a holiday cocktail.

The door opened and Spencer entered the suite. He wore a white silk robe and carried a bottle of sparkling water.

"Where have you been?" Ian turned around.

"Getting a deep-tissue massage at the spa." Spencer unwrapped a towel from around his neck. "First the aesthetician examines your skin and asks you all sorts of questions. To be honest, it felt like being interrogated by the sports master at Harrow. Then she lathers your body with hot oils and kneads your muscles. By the time she was finished, I could have solved all the world's problems."

"You should suggest installing a massage table in Parliament," Ian grunted.

"That's an excellent idea." Spencer beamed. "I'll bring it up the next time I'm at Ten Downing Street."

"At least you weren't still with Tabitha." Ian knotted his tie. "I was afraid you'd eloped."

"Tabitha had some errands to run." Spencer poured a glass of orange juice. "I can't wait for you to meet her, we have so much in common. She's a huge fan of British punk rock. Her main area of historical research is seventeenth-century England. That's when Braxton Hall was built! And we both love tennis. She used to be a ball girl at Forest Hills and I haven't missed a Wimbledon in ten years."

"I hope you didn't mention you sit in the royal box," Ian said worriedly. "She'll try to wrangle an invitation."

"Honestly, Ian, you're worse than Scrooge," Spencer said irritably. "Tabitha barely let me buy her a hot chocolate in Central Park. And charity is very important to her. On Christmas day, while you and I were griping that we had to miss the plum pudding to catch our flight, Tabitha was serving turkey and mashed potatoes at a homeless shelter in the Bronx."

The only British Airways flight that could accommodate the Braxton jewels departed on Christmas night. Ian felt bad grumbling about it. But Christmas at Braxton Hall was his favorite day of the year. Yule logs wrapped in hazel twigs burned in the fireplaces and there were crystal bowls of Christmas punch.

The best part was the church service in the village. Lady Violet insisted everyone in the household attend. Last year Ian saw Holly with her mother, Mary. Holly had *Anne of Green Gables* tucked under her hymnbook and Ian felt a jolt of happiness.

"I'm sure Tabitha is lovely," Ian acknowledged. "But you just met. When it comes to women, you're like the bullet train from London to Paris."

Spencer put down his glass and looked at Ian curiously.

"You're all dressed up! Don't tell me you have a date with the woman from the Met. That would be the best news I've heard since we arrived."

"The woman from the Met is in her mid-fifties," Ian remarked.

"You're going somewhere." Spencer glanced at Ian's crisp white shirt and slacks. "You're wearing the gold cuff links! You swore you'd never wear them again after Annalise stood you up."

"Annalise did not stand me up," Ian snapped. "She didn't return to Oxford, there's a difference."

"You didn't think so at the time," Spencer reminded him. "Your heart was shattered and you didn't attend another dance freshman year."

Ian and Annalise had met in a freshman geography seminar. Annalise was from a mining town called Koolyanobbing in Western Australia. Ian had never heard of the tiny town with the long Aboriginal name. Annalise took Ian's hand and traced the distance from Oxford across the Indian Ocean to Australia on a map. She laughed that she couldn't be farther from home if she went to the moon but Ian wasn't listening. He felt the warmth of her palm on his and something shifted inside him.

They became inseparable and Ian marveled that life could be so good. They saw concerts at the Sheldonian Theatre and volunteered at Teach Green. In the evenings they strolled around Oxford and Annalise listed the things she never experienced at home: Exploring one-thousand-year-old Oxford Castle when the oldest building in Western Australia was built in 1830. Thousands of volumes at the Bodleian Library when her town was so remote that prop planes bringing jars of Vegemite delivered books.

Annalise went home for Christmas and Ian couldn't wait for her to return for the new term. They'd go boating on the Cherwell and Lady Violet suggested they stay at the Braxton flat in London and see a play.

On the first day of term there was a knock on his door. Ian expected it to be Annalise with a fresh tan from three weeks in the Australian sun. Instead, the houseman handed him a letter. Ian tore open the envelope and read out loud.

Dear Ian,

You're probably standing at the window of your rooms, gazing at a snowy field. You're wearing the scarf I knitted you for Christmas and the sweater with the snowflakes we bought at the thrift shop. I'm so jealous. The temperature here hasn't dipped below 40 Celsius since I arrived. The bathwater comes out so hot, you could make a cup of tea.

For the first week I missed everything about Oxford: Professor Higman's Latin lectures and late-night study sessions at Radcliffe Camera. Mostly I missed you. I lay in bed and couldn't imagine how I'd survive three weeks without you.

Then a funny thing happened. When I was packing to return to Oxford I kept forgetting things. First, I forgot my jeans and then I forgot my iPad. I realized I had forgotten how much I missed being at home.

I remember watching the fortieth anniversary of the moon landing with my parents. The only thing more exciting for the astronauts than walking on the moon was being reunited with their families on Earth.

Attending Oxford was my dream since I was fourteen, but it's easy to dream when your parents are just across the hall.

There was another paragraph of apology but Ian couldn't read it. He considered selling the gold cuff links he'd received from Lady Violet for Christmas and buying an airline ticket to Australia. But what good would it do? He could as easily imagine moving to an Australian mining town as he could living with penguins in the South Pole. If he felt that way about leaving England, how could he fault Annalise for feeling the same?

"All right, I met someone." Ian pulled his attention from his thoughts. "I invited her for a cocktail."

"What does she do?" Spencer asked.

"I don't know, she didn't tell me."

"You must know!" Spencer exclaimed. "You're not the kind of guy who's attracted to a woman because she's got good legs."

How could Ian explain that Sabrina was special? She had a sparkle coupled with a warmth he hadn't experienced before.

"I don't need her curriculum vitae, it's one drink," Ian said. "I'll be done in plenty of time to meet you at Tiffany's."

Spencer took a bottle of vodka from the bar and poured it into the orange juice.

"Would you like one?" He raised his glass.

Ian shook his head and turned back to the mirror.

"You don't need to cut your date short for us," Spencer assured him. "Tabitha and I will be fine."

Ian gave his tie a final yank. "I'll be there. And go easy on the vodka. You become as generous as Santa Claus when you've had too much to drink."

Ian tapped his foot on the marble floor and glanced around the Plaza's lobby. Maybe this was a mistake. He should go upstairs and tell Spencer he'd changed his mind. Then he'd send Sabrina a message apologizing and saying he had to catch up on work.

The elevator door opened and Sabrina stepped out. She looked more beautiful than he had seen her: her hair was pinned back and she wore a cashmere coat with a pink turtleneck underneath.

"Am I late?" Sabrina approached him.

"I was early," Ian admitted, taking her arm. She smelled of perfume and he was glad he hadn't canceled the date. "Let's go. Tonight, I want to see your New York."

"I hope the bar isn't too cheesy," Sabrina said, when the waiter set their drinks on the table. "It got a rave review in *New York Magazine* as one of the best Christmas spots in New York."

The Roof was on the twenty-ninth floor of the Viceroy Hotel.

When they entered, Ian thought the space resembled a winter wonderland. There were huge floral bouquets and branches wrapped in silver and gold lights. Banquettes were outfitted with fuzzy pillows and fake icicles hung from the ceiling.

"It's perfect." Ian admired the twinkling lights and the view of Central Park.

"I'm sure it's not what you're used to. . . ." Sabrina said and stopped.

She had been quiet while they were walking and Ian wondered if something was wrong.

"What I'm used to?" he asked.

"I overheard you talking at the Palm Court," she said, blushing. "I didn't mean to, but I couldn't help it. It's so exciting that your family jewels are going to be displayed at the Met. I wasn't sure where a British lord would go for cocktails, and now I've taken you somewhere where the waiters dress as elves." She pointed at a waiter wearing a red satin vest and green slacks.

"The family jewels?" Ian repeated.

"The Braxton collection," Sabrina prompted. "I was going to look them up online but I didn't have time. I've brought you to a place that serves candy cane hot toddies with red and green marshmallows. You probably want to go straight back to the Plaza."

Ian's cheeks paled and he wished he had accepted Spencer's offer of a vodka and orange juice before his date. Sabrina had heard him talking to the woman from the Met! She thought he was Lord Braxton and the Braxton jewels belonged to him.

Sabrina had a suite at the Plaza and thought nothing of shopping for expensive jewelry. She was probably used to dating important men. What if he told her he was Spencer's personal secretary and she wasn't interested in him?

Sabrina was still talking. She leaned forward and touched his arm.

"You have to tell me about growing up at Braxton Hall. I'm a huge fan of the royal family. I watched both royal weddings and all the christenings."

Ian wasn't sure what stopped him from telling the truth. Was it the smell of her perfume—a scent that was so rich it was almost buttery—or the excitement in those round blue eyes?

"Braxton Hall is my favorite place in the world," he said before he could stop himself. "Besides being here with you, of course." He gulped the hot toddy so fast it burned his throat. "And this is perfect." He waved around the room. "You'd be surprised at how cheesy members of the British aristocracy can be. Every Wednesday, students at Oxford go to the Zodiac for 'Cheesy Listening.' They see who can play the corniest songs on the jukebox."

"That sounds awful." Sabrina rolled her eyes.

She leaned back in her seat and smiled mischievously.

"Did you do all the things at Oxford they show in movies? Skinny dipping in the Thames and running naked across the commons in the snow?"

"Some of them," Ian admitted. "I also studied a lot. I wanted to do something with my education."

"It must be a big responsibility being a lord." Sabrina ran her fingers over the rim of her glass.

"It is," Ian agreed. "But there are perks too."

"Like staying at the Plaza and wearing John Lobb shoes?" she teased.

"Those are nice," he agreed. "And I love to travel. But the best part is helping others. The Braxton Foundation builds libraries in towns that don't even have bookstores. And we're making a difference in schools—" He stopped. "I'm boring you."

"I think it's wonderful," she answered. "Helping others is the best part about Christmas. If you came to New York in January, you'd see people fighting over Ubers and pulling things out of each other's hands at the department store sales. At Christmas, everyone is nice to each other. If I could make one wish, it would be that the Christmas spirit lasted all year." She looked at Ian. "What would you wish for?"

"I hadn't thought about it," he said.

"You must wish for something," she said and her smile was as radiant as the colored lights strung over the fireplace. "Not even British lords can have everything they desire."

He pointed at the waiter in his red-and-green elf's costume. "I'd wish that our waiter took forever to bring our check so we had to sit here all night."

"New York is so lively," Ian said, buttoning his coat.

They had left the Roof and were strolling down Fifth Avenue. A man banged a bell on a Salvation Army bucket and a group of tourists took selfies in front of the window at Bloomingdale's.

"When I was in high school my friends and I had pajama parties and watched classic Christmas movies set in New York. My favorites were *Miracle on 34th Street* and *You've Got Mail*." Sabrina walked beside him. "I thought New York was the most exciting city in the world."

They stopped to admire the window at Bergdorf's. Snow White sat at a table with the seven dwarves. The table was set with pumpkin pie and glasses of eggnog. The window at Saks had an ice princess perched on a frozen sleigh, and Macy's windows were filled with musical polar bears.

Ian's arm brushed Sabrina's sleeve and he wanted to keep walking. But Sabrina raised her hand and hailed a taxi.

"Where are we going?" he asked when they were seated in the cab.

"You said you wanted to see my New York." She leaned forward and gave the driver the address.

Ian took his phone out of his pocket and checked the time. What if he was late to meet Spencer and Tabitha at Tiffany's? But he had plenty of time. Spencer always ordered three courses at dinner, and he loved to linger over coffee and dessert.

Ian put the phone away and nodded. "You're right. I did."

"That's the Hudson River." Sabrina pointed at the view. "And over there is the East River and the Brooklyn Bridge."

They were on the observation deck on the eighty-sixth floor of the Empire State Building. The night sky was full of stars and they had a 360-degree view of the city.

"I'm lucky, I have a friend who works here. He gets a certain number of free passes a year. It's one of my favorite places in New York. Every night the lights turn different colors," she continued. "On Valentine's Day they're red and white, and on the Super Bowl they're the colors of the winning team. Last year the lights were pink in honor of Barbie's sixtieth anniversary."

The air was freezing on Ian's cheeks and he dug his hands into his pockets.

"In *Sleepless in Seattle,* the main characters have a series of misunderstandings and never connect," Sabrina said dreamily. "But then Meg Ryan realizes she's loved Tom Hank's character all along. She follows him to the top of the Empire State Building but he's disappeared. Then she discovers the teddy bear his son left on the observation deck. At the same moment Tom and his son step out of the elevator to rescue the teddy bear. Meg and Tom look at each other and know they're meant to be together." She grinned. "I've watched the scene a hundred times."

Times Square glittered like a brightly wrapped present and the Statue of Liberty was the color of burnished gold. Suddenly Ian had the urge to kiss her. He leaned forward as music blared over the loudspeaker.

Ian jumped back in surprise and Sabrina tried not to laugh.

"Every night during Christmas there's a light show set to music." She smiled. "They're playing Mariah Carey's 'All I Want for Christmas Is You.'"

"It's brilliant," he conceded. He wondered if Sabrina knew he wanted to kiss her. "Even better than the lights on Big Ben in London."

They took the elevator back to the ground floor and climbed into a taxi. The traffic on Fifth Avenue was at a standstill and cars honked their horns.

"The best thing about New York is it means something different to everyone." Sabrina peered out the taxi's window. "When I got my first job in Manhattan, I wanted to be Audrey Hepburn in *Breakfast at Tiffany's*. I stood at the Tiffany's window holding a croissant and a cup of coffee and wished all my dreams would come true." She turned to Ian. "That might sound as corny as playing 'Cheesy Listening' on the jukebox, but I felt if I worked hard enough, I could make anything happen."

An icy fear crept down Ian's spine. He took his phone from his pocket and glanced at the time.

"Tiffany's!" he exclaimed.

"It's a dozen blocks from here." Sabrina waved at the street. "At Christmas, Tiffany's windows are littered with diamonds and lit with blue and silver lights."

"I'm meeting someone there and I'm late."

"Meeting someone at Tiffany's?" Sabrina's voice wobbled.

How had Ian lost track of time? It was 8:30 P.M. when they took the elevator to the observation deck and now it was almost 10:00 P.M.

Ian opened his wallet and took out a hundred-dollar bill.

"This is for you." He handed it to the driver. "Please take the lady wherever she wants to go."

Sabrina looked so beautiful. Her cheeks glowed from the cold and there were snowflakes in her hair.

"I don't have time to explain." He opened the door and jumped out. "Thank you for a perfect evening. I had a wonderful time."

Seven

It was 9:00 A.M. the next morning and Sabrina had already clocked forty minutes on the treadmill followed by twenty minutes on the elliptical machine.

When she'd checked in to the Plaza's spa, the perky young attendant had handed her the spa menu and asked which service she would prefer. The Stone Soother used water-heated basalt stones to massage her muscles, and Touch of Sun captured the spirit of summer with a moisture massage followed by a light spray of self-tanning lotion. Sabrina couldn't even remember what summer felt like. Walking out with a tan seemed as foreign as celebrating Christmas in a tropical climate.

She'd returned the menu and headed straight to the gym. She wouldn't dream of charging a spa treatment to Grayson's account, and it wouldn't help the way she was feeling. She needed to distract herself with exercise until every muscle ached.

How could she have made a mess of her date with Ian? She had gushed over Braxton Hall like her college roommate, Amy, when she returned from a semester in London with a crush on Prince Harry and a suitcase of Cadbury Flake bars. Amy had subscribed to every Instagram account about the royal family and started eating baked beans and bangers for breakfast.

Then Sabrina took Ian to the top of the Empire State Building and described the final scene of one of the most romantic movies she'd ever seen. It made her blush just thinking about it. There had been the moment when they were leaning against the railing and she thought Ian was going to kiss her. Then the light show started and the mood changed.

She'd spent all her money on taxis, but she could hardly show Ian New York from the subway. In the taxi going uptown she thought things were going to be all right. But Ian announced he was meeting someone at Tiffany's and jumped out of the cab. Why had he been in a rush, and why hadn't he mentioned it before?

Ian didn't seem the kind of guy who would schedule two dates on the same night. It was more likely that Tabitha was in England and he had some magnificent piece of jewelry made for her: a ruby and emerald Christmas pendant or diamond earrings that would glitter like icicles.

But Sabrina had been a journalist long enough to know one couldn't trust circumstantial evidence. Maybe Ian and Tabitha had known each other since they were children. They had taken dancing lessons or whatever members of the British aristocracy did and ended up as a couple. He wanted to break up with her but didn't know how to let her down easily.

She wiped a trickle of sweat from her forehead and groaned. Ian had made it clear he had no intention of seeing Sabrina again. He'd bolted out of the taxi faster than a horse at the Kentucky Derby.

She was meeting Grayson in an hour and she still wanted to get in fifty push-ups and ten minutes of abdominal crunches. Abdominal crunches were the worst. After twenty-five crunches she would be in so much pain, she wouldn't have the energy to worry about Ian.

"Sabrina, please come in." Grayson opened the door of his suite. Logs crackled in the fireplace and the dining table was set with a bowl of muesli and slices of fresh fruit.

"I had a breakfast call with a client in Zurich and got nostalgic for Swiss muesli." He waved at the bowl. "It's much tastier than the instant oatmeal we eat in America."

"I've never been to Switzerland." Sabrina sat opposite him on the velvet love seat. "I've never been to Europe at all."

"Never?" Grayson raised his eyebrows. "Each European country has a different personality. The Italians do everything for love and the French lounge around in cafés all day and the Spanish find a way to make every day a celebration."

"And the British?" Sabrina asked before she could stop herself.

Grayson considered her question.

"The British know who they are, I admire that about them. There's nothing more important than having confidence in one's opinions." He stirred cream into coffee. "People think an art dealer should influence a client's taste, but the client has to live with the painting. Last year Miley Cyrus asked me to choose art for her house in Malibu. She wanted to be seen as an independent woman, and someone suggested she buy a Frida Kahlo. I bought a painting from Monet's Gardens in Giverny series instead." He smiled at the memory. "I showed her a print of a Kahlo and asked if she would rather look at a woman with eyebrows as thick as caterpillars or study the way Monet made every brushstroke a symphony.

She hung the Monet in her bedroom and bought two more for the living room."

Sabrina opened her laptop and started typing.

"Kay taught me the importance of self-confidence. She said that sometime between childhood and becoming an adult, people stop believing in themselves." He sipped his coffee. "That's why everyone loved Eloise. Eloise knew who she was and what she wanted. Nothing could sway her."

Plaza Hotel, December 1960

"What do you think Eloise wants to be when she grows up? An astronaut or a firefighter?" Kay asked Grayson, glancing up from her typewriter.

It was the first week of December, and Fifth Avenue was so crowded it took Grayson thirty minutes to walk from the subway to the Plaza Hotel. He couldn't get through the lobby without bumping into valets juggling boxes. And children cramming their mouths with gingerbread snaps and spinning in circles around the giant Christmas tree.

Kay was oblivious to the Christmas frenzy. She was working on a new book, *Eloise Takes a Bawth,* and for the first time since they'd met, she was suffering from writer's block. Every day for the last week she had sat with a Coca-Cola and a bowl of pretzels and stared at the blank page in the typewriter.

"Well, neither." Grayson opened the bottle of Coca-Cola. "A woman isn't strong enough to be a firefighter. And the seven astronauts NASA hired last year have to live together in a training center in Houston. A woman couldn't leave her family for that long, and she couldn't live with other men."

"Can you imagine going into space?" Kay ate a handful of pretzels. "Last year they sent a satellite. One day we'll be able to take pictures of the moon. I bet it resembles a piece of Swiss cheese."

"Why does Eloise have to want to be anything?" he inquired. "My sister married her high school sweetheart and they have two children. Artie works in a garage and they're saving up so he can buy his own shop."

"No one wants to be someone's wife or mother without being something that doesn't include an apostrophe in her name first. Why do you think Barbie dolls are popular?" Kay asked. "Little girls play with Barbie and dream of becoming high-fashion models."

"My sister doesn't let her daughters play with Barbies." Grayson set the bottle on the coffee table. "It puts ideas in their heads."

"It isn't the 1950s anymore, girls should form their own ideas. If Eloise is going to sit in the bathtub and only think about styles of wedding dresses, she may as well drown. Eloise wants to be something special, that's who she is."

Kay typed a few words and then crumpled the page and threw it to the floor.

"I just don't know what she wants to be. I'm as stuck as peanut butter on the roof of my mouth after a peanut butter and jelly sandwich."

Grayson had to smile. Kay was the only middle-aged woman he knew who ate peanut butter and jelly sandwiches. They were her favorite midnight snack, and she often asked him to make a stack and leave them with a glass of milk.

"Eloise could be a scientist at NASA," he suggested. "She wouldn't have to live with astronauts or go up in a rocket but she'd still be involved in the space program."

Kay looked at Grayson and her eyes twinkled.

"Eloise loves playing with knobs! That's why she visits the hotel telephone operators in their booths." She fed a fresh page into the typewriter. "I don't know what I'd do without you. I might get this manuscript to my publisher by New Year after all."

"Is there anything else I can do for you, Miss Thompson?" Grayson asked.

"*Eloise Takes a Bawth* isn't only going to be about what Eloise wants to be when she grows up," Kay continued. "It's going to be about Eloise's favorite things now. If Eloise wants to wear pink pajamas and slippers to afternoon tea at the Palm Court, that's what she's going to do. Who says she needs to wear a dress to dine in public, as long as she's wearing clothes? And if she wants to flip through Nanny's gossip magazines instead of reading *Anne of Green Gables,* who cares? Magazines have words; she'll still be practicing her reading. Eloise knows who she is, and perhaps adults reading the book will learn to believe in themselves."

"I'm sure they will," Grayson agreed diplomatically.

"Good heavens, it's six thirty!" Kay said, glancing at her watch. "Didn't your shift end at six?"

"I'm not in a hurry."

"You're twenty years old. You should always be in a hurry—to meet a pretty girl or advance your career," Kay admonished. "Please tell maid service I can't be interrupted." She swept the last pretzels into her palm. "And leave me some peanut butter sandwiches. I'll be starving when I'm finished."

Grayson pointed at a silver dome on the dining table.

"I already made them. Plus a glass of Ovaltine. Eight ounces of Ovaltine has a hundred percent of your daily vitamins and minerals."

Kay's fingers clacked over the typewriter keys and she beamed.

"You take good care of me. You'll make a wonderful husband and father someday." She waved one hand. "Now I need to be alone. Or I'll never write the next chapter, and Eloise will be sitting in the bawth so long, her skin will become as wrinkly as her mother's neck before she went to Paris for those expensive beauty treatments."

Grayson guessed the subway would be too crowded during evening rush hour. Office workers spent their lunch hours doing their Christmas shopping and yesterday he had almost sat on a Tiny Tears doll. When he moved to the next seat, a package started meowing. The package's owner pulled back the opening and Grayson agreed it was the cutest kitten he had ever seen. But he still had to move. He couldn't get cat fur on his uniform.

He decided to help out in the Grand Ballroom instead. There was a Christmas ball and empty martini glasses were stacking up faster than waiters could collect them. He crossed the floor and noticed a pair of heels sticking out from under a table.

He kneeled down and saw a young woman hunched in the corner. Her ball gown billowed around her and she held a martini glass.

"It is you. I thought I recognized those ankles." Grayson climbed under the table. "Don't tell me you lost your father's car keys again."

"That would be impossible," Veronica replied. "My father's

train was early that day and he was home when I arrived. Now he drives the Jaguar into the city and parks in a garage. He said it's so I don't get into trouble, but I think he was dying to get behind the wheel."

"Then why are you under a table?" Grayson asked.

"I'm hiding from my date," Veronica said.

"Is he drunk?" he inquired. "I can tell the banquet manager to ask him to leave."

"Kevin never has more than two martinis." Veronica shook her head. "A Tiffany's box fell out of his pocket when he stood up to dance. I'm afraid it was for me."

"You're hiding from your date because he was about to give you jewelry from Tiffany's?"

"He's not just my date, we've been going steady for a year. And it was a square box. The kind that holds an engagement ring."

Grayson had forgotten how pretty she was. Her hair curled around her shoulders, and she had narrow cheekbones like Grace Kelly.

"Don't your parents approve of him?"

"On the contrary, they like Kevin more than they like me," Veronica said thoughtfully. "Kevin studies law at Columbia and he's so handsome, he reminds my mother of Montgomery Clift before he got that scar in a car accident."

"I don't see the problem. He sounds perfect."

"I'm only twenty, I don't want to marry anyone!" Veronica's mouth formed a pout. "My mother has been planning my wedding since I was six years old. She thinks everything I do is to get ready for my big day. As if I'm William Tell's arrow pointed at a shiny green apple."

"Isn't that the point of debutante balls?" Grayson gave a small smile. "So girls whose parents are in the New York Social Register meet boys from Princeton and Yale? You'll have the wedding ceremony at St. Patrick's Cathedral followed by a reception for five hundred right here in the Grand Ballroom."

"You make it sound even worse than it is," Veronica groaned. "Every life event celebrated at the Plaza!"

"It is the best hotel in New York," Grayson said loyally.

"I want to do more than eat cucumber sandwiches at the Palm Court before I get married." She waved her long white glove. "I wouldn't marry Rock Hudson if he asked me, and he was so handsome in *Pillow Talk* I was envious of Doris Day."

"What do you want to do instead?" Grayson asked.

"I want to go to London and study art," she declared. "But if my parents find out Kevin proposed, they'll never let me go. My mother will be on the phone to the wedding planner at the Plaza faster than she can run up her Bergdorf's charge card."

"You can't stay under here forever," Grayson pointed out. "Besides, you were on the planning committee. Don't you want to attend your own ball?"

Veronica stroked the folds of her skirt.

"You can dance with me!" she announced.

"That won't stop Kevin from proposing," Grayson argued. "A pretty girl isn't going to dance with one guy, even if he is her date."

"Then we'll dance all night," she urged. Her eyes resembled fireflies in the dark. "Kevin will get bored and leave without me."

Veronica's perfume wafted toward him and he felt strangely intoxicated. As if he had drunk a whole tray of martinis.

"I'm a butler, I can't dance with guests," Grayson remarked. "And what if Kevin gets angry? I weigh one hundred sixty pounds and I've never fought in my life. I bet Kevin played football in college."

"The first rule of being a butler at the Plaza is doing whatever a guest says," she said mischievously. "And Kevin wouldn't kill a spider. He puts them outside."

Kay had been saying the same thing for years. And Grayson received many strange requests. Mrs. Gould on the fifteenth floor asked him to find earplugs for her dog, Howell, because he was sensitive to noise. Max Thurston in the Vanderbilt Suite insisted Grayson do the *New York Times* crossword puzzle every Sunday. Max and his wife, Mitzi, did the puzzle for fifty-three years before she died.

The difference was, Grayson wanted to dance with Veronica. Just looking at her milky white shoulders made him incapable of thinking of anything else.

"I guess I don't have a choice," he conceded.

"Don't look so glum." Veronica pulled back the tablecloth and light from the chandeliers twinkled on the marble floor. "I'm a good dancer. You might enjoy it."

Grayson stood up to refill his coffee cup and Sabrina waited for him to continue. He had been talking for hours, but Sabrina was so engrossed she had barely looked up from her laptop.

"Did Veronica go to England and become an artist?" she prompted.

"That's another story. We'll have to continue tomorrow," he said. "I promised Ralph Lauren I'd help him pick out a Christmas present for his wife, Ricky."

"Christmas was two days ago," Sabrina reminded him.

"Ralph was on a fashion shoot and his plane home got delayed." Grayson smiled. "That's why the gift has to be special. Ricky gets furious if Ralph misses holidays with the family."

"It must be intimidating working with such famous people," she commented.

"It was in the beginning, but Kay taught me to believe in myself. She told me a story about how the first time she performed at the Persian Room, Jerry Lewis and Dean Martin were in the audience. They were the biggest stars in America, and she got so nervous, she begged her manager to claim she had food poisoning so she wouldn't have to go on. He argued that Jerry and Dean wouldn't have paid twenty-five dollars a ticket if they didn't think they'd be entertained. She went out there and gave the best show of her career."

Grayson picked up an envelope from the sideboard.

"I have two tickets to the UNICEF Snowflake Ball tonight in the Grand Ballroom. Why don't you take them?"

The UNICEF Snowflake Ball was one of the most coveted holiday events in New York. A ticket cost a thousand dollars and last year Mariah Carey had performed.

"Thank you, but I don't have a date, and it's not the kind of event you go to alone." Sabrina shook her head. "Even if I did, I don't have anything to wear. All the women wear couture gowns and jewelry from Harry Winston."

"When I was a butler, the Plaza had a storeroom full of ball gowns and tuxedos," Grayson recalled. "Guests could get practically anything without leaving the hotel. There was even a tricycle garage where children could borrow tricycles like Eloise. One day, Kay decided she was going to borrow one. But she was too tall, her legs didn't fit under the handlebars."

He handed her the envelope.

"Take it in case you change your mind. You never know what might happen." His tone was thoughtful. "I was at the Christmas ball all those years ago to collect empty glasses, and it turned into the most important night of my life."

It was midafternoon and Sabrina was curled up on the sofa in her suite's living room. She was wearing her favorite fuzzy socks and there was a pot of tangerine tea and a plate of scones on the coffee table.

She should have been transcribing her notes but she couldn't stop thinking about Ian. She spent an hour googling the Braxton family and came up with nothing except a mention of the Braxton Foundation's annual Christmas ball at the Savoy in London. It wasn't surprising. Not all members of the royal family had Instagram accounts like William and Kate's @kensingtonroyal.

Ian had asked her to show him her New York, but he thought she could afford to stay at the Plaza. He probably assumed she had tickets to a Broadway show. Afterward they'd have supper at Sardi's and mingle with actors and producers. They'd end the night drinking White Russians at the St. Regis and a Bentley would drive them back to the Plaza.

Suddenly she had an idea. What if she invited him to the Snowflake Ball? It was just the sort of thing he would expect her to attend. And how could he resist an invitation to the most sought-after event of the holiday season?

She scribbled on a piece of stationery. Then she picked up the house phone and pressed the number for the operator.

"Could you send a butler to the Fitzgerald Suite?" she said. "I need a letter delivered."

Sabrina hung up and watched snowflakes dance outside the window.

Grayson said Kay had taught him to believe in himself. Eloise was so confident that anyone would enjoy her company: from the doorman who said he was too busy but stopped to talk to her when she and Weenie skipped through the revolving doors, to the manager, Mr. Salomone himself, who was often on his way to an appointment when Eloise stopped by his office and ended up playing checkers for hours.

She had to believe that Ian wanted to see her again. She sank onto the sofa and waited for the butler to arrive.

Eight

It was midmorning and Ian stood on the corner of Forty-Second Street and Lexington Avenue, gazing at the Chrysler Building. It really was one of the most beautiful buildings he had seen. The top floors formed a crown, and the sunburst pattern caught the winter sun.

He had woken up early and sat at the desk in the suite's living room, writing descriptions of each piece in the Braxton collection. But he couldn't concentrate and everything seemed to irritate him: Spencer's soft snoring from the bedroom and the Christmas music that played on a hidden speaker. He almost called a butler and asked him to turn off the music but that wouldn't solve anything.

How could he have been so rude to Sabrina last night? He played it back in his mind: the taxi crawling up Fifth Avenue and the sick feeling in his stomach when he realized he was late and then jumping out of the cab.

This morning it took all his willpower not to call Sabrina and admit that he wasn't Lord Braxton, he was actually Spencer's personal secretary. The reason he had to get to Tiffany's was because at that moment Tabitha might be trying on a rare yellow diamond that Spencer might find so alluring he would whip out his American Express card and buy it on the spot.

But Sabrina would be furious that he had lied and he couldn't blame her. Ian always told the truth except for the small fibs he made up about Spencer. Like when he told the flamenco dancer he found in Spencer's hotel room in Barcelona that Spencer had a rare skin disease. Maria ran off so quickly she forgot her castanets on the bedside table.

Ian had closed his laptop and grabbed a warm jacket. Then he took the elevator to the lobby and asked the concierge for a map of New York's must-see buildings.

The Seagram Building was built in 1958 and had thirty-eight floors of tinted black glass. One World Trade Center was sharp and pointy and reminded him of a steel porcupine. But it was the older buildings that drew him: the Woolworth Building's burnished gold façade and the marble lions in front of the New York Public Library.

Lady Violet had instilled in him a love of architecture. She said that houses were like people: the more love you gave them, the more they shined. He remembered the time he found her kneeling in the drawing room with a bottle of Pledge and a cloth.

"You must think I'm ridiculous, there's a whole staff whose job is to polish the fireplace mantels and dust the window ledges." Lady Violet straightened up. She blushed as if she were a young woman and Ian had discovered her having an assignation with the stable boy. "I can't fire them. Then they wouldn't be able to support their families. But few things are more satisfying than making a brass candlestick gleam so brightly you can see your reflection." Her face broke into a smile. "Though I might change my mind soon. I'm starting to see too many wrinkles."

"It's a beautiful house," Ian said with a nod. "I'm fortunate to work here."

"I was lucky that Spencer's father loved Braxton Hall as much as I did. I couldn't have married someone who wanted to live in a high-rise in London. Now that Peter is gone and Spencer is grown up, I give Braxton Hall all my attention." Violet's dreamy expression disappeared and her eyes twinkled. "You're in your twenties. You should be in love with girls, not houses."

"Dating is time-consuming." Ian waved the papers clutched in his hand. "If I don't get the planner at the Savoy a head count by tomorrow, we'll be holding the Christmas ball here in Braxton Hall."

Lady Violet let out a little laugh.

"And have some seventy-year-old dowager spill cranberry sauce on my rugs?" She shivered dramatically. "Give me the list, I'll call the guests who haven't replied. I'll tell them if they don't give us an answer they won't be invited next year."

Ian studied the winter sun reflecting off the Chrysler Building. Lady Violet was right: one of the most important parts of a relationship was having things in common. He had to tell Sabrina the truth. How could he know if they shared the same dreams if he lied about who he was?

He turned down Lexington Avenue toward the Plaza Hotel. He'd send her a note asking her to have dinner with him. They'd get pizza in Little Italy and he'd tell her everything about himself: How he got his first after-school job at a newsagent, and the owner used unsold newspapers to wrap fish and chips. How when he was eight, his school arranged a trip to London at Christmas to see the pantomimes. He still remembered returning home after seeing *Jack and the Beanstalk* and wanting to plant a seed and watch it grow. But the ground was covered in snow and he had to settle for placing a seed and some dirt in a glass jar. Every night when he went to sleep, he was certain that by morning there would be a tree so tall, it would push through his ceiling. Instead, he'd wake up relieved and disappointed that the seed had only turned into a small green sprout.

Then he would ask everything about Sabrina: Did she have a pet when she was growing up? What was her first concert? If she could meet anyone who could make a difference in the world, who would it be?

Spencer was eating breakfast when Ian arrived in the suite. Ian took off his jacket and had to smile. Spencer insisted on a full English breakfast no matter where they traveled: scrambled eggs, back bacon, grilled tomatoes, and black pudding. It reminded Ian of school holidays at Braxton Hall when the cook ladled so much food onto his plate, he could hardly move for hours.

"Where have you been?" Spencer waved at Ian's untouched plate. "You didn't eat your breakfast."

"I wasn't hungry. I took a walking tour of famous buildings in Manhattan."

"At nine a.m. and without your morning coffee?" Spencer stirred two sugars into his cup.

"New York has some exceptional architecture. St. Patrick's Cathedral is every bit as imposing as Westminster Abbey." Ian sat opposite Spencer and poured a cup of coffee.

"It will still be there after you've had a plate of bangers." Spencer looked at Ian curiously. "You're acting strangely. Last night you were late to Tiffany's. You haven't been late for anything since algebra at Harrow. And you were only late then because a cat got stuck in a tree and you climbed up to save it."

"I lost track of time," Ian admitted. "We went to the Empire State Building, and traffic was stopped on Fifth Avenue."

Spencer's eyes lit up.

"That's right, you were on a date!" He leaned forward. "I knew something was different about you. You went to her place for breakfast this morning and you're just coming back."

"I didn't go to her place," Ian grunted. "And for your information, Sabrina is staying at the Plaza."

Spencer leaned back in his chair and whistled. "She must be a famous actress or the CEO of some Silicon Valley start-up."

Ian was feeling worse by the minute. He didn't want to talk about Sabrina with Spencer.

"I still don't understand why Tabitha was gone when I arrived at Tiffany's," he said instead.

"I told you last night," Spencer replied. "Tabitha's little brother is home from college and she had tickets to see *Home Alone* in concert at Lincoln Center. It's quite the production. The movie plays on a giant screen while an orchestra performs music from the soundtrack."

"That must have cost a fortune." Ian drank his coffee. "I hope you didn't pay for it."

He didn't know why everything Spencer was saying annoyed him. And the coffee wasn't helping his mood. He should switch to tea with honey.

"Tabitha gets student tickets," Spencer said. "She's very close to her family. It's one of the things we have in common."

Spencer spread marmalade on toast.

"I've never met a girl quite like her," he continued. "She wouldn't even try on earrings at Tiffany's until the saleswoman promised that their diamonds are ethically sourced. And those sapphire and diamond teardrop earrings looked so lovely on her. She has the most beautiful earlobes."

"Earlobes can't be beautiful," Ian said in alarm.

Spencer's tone had changed and that dreamy expression came into his eyes like when he was falling for a girl.

"You can see her earlobes for yourself," Spencer returned. "We can double date tonight at the Winter Village at Bryant Park. There's ice-skating and you can dine inside your own personal igloo under the stars."

If Ian and Sabrina had dinner with Spencer and Tabitha, Sabrina would know that Ian wasn't Lord Braxton. But Ian had planned on telling her anyway. This might make it easier and he could keep an eye on Spencer at the same time.

"That's not a bad idea," Ian agreed cautiously.

"Excellent, I'll call Tabitha." Spencer stood up and walked to the bedroom. "Then I'll take a nap. A full English breakfast always makes me sleepy."

There was a knock at the door and for a moment Ian thought it was Sabrina. He opened it but a butler stood in the hallway.

"I have a letter for Lord Braxton." The butler handed Ian an envelope.

Ian fished two dollar bills out of his pocket. He put the envelope on the coffee table and sank onto the sofa.

He couldn't invite Sabrina to dinner without explaining who he was first. And it wasn't the sort of thing he could say over the phone; he had to tell her in person.

"Who was that?" Spencer appeared from the bedroom.

"There's a letter for you." Ian pointed to the envelope.

Spencer opened it and scanned the page.

"It's for you," Spencer said. "It's an invitation to the UNICEF Snowflake Ball."

"It can't be for me." Ian grabbed the paper. He read the unfamiliar handwriting and there was a sticky feeling in his throat, as if he'd eaten too much nougat.

> Dear Ian,
> I know it's short notice, but I have two tickets to tonight's Snowflake Ball. I wondered if you'd like to be my guest. Dress is formal but I'm sure you have something in your closet. After all, you own a pair of John Lobb shoes. Please give your answer to the butler.

For a moment Ian's heart lifted and he walked to the window. The sky was pale blue and the Manhattan skyline was as bright and shiny as the brass buttons on the butler's uniform.

The butler! Ian had let him leave without giving his reply. His eyes rested on the envelope and he groaned. Sabrina had invited him because she thought he was Lord Braxton. Would she still want to take him when he revealed he was Spencer's secretary?

"I'll tell Tabitha that the double date is canceled," Spencer said cheerfully. "There'll be more mulled wine and fondue for us. It reminds me of the holiday in Gstaad when we were at Oxford. Marjorie and I spent one night eating fondue and talking about everything." His brow furrowed. "I loved watching her mouth when she talked. Sometimes I wonder what would have happened if she hadn't run off with that Arabian prince."

"I didn't say I was going." Ian turned his attention to Spencer. "And you're not going to sit in an igloo with Tabitha by yourself.

You've seen her every day since we arrived. Why don't you and I do something together? We can see the Rockettes at Radio City Music Hall."

"No offense, but Tabitha's legs are better than yours." Spencer punched Ian playfully. "And of course you're going. Think about the good you'll do for the foundation. The most important people in New York will be there."

Spencer had a point. One of the reasons Lady Violet had agreed to the Met exhibit was it opened up a new circle of potential donors.

He could accept Sabrina's invitation and tell her the truth tonight at the ball.

"Trust me on this one." Spencer picked up a slice of toast and walked to the bedroom. "Love is as unpredictable as holiday traffic on the M5, but you can't ignore it. If you do, it might never happen again."

Ian stood at the window and admired the view: the white blanket covering Central Park and the department store windows that even from this height were as colorful as the bags of sweets he used to buy after school. Only Spencer would mention the word "love" about a girl he met two days ago.

Lady Violet had said he was too young to fall in love with buildings, and even planning the Met exhibit didn't fill up his thoughts. He pictured Sabrina sitting in the cab on the way to Tiffany's. Her cheeks were bright from the cold and he wanted to kiss the snowflakes that had settled on her nose.

He took a piece of stationery from the desk drawer and scribbled a reply. Spencer was right about one thing. At this moment, seeing Sabrina again was the most important thing in the world.

Nine

Sabrina studied her reflection in the suite's mirror and felt a surge of anticipation. The silver ball gown looked even more breathtaking than when it was hanging in the Plaza's storeroom. The bodice was sewn with pearls, and there was a wide sash.

She had been so nervous when the butler brought Ian's reply, she almost didn't open the envelope. The butler waited patiently and it took her a few minutes to realize he wasn't interested in Ian's response. He was only waiting for his tip.

She twirled in front of the mirror and felt like Cinderella. The gown had to be returned by tomorrow, and even the evening shoes were borrowed from Chloe. Sabrina had told Chloe she had nowhere to wear them, but Chloe insisted she pack them anyway. A woman should always travel with a pair of stilettos; they were as essential as extra underwear.

Everything about her outfit was perfect, so why was there an unsettled feeling in her stomach? Grayson had insisted she use the tickets; she should relax and enjoy herself. After all, in six days Ian would be on his way back to England. And Sabrina would be in her apartment, moving the space heater around because it only produced enough heat to warm what was directly in front of it.

The Plaza's lobby was as crowded as the Metropolitan Museum on the night of Anna Wintour's Met Gala. Sabrina had never attended, but she had seen photos in *Page Six*: society women wearing gowns with skirts as wide as Scarlett O'Hara's, mingling with waiflike models in sheaths so tight they could have been sprayed on. And the jewelry! Diamonds as bright and sparkly as the ball that dropped in Times Square on New Year's Eve.

She passed Maurice Fine Jewelry just as a woman dressed in black stepped out of the store. It was the salesgirl who had tried to sell her the pendant.

"Sabrina! I saw you through the window and had to say hello. That dress is beautiful on you," the salesgirl gushed. "Is that tulle? I've never seen such gorgeous fabric."

"Do you like it?" Sabrina ran her fingers over the waist. "I was afraid it was too much. But it is the Snowflake Ball."

"It's lovely." The salesgirl eyed her critically. "But you're not wearing any jewelry."

Sabrina brought her hand to her neck. She didn't own any proper jewelry, and it was hardly the kind of gown you could pair with a heart necklace from Target.

"The gown is so elegant, it doesn't need anything else," Sabrina said.

"Trust me, every woman is more alluring with something glittering around her neck." The salesgirl pursed her lips. "That diamond and emerald pendant you tried on yesterday would be perfect. Why don't you borrow it?"

"I couldn't do that." Sabrina was shocked. "What if I lose it?"

"Guests do it all the time. It's like taking a car home from the showroom before you decide to buy it." The salesgirl gently propelled Sabrina into the store. "Let me show you what it would look like with the dress."

Sabrina tried to stop her, but the woman fastened it around her neck. She glanced in the mirror and almost didn't recognize herself. The emeralds brought a glow to her complexion and the diamonds shimmered against her skin.

"Oh, it's beautiful." She caught her breath.

"It's exactly what the dress needs," the salesgirl said knowingly. "Your boyfriend will love it."

"I don't have a boyfriend." Sabrina turned around.

"The guy with the brown eyes and sexy British accent," the salesgirl said and smiled. "Trust me, he'll be your boyfriend after tonight. He couldn't possibly resist you."

The minute Sabrina returned to the lobby, she wondered what she had done. What if the pendant slipped off? She'd never be able to pay for it. She was about to turn back to the store when Ian stepped out of the elevator.

"Sabrina." He crossed the marble floor. "You look . . ."

His mouth dropped open and he slipped his hands in his pockets. Sabrina had never seen him look so handsome. His tuxedo fit him perfectly and he wore a black bow tie and gold cuff links.

"Not overdressed, I hope." She let out a little laugh. "I wouldn't want you going back to England thinking American women are too showy."

"That's not what I was going to say." His voice was serious, and Sabrina suddenly felt self-conscious.

She looked up and their eyes met. There was a new expression on his face: a mix of wonder and admiration. He moved closer and for a moment she thought he might kiss her.

"What were you going to say?" she asked.

Ian opened his mouth to answer, but a choral group started singing "God Rest Ye Merry Gentlemen."

Ian started and gave Sabrina his arm. He turned to her and grinned.

"We better go into the ballroom, or we'll be crushed by a bunch of singers dressed as Victorian carolers."

Urns of white roses were scattered around the ballroom and all the decorations were silver and blue. Ballet dancers in silver tutus posed on marble pedestals and pine trees were strung with silver and blue lights. The tablecloths were powder blue and a Tiffany box sat at each table setting.

"I can't believe those ballet dancers are real," Ian said when they took their seats. "What if they sneeze or get a cramp in their foot?"

"The Snowflake Ball is known for its fabulous décor," Sabrina said. "Every year they try to outdo themselves."

Her nervousness ebbed after her first glass of champagne and she started to enjoy herself. Ian was warm and attentive, and just being in the ballroom was like entering some magical fairyland.

"Last year the ballroom resembled a scene from *The Nutcracker*. Dancers wore pinafores from Burberry and the toy soldiers were dressed in uniforms with gold buttons. Clara's costume was hand stitched with Swarovski diamonds, and guests took home silver nutcrackers engraved with their initials."

"You know everything about it; you must attend this kind of event all the time," Ian commented, sipping his champagne.

Sabrina couldn't say she'd read a piece on the Snowflake Ball in *The New York Times*. The trick was to turn the conversation to him.

"I'm sure you do too." A smile played on her lips. "Between royal weddings and attending Ascot and Wimbledon, how do you have time for anything else?"

Ian put down his champagne flute and his expression was thoughtful.

"Some of those things get tiresome, but there's also a lot of opportunity to do good," he began. "The Braxton Foundation takes a box at Wimbledon and invites underprivileged children. Many of them have never seen a tennis racquet. And every year we hold a Christmas party in the food hall at Harrods. There's a Santa Claus and each child receives a stocking stuffed with socks and mittens knitted by Mrs. Claus." He paused. "I was afraid they'd eat too many sweets and get stomachaches. But they were more excited about the socks and mittens. They'd stay warm all winter."

Ian's eyes lit up when he spoke and Sabrina felt a lump in her throat. The champagne made her bold and she asked the question she had been thinking about all night.

"Does Tabitha enjoy society events?"

"Tabitha?" he repeated.

"It's none of my business, we've only known each other three days," she went on hurriedly. "But the second day we met, you got a call from someone named Tabitha and it sounded urgent."

Her cheeks flushed with embarrassment and she picked up her champagne flute. If she drank any more she might get drunk, but if she didn't she wouldn't have the courage to continue.

"And last night you had to meet someone at Tiffany's and jumped out of the cab. I thought . . ." she stammered.

"There is a woman named Tabitha who is important to members of the foundation." Ian seemed to choose his words carefully. "But I'm not involved with her. I'm not involved with anyone."

The tightness in her chest dissolved and she tried to sound playful.

"Not a duchess who is Prince Louis's godmother or some high-flying stockbroker?"

"The foundation keeps me busy, I haven't had time to date." Ian leaned forward and touched her hand. "Besides, I never met the right woman."

Ian's palm was warm and she leaned toward him. Suddenly a flash went off and she blinked.

"Could we get another photo?" a man holding a camera asked. "UNICEF wants us to get every table for their Instagram."

The master of ceremonies stepped on the stage and welcomed everyone to tonight's ball. Waiters brought the first course: poached pear and a mousse that was so delicate, Sabrina was afraid it would slip off her spoon and dissolve onto the plate.

Even Ian seemed impressed by the menu: roasted goose with crunchy skin and a rice pilaf with raisins imported from South America.

Sabrina teased him that, with all the Christmas house parties he was invited to, he must eat like this all the time.

"We don't all live like characters in a PBS special," he said when the waiter brought dessert: plum pudding laced with sugar that resembled a golden spiderweb. "Most of the young members of the British aristocracy work ordinary jobs."

"If you call being a member of Parliament or running a multinational hedge fund normal." Sabrina smiled.

"I still don't know what you do," Ian countered. "If you're the

CIA or Interpol, you're wasting your time. I don't know any state secrets, and I haven't been inside Ten Downing Street in years."

"I'd be a terrible spy, I'm not good at keeping secrets," she said flippantly. Her eyes grew serious and she fiddled with her dessertspoon. "I've always wanted to educate people. Not teach math or physics or anything you learn in a classroom. I want to find ways to open their minds to all the world's possibilities."

"That's the way I feel about books," Ian agreed. "A book is just three hundred pages, but it makes you believe you can do anything. Pip in *Great Expectations* was a penniless orphan. Then he got a surprise inheritance and became a proper gentleman who helped so many people."

"And you can find love," Sabrina said before she could stop herself. "The greatest love stories are in books."

Ian was quiet, and Sabrina wondered what had made her say that.

"Sabrina, there's something I want to tell you. . . ." he began.

Sabrina waited for him to continue, but the lights dimmed and the master of ceremonies bounded onto the stage.

"I hope everyone enjoyed dinner. And remember, donating has never been easier. In the old days, you couldn't get too drunk because you had to write a check. Now your phone will transfer the money directly into UNICEF's bank account."

Everyone laughed and he continued.

"But I'm not here to talk about money. The Snowflake Ball is in its fifteenth year, and we're so grateful for your support. So without further ado, I'd like to introduce our surprise guest." He waved toward the curtains. "He's just some red-headed elf I met in Santa's workshop, but he can sing!"

A strobe light scanned the stage and Ed Sheeran appeared

wearing a red-and-green-striped hat and pointy shoes with bells. Ian impulsively took Sabrina's hand and Sabrina let it rest there.

What was Ian going to tell her? Candles flickered on the white tablecloth and the air smelled of pine needles and sugary desserts. It didn't matter. She was sitting beside him at the Snowflake Ball and she couldn't ask for anything more.

They left the ballroom and were standing near the elevator. Ian moved closer and his tuxedo brushed against her dress.

"I had a wonderful time." He pressed the button. "Even if I will regret the extra glasses of cognac."

"I did too," Sabrina said.

The elevator doors opened and Ian waited for Sabrina to step inside. Suddenly she panicked. What if he wanted to come into her suite for a nightcap? There were none of the things that a high-earning executive might own: expensive luggage or a winter coat by some designer brand. One look at her Payless running shoes or her aging laptop and he would suspect she couldn't afford her suite.

"I'm not going upstairs yet," she said quickly. "I have to send some faxes."

"At midnight?" Ian asked. "The business center isn't open."

"The concierge will open it for me," she answered. "It really can't wait."

Ian entered the elevator and turned to face Sabrina.

"Sabrina, I'm glad you invited me." He paused as if he was thinking. "It was the most magical night."

The doors closed and Sabrina sank onto an armchair in the

Plaza's lobby. She'd wait a few minutes and then go up to her suite. Tomorrow she'd return the emerald and diamond pendant and take the ball gown to the storeroom. But right now she would watch the valets in their gold uniforms and listen to "Silent Night" over the speakers. The night had been perfect, and she wasn't ready for it to end.

Ten

It was 9:00 A.M. the next morning and Sabrina knocked on the door of Grayson's suite.

She had expected to wake up groggy and hung over but she jumped out of bed before her alarm went off. Everything seemed easy: the gym was warm and inviting, and she finished her workout before her calves started to ache.

There was a different salesgirl at the jewelry store, and Sabrina didn't have to explain why she wasn't going to buy the pendant. And the butler collected the ball gown and promised to have it dry cleaned before it was returned to the storeroom.

She had been tempted to text Ian, but there wasn't time. She had to get Grayson to tell his story by New Year's, and there was so much material to cover. If he didn't finish, she wouldn't be able to fill three hundred pages and she'd be out of a job.

"Sabrina, please come in." Grayson opened the door and motioned for her to sit down. "I'm afraid I told the butler to take away the pastries." He sat opposite her. "If I start every day with the Plaza's apple turnovers, I'll leave five pounds heavier."

He poured two cups of coffee and handed one to Sabrina.

"And it didn't help eating dinner at Ralph and Ricky's townhouse. Ricky is the most accomplished chef I know." His eyes twinkled. "We had stuffed Cornish hens and a croquembouche she learned to make at a pastry school in Switzerland."

"It sounds heavenly," Sabrina said dreamily.

She had seen photos of Ralph Lauren's New York apartment: a three-story brownstone with views of Central Park and an indoor pool. But she had never known anyone who had been there.

"Did you know they've been married for fifty-six years? It was love at first sight." Grayson grinned. "Ricky was working at an optometrist's and Ralph came in for an appointment. I kidded him that if he had perfect vision, they wouldn't have met. He said his eyesight was perfect for him: it led him to the most wonderful girl."

"That's a lovely story." Sabrina opened her laptop and started typing.

"Ralph always says that Ricky is the talent in the family. Ralph only designs clothes, but Ricky paints watercolors and furnishes their houses and she's even a licensed psychotherapist." His voice grew thoughtful. "Kay believed that being in love is like drinking a special tonic; it makes you better at everything you do. But first you have to find it, and true love can be elusive. You never know when it's going to appear. And sometimes you don't do anything to keep it until it's too late."

Plaza Hotel, December 1960

It had been two weeks since the Christmas ball when Grayson danced with Veronica. He had helped the waitstaff in the Grand Ballroom almost every night after his butler shifts ended.

He told himself it was because he needed the extra money. Christmas was in four days, and he had to buy presents for his nieces. But truthfully, he was hoping to see Veronica. Every night he scanned the ballroom for a girl in a billowing white gown. A few times he thought he saw her drinking champagne or dancing to a Frank Sinatra song. But the girl would turn around and she didn't have Veronica's high cheekbones or luminous smile.

Tonight he noticed a girl standing by herself at the buffet table. Her back was to him but she had Veronica's silky dark hair.

He crossed the room as she turned around. Veronica's eyes lit up and she waved.

"It's good to see you." Grayson walked over to join her. "I thought you'd retired from the party circuit. I haven't seen you at any balls."

"Hardly retired." She gave a little laugh. "I've been to parties at every ballroom in New York. The Carlyle places the tables too close together; you bump elbows with your neighbor. The Plaza is the most elegant, but sometimes the silverware isn't polished." She leaned forward conspiratorially. "My dessertspoon is tarnished. I couldn't finish my sorbet."

"That's impossible!" Grayson started toward the kitchen. "I'll find a new spoon and get another dish of sorbet."

"Don't leave." She put her hand on his arm. "You're the only guy here wearing a tuxedo who isn't too drunk to remember my name." Her eyes widened in a question. "Do you remember my name?"

"Of course I do. It's Veronica." He glanced at her ring finger. "I see you've managed to avoid getting engaged."

"Kevin dumped me," she said matter-of-factly. "He's engaged to a girl he met at Columbia."

Grayson remembered dancing with Veronica all night at the debutante ball.

"I hope it wasn't my fault."

"It had nothing to do with us. Gladys works in the cafeteria at Columbia. She's not from the proper background, so Kevin never let himself fall in love with her. But when the diamond ring fell out of his pocket, he realized he couldn't go through with proposing to me." She smiled guiltily. "I was so relieved I almost kissed him when he told me. But I pretended to be upset. My mother was devastated. She insisted I accept invitations to every ball. Finally I told her that my heart isn't in it. What I need is to get out of New York," she finished triumphantly. "I leave on January twentieth for London. I'm going to study at the Royal Academy of Arts."

"That's great news," Grayson said, wondering why his chest tightened and he felt like he had the worst kind of heartburn.

"My mother thinks I'm going to snag some British lord, but I have no interest in balls and garden parties. London is years ahead of New York, there's a whole wave of pop art and new music."

"England will be lucky to have you," Grayson said diplomatically.

Veronica ate a bite of melba toast and pâté and put down her plate.

"The fraternity who put on tonight's gala skimped on the food and I'm starving." She picked up her purse. "Why don't we get out of here and share a burger?"

"Employees aren't allowed to eat at the Palm Court," Grayson said as he shook his head.

"There are other places to grab a burger in New York. Let's go to Sardi's." She took out a set of keys. "I have a car."

"I thought your father wouldn't let you drive it."

Veronica was already walking toward the exit. She turned and smiled cheekily.

"I found a ticket to the horse races in the glove compartment. I won't tell my mother if he lets me borrow the car. It's a mutually beneficial agreement."

They sat in a booth at Sardi's and drank vanilla milkshakes. The other diners were dressed casually, and Grayson felt self-conscious in his butler's uniform and Veronica's ball gown. But Veronica didn't seem to mind. She laid her long satin gloves on the table and bit into her burger.

"My mother hasn't let me eat a burger since Kevin broke up with me," she said. "She's afraid I'll get fat."

"That doesn't seem likely." Grayson's eyes traveled from her slender neck to the small waist of her dress.

"I only have to keep her happy until I leave for London." She dipped a fry into ketchup. "Then I can eat fish and chips anytime I want."

"Have you always wanted to be an artist?" Grayson asked.

"I'm not talented enough to be an artist," Veronica corrected him. "I want to be an art collector. I thought if I attend art school,

I'll discover great artists at the beginning of their careers. One day I'll have a collection that's so impressive, every museum will want to acquire it."

Suddenly Grayson couldn't imagine never seeing her again.

"One of the guests at the Plaza gave me tickets to the New Year's Eve ball. Would you be my date?"

She shook her head. "I don't think so."

"Why not? You must like me. We danced all night and tonight you invited me to Sardi's," he said, perplexed. "And it's the party of the year."

"I do like you, but I don't want to date anyone," she cut in. "I'm sick of spending my afternoons at the beauty parlor getting my hair done. And I don't want to have to worry about fitting into this dress."

"I don't care about your hair. And you could wear a bathrobe to the ball and I wouldn't mind."

"You say that now, but you'll feel differently when you come to pick me up and you've spent ten dollars on a box of chocolates."

Grayson drank his milkshake and tried to hide his disappointment.

"I'll tell you what." Veronica had noticed his expression. "If you think of some fabulous gift to give me, I'll go on a date with you."

"I don't make much money," Grayson said truthfully. "I can't afford jewelry."

"I'm sick of jewelry and I'm sick of perfume. I'm even becoming allergic to roses," she sighed. "I don't mean anything extravagant. Something completely original, something I would never buy for myself."

"Then you'll go to the ball with me?"

She leaned closer and Grayson could smell her fragrance.

"Then I'll do anything you want."

Grayson stopped talking and Sabrina looked up from her laptop. She was so engrossed in the story, she hadn't realized how long they had been working.

"What did you get her?" she asked.

"That's not a simple answer." Grayson stood up and moved to the window. "You know what I love about Manhattan?" He pointed outside. "Every time I visit, Central Park could have been painted by a different artist. Today it's as gray and somber as a J. M. W. Turner. In spring when the cherry blossoms bloom, the pastel colors remind me of a Seurat."

He turned and looked at Sabrina.

"I don't know what I'd do without art. Love can disappoint you and friends come and go. Art lasts a lifetime."

Sabrina wanted to ask more questions, but there was something in his eyes that made her remain quiet.

"I've got a meeting," he said finally. "Why don't we continue this evening?"

"Of course." She stood up and gathered her laptop. "I'll transcribe my notes."

She hesitated at the door and turned around.

"I didn't thank you for the tickets to the Snowflake Ball." She smiled. "I ended up going after all. I had a wonderful time."

Sabrina sat on the love seat in her suite and glanced at her phone. She kept waiting for Ian to call or text, but her phone stayed silent.

What if Ian thought it was a bad idea to see each other again because he was going back to England?

She scrolled through her notes and stopped. Grayson said true love could be elusive. Sometimes you didn't do anything until it was too late. She stared at the fire crackling in the fireplace. Why should she wait for Ian to text when she could do the same? She tapped out a text and pressed Send.

Eleven

It was the morning after the Snowflake Ball and Ian stood at the edge of Central Park. When he woke up his head was pounding from last night's champagne, and he contemplated staying in the suite. But then Spencer made rustling noises in the bedroom and the unfinished document blinked on his laptop and he had to go outside and clear his head.

Central Park was even more beautiful than the photos in the visitors' guide. Bridges were blanketed in snow and pine trees formed a tapestry of icicles. Later in the day, horse-drawn carriages would take tourists on the bridle paths and children perched on sleds would spin down the gentle slopes. But for now the sun had barely pushed past the skyscrapers, and even the little huts that sold hot dogs were closed.

Last night was the best he could remember. Sabrina resembled a movie star with her red lipstick and dark hair curling around her shoulders. And she was so easy to be with: he could have talked to her for hours about books and philanthropy.

He had been so close to telling her that he was Spencer's personal secretary, and then the photographer had interrupted and he'd lost his nerve. Her silver gown was almost definitely couture, and the emerald and diamond pendant must have cost more than his year's salary. Would she be interested in him if she discovered he had been a scholarship student and now earned enough to rent a bedsit in Sussex?

What if it was too late to tell her the truth? He crossed Fifth Avenue and entered the Plaza's lobby. There wasn't time to think about it now. First he had to finish cataloging the jewels for the exhibit, and then he could worry about Sabrina.

"Would you like a cup of tea while you work?" the woman asked.

Ian sat in the Plaza's vault where the Braxton collection was being kept until the exhibit opening. He wondered what other objects had been stored in the hotel safe over the years. Secret papers belonging to a Russian spy who tried to infiltrate the United Nations during the Cold War? A rare emerald owned by an Arabian princess that could pay for a whole year in the Royal Suite?

"No, thank you," he answered, chuckling to himself. He had to stop reading James Bond books.

Ian spread the jewels in front of him. There were diamond teardrop earrings that glittered like ornaments on the Plaza's Christmas tree. He picked up the jewel-encrusted sword that had been given to the Earl of Braxton when he returned from fighting the Spanish Armada, and a brooch the Duchess of Braxton had received from Queen Victoria after the birth of her first child.

A silver charm bracelet caught his eye, and he remembered when he first saw it. It was his third year at the foundation and he had been sorting through the endless invitations Spencer received at Christmastime. He'd peered into the billiard room where Spencer often spent his evenings. Lady Violet was sitting at the desk and fiddling with a charm bracelet.

Braxton Hall, December 2017

"I'm sorry, I didn't mean to interrupt." Ian stood at the door of the billiard room. It was one of his favorite rooms in Braxton Hall. The walls were covered with portraits of Braxton ancestors and there was a great stone fireplace.

"If you're looking for Spencer, he's playing Santa Claus at the elementary school. I thought he wouldn't want to strap a pillow around his stomach and wear a gray beard. He can be a little vain," Lady Violet laughed. "But he was thrilled. He asked the cook to make extra gingerbread cookies because he didn't want any of the children to go home hungry."

"I wondered which invitations Spencer wants to accept for New Year's Eve." Ian waved at a stack of card stock. "He's been invited to balls at the American Embassy and the Dorchester. An Australian fashion company even offered to fly him to see the fireworks over the Sydney Harbour Bridge. I declined that one. It's summer in Sydney and the beaches are full of pretty girls. He might not come back."

"No wonder he's popular, there aren't many earls in their twenties." Violet pointed to a wooden jewelry box. "Most are Spencer's father's age. If he was alive, he'd be choosing which cuff links to wear with his tuxedo."

"I'm sorry, I didn't mean—"

"You don't have to apologize." She tried to keep her voice light.

"I was deciding which necklace to wear to the annual Christmas lunch at Buckingham Palace." She examined a sapphire choker. "One doesn't want to outshine the Queen. It's a lovely event. Everyone gets tipsy on sherry and takes home a Christmas pudding stamped with the royal crest."

Ian noticed a silver charm bracelet. "What an unusual bracelet."

Violet turned over the charm of a horse. "Peter gave it to me . . . twice."

"I don't understand." Ian frowned.

"I was eighteen and my parents wanted to marry me off. So I attended my first summer of house parties. I wasn't beautiful and I didn't know how to flirt. Instead, I tried to participate in all the events: croquet and fox hunting." Violet's eyes danced. "But I fell off a pony as a child and was terrified of horses. I pretended I twisted my ankle and while the other guests hunted, I stayed behind and chatted with the groom. Peter was different from the other boys who were only interested in cars and girls. He was serious and kind." She touched the bracelet. "By the end of the week, I was in love."

"What happened?" Ian prompted her.

"The last day of the hunt, Peter would hardly talk to me. I asked if I'd offended him and he said quite the opposite. It was completely inappropriate but he couldn't help it: he had feelings for me. Then he presented me with a small box.

"Inside was the bracelet. Peter's whole life was horses." Violet's voice thickened. "I thought that when he found out that I lied and was afraid of them, he wouldn't be in love with me anymore. I didn't want to hurt him by not accepting the bracelet, so

I took it to a pawnshop. I was going to give him the money with a note saying I couldn't keep it. I didn't want him to lose twenty pounds.

"He stopped me on the way to dinner and insisted on speaking to me. He had passed the pawnshop and saw the bracelet in the window. The owner told him that a young woman brought it.

"I started to explain and Peter interrupted and said he guessed I was afraid of horses. He saw me running across the field when I was supposed to have twisted my ankle. He didn't care if I never rode a horse in my life, he was still in love with me." She twirled the bracelet around her wrist. "Then he gave me the bracelet again."

"That's a wonderful story." Ian beamed.

"It wasn't easy," Violet ruminated. "My parents didn't approve, and my friends thought I was playing at being some modern version of Lady Chatterley."

She put the bracelet in the box and said thoughtfully, "You can come from different backgrounds and disagree about a million things. But if you're in love, you find a way to make it work." Her eyes misted over. "There's nothing else you can do."

Ian slipped the Braxton jewels into their velvet pouches and rang the bell.

Lady Violet had been terribly rich and Peter only a groom when they met, and they were happily married for twenty-five years. Maybe he and Sabrina had a chance. But what would happen when Sabrina discovered he'd lied about who he was?

There was only one way to find out. He had to see her again. He returned the jewels to the woman in charge of the vault and took the elevator to his suite. He was about to punch in Sabrina's number when the house phone rang.

"Is that Lord Braxton?" a male voice asked before Ian could speak. "I'm confirming your luncheon reservation at Tavern on the Green. We have you in the private dining room. The chef created a special menu: roasted wild mushroom soup and Long Island duck with Chinese noodles." The voice paused. "And a pumpkin cheesecake wedding cake, just as you requested."

Ian's cheeks paled and he clutched the phone.

"Did you say wedding cake?" he repeated.

"It's a six-inch cake, perfect for five people. Does the bride like cherry? The pastry chef thought it might be nice to serve it with a cherry sorbet."

"The bride?" Ian repeated, frowning. "Are you sure you have the right suite?"

"The Pulitzer Suite at the Plaza Hotel. You called a few hours ago. We were very pleased to be able to accommodate you." The voice chuckled. "I hope no one's having a case of cold feet. It goes away with a shot of bourbon before the ceremony."

Ian thought quickly. "Where did I say the ceremony was going to be?"

"Well, you didn't." The voice hesitated. "As long as your party arrives by two p.m., there'll be plenty of time for the luncheon. Is something wrong, Lord Braxton?"

"Nothing at all," Ian said. "Thank you, I have to go."

Ian hung up and strode to the window. He barely noticed the crowds jostling on the sidewalk or the carriages lined up in front of Central Park.

Spencer couldn't be getting married! Then he remembered Gstaad: Spencer had booked the wedding chapel at the Palace

Hotel followed by dinner at La Bagatelle. It had the best views in Gstaad and a zither player to serenade the bride and groom.

That was before the Arabian prince seduced Marjorie. Prince Amet had given her a flawless seven-carat diamond and the promise of a private jet to whisk them to their honeymoon in the Seychelles.

Ian remembered sitting in a bar with Spencer the evening after Marjorie left. Spencer downed schnapps and moaned that Marjorie didn't know what she was doing. Her fair British skin would never survive in the Arabian sun.

Ian called Spencer's phone but it went straight to voice mail. That wasn't a surprise. If Spencer thought Ian approved, he would have made him the best man.

Even if Ian only searched the Protestant churches in Manhattan, it would take him days to find them. And what religion was Tabitha? Spencer could be getting married at a Mormon temple or a synagogue.

"I'm not doing any good standing here," Ian said out loud, grabbing his coat.

He had to find them before Spencer kissed the bride and the officiant announced the new Lord and Lady Braxton.

"My name is Ian Westing in the Pulitzer Suite." Ian approached the concierge desk. "Did Lord Braxton see you about making arrangements?"

"Arrangements?" the concierge repeated.

"For a wedding this afternoon."

"I'm sorry, sir." He shook his head. "I haven't seen Lord Braxton."

Ian had to try something different. "What's the closest church to the Plaza?"

The man tapped on his computer.

"That would be St. Patrick's Cathedral on Fifth Avenue," he said to Ian. "It's one of Manhattan's most famous landmarks. It takes up an entire city block."

Spencer would hardly hold an intimate ceremony at the largest cathedral in New York.

"Something smaller, somewhere you could hold a last-minute wedding."

"First you'd have to get the wedding license. That would be from the city clerk. . . ."

The wedding license! Surely they would have to write on the wedding license where the ceremony was going to be held.

"Is there a car that can take me to the city clerk's office?"

"Of course." The man smiled, relieved to be able to help. "Would you like a Bentley or one of the new Teslas?"

Ian jumped out of the Bentley and opened the door of the Office of the City Clerk.

"Can I help you?" An older woman sat behind a desk. A sandwich bag was open in front of her and she was reading *People* magazine.

"I need to speak with the city clerk," Ian replied.

"Gerald is at lunch." She pointed at the empty desk. "He'll be back at two p.m."

Ian glanced at the clock on the wall. A lump formed in his throat and he felt slightly sick.

"That's a two-hour lunch!" he exclaimed.

"He had cataract surgery and had to see his eye doctor." She took a bite of her sandwich. "You can't sign a marriage license if you can't read the applicants' names."

By 2:00 P.M. Spencer and Tabitha would be eating duck at Tavern on the Green. Spencer would probably be wearing the navy suit Ian had ordered for him from Liberty London. Ian shuddered to think what Spencer was giving Tabitha as a wedding present: a diamond Cartier watch, or a rare vase he'd seen in the window at Sotheby's?

"Did a couple come in earlier?" he asked hopefully.

"All we get is couples," the woman responded. "We provide marriage licenses."

"The man had sandy blond hair and a British accent and the girl . . ." He couldn't quite remember what Tabitha looked like.

"I wouldn't have heard his accent. I listen to podcasts while I work." She held up a pair of headphones.

Ian started to say something and stopped. It wouldn't help to snap at the clerk's secretary.

"Thank you." He opened the door. "You've been most helpful."

"It doesn't sound like I have," the woman said cheerfully. "Come back when you're getting married. I give candy to the bride and groom." She opened her desk drawer to reveal a selection of candy bars. "Reese's Peanut Butter Cups are the most popular."

Ian spent the next two hours searching churches in Manhattan. Every time he climbed back into the Plaza's Bentley, he knew it was pointless. Finding the right church was as likely as picking out a particular guard at the Changing of the Guard at Buckingham Palace.

He wondered what Sabrina was doing. Perhaps responding to the faxes she'd sent last night or having lunch at the Palm Court. Suddenly he longed to be sitting opposite her. He'd show her how to pour a proper cup of tea and they'd talk about New Year's celebrations in London and New York.

The Bentley let him off on the corner of Sixty-Seventh Street and Central Park West. Tavern on the Green resembled a British tavern with red brick walls and a peaked roof. A red awning covered a walkway and there was a live Christmas tree.

The main room had rounded walls and a beamed ceiling. An open kitchen revealed a wood-burning stove and pots of chrysanthemums dotted the floor.

"Do you have a reservation?" the hostess asked politely.

"No, I'm—" Ian started walking into the restaurant.

"I'm sorry, we're completely full." The hostess stopped him. "The week after Christmas is our most popular time."

"I don't want lunch," Ian grunted. "I'm looking for a wedding party. The name is Braxton, Lord Spencer Braxton."

The hostess peered at her computer screen.

"You should have said so." She inspected Ian's casual shirt and slacks. "I don't see you on the guest list, and the other members of the party are dressed quite formally—"

"I don't care if they're dressed to visit Buckingham Palace and I'm wearing my birthday suit," Ian spluttered.

The hostess bit her lip.

"We do have a dress code. But Lord Braxton was quite charming, and he did tip generously." She motioned him to follow her. "So you can come with me."

There were sounds of laughter followed by clapping and clinking glasses. Ian opened the door and Spencer was standing and holding a champagne flute. Spencer was wearing a navy blazer with a red handkerchief tucked in his breast pocket. Ian recognized Spencer's father's gold watch.

"What are you doing here?" Spencer asked in surprise.

"What am I doing here?" Ian retorted. "What have you done and why didn't you tell me?"

Tabitha sat on one side of Spencer and there was an older couple and a boy of about twenty at the table.

"Who did you even have as the best man!" Ian exploded. "A Salvation Army Santa Claus or the driver of the Rolls-Royce parked out front?"

"I didn't invite you because you don't know anyone in the wedding party except Tabitha," Spencer said, perplexed. "And I don't know what you mean about the best man." He rubbed his forehead. "I'm the best man. That's why we're here."

Ian glanced around the table more slowly. The older man was wearing a gray morning suit with a carnation in his buttonhole. The woman was dressed in an ivory pleated skirt and matching jacket with a small hat perched on her head.

"I don't understand," Ian said.

Spencer's eyes lit up with understanding and he let out a laugh.

"You thought Tabitha and I got married!"

Spencer waved around the table.

"This is Tabitha's father, Scott." He grinned. "Scott and his fiancée, Trina, are visiting from Milwaukee and decided to get married. It was very last minute, but Tavern on the Green did a wonderful job. Sit down and have a plate of duck."

Tabitha's father stood up to shake Ian's hand.

"It's a pleasure to meet you," Scott said. "Spencer told us all about you."

"It's a pleasure to meet you too." Ian let the man squeeze his hand.

"We were supposed to get married in Niagara Falls, but Scott hurt his back," Trina piped up. "Spencer arranged everything. We drove in the swankiest car I've ever seen. And the people at the city clerk's office were so kind." She reached into her purse and brought out a Reese's wrapper. "They even give out candy when you sign the license."

Ian remembered the secretary at the city clerk's office. His throat was dry and his stomach ached and he had to sit down.

"I will have that duck after all," he groaned. "And a large gin and tonic, heavy on the gin, light on the tonic."

Tabitha's father owned a menswear store in Milwaukee and he peppered Ian with questions about British fashion. Trina wanted to know if Ian had met little Louis and whether he was as cute as the photos on the internet. Even Tabitha's younger brother, Stephen, was pleasant. He was a theater major and dreamed of being a star on Broadway.

They ate pumpkin cheesecake and toasted the bride and groom with a bottle of Moët & Chandon. Each member of the wedding party received a Tiffany's Christmas ornament, and there were bags of rice to toss at the happy couple.

"You should visit us in Milwaukee," Trina said to Ian as she climbed into the Rolls-Royce. "It's the Big Apple of the Midwest."

"I'd love to." Ian nodded politely.

"I gave Spencer my email." Scott squeezed Ian's hand even harder than before. "Maybe you'd be interested in starting an export business. I could sell John Lobb shoes at my store."

Spencer tucked his gold American Express card into his wallet and turned to Ian.

"Tabitha and Stephen and I are going to take a cruise of the harbor," Spencer said. "Would you like to join us?"

"I'm going back to the Plaza." Ian looked sternly at Spencer. "Somebody needs to alert Lady Violet's accountant about the incoming charges."

"Good idea, I wouldn't want them freezing my card." Spencer took Tabitha's arm. "They can be so finicky about overseas charges. You buy one thing that seems a bit odd and they think it was stolen."

It was late afternoon and Ian sat in the suite's living room. A sheath of papers was spread out in front of him and there was a tray of Christmas cookies.

The door opened and Spencer entered the suite. His handkerchief was missing and his tie hung loosely around his neck.

"I do love weddings, but I can't stand wearing a tie during the day." Spencer yanked off the tie. "It reminds me of our days at Harrow."

"Is that all you have to say?" Ian demanded.

"I'm sorry I didn't invite you." Spencer sat on the love seat. "Tabitha's father is quite shy. Tabitha thought he wouldn't be comfortable reciting his vows with a stranger."

"*I'm* a stranger. You've known Tabitha for three days, and you spent five thousand dollars on her father's wedding!" Ian grabbed a paper. "Two thousand on the bride's outfit from the bridal salon at Bloomingdale's, and a thousand on the groom's suit. *You* don't own a morning suit that costs that much."

"Scott has very good taste. He would have brought a suit, but he thought they were getting married at Niagara Falls," Spencer explained. "And Trina fell in love with the hat. It's Christian Dior."

"I don't care if it was made by the Queen's hatter. We're leaving in five days, and you'll never see these people again." Ian picked up another sheet. "Not to mention the corkage fee for the Moët & Chandon from the Plaza's cellar. I don't know what that costs. I haven't received the Plaza's bill."

"What were you doing at Tavern on the Green anyway?" Spencer said irritably. "I thought you were going to spend the day with Sabrina."

"I was going to see Sabrina. But then someone called to go over the wedding menu." Ian glowered.

Spencer poured a glass of whiskey and looked at Ian.

"Do you ever think you spend so much time thwarting my romances because you're too afraid to have one of your own?"

"What are you talking about?" Ian asked.

"When have you ever been in love?"

"Well, I haven't," Ian replied. "I've been too busy. And I can't afford—"

"You make a decent salary. And a school can live with fewer library books so you can take a girl to the movies," Spencer fumed. "You seem to be taken with Sabrina, but you won't give it a chance. What if she's the one and you let her get away?"

"That's ridiculous. We just met."

"My mother taught me that love can happen anytime." Spencer walked to the bedroom. "That's what makes it magic. And what could be more magical than Christmas in New York?"

Ian waited until Spencer closed the door and then he picked

up a paper. Of course he wanted the things that came with love: someone to share things with, marriage and a family.

He pictured Sabrina in the silver gown with the diamond and emerald pendant around her neck. Even if he was falling for her, she wouldn't be interested in him when she learned he wasn't Lord Braxton.

But Lady Violet had been afraid of horses and Peter fell in love with her anyway. He couldn't give up if there was a chance Sabrina had feelings for him too.

His phone lay on the coffee table and he scrolled through and found Sabrina's number.

Spencer was right; it was Christmas. Anything could happen.

Twelve

For the third time since Ian called, Sabrina searched through the clothes in her closet. She wished she had taken Chloe up on her offer of the Alice + Olivia gold V-neck dress or the Kate Spade boots with stiletto heels. Ian had asked her out tonight and she wanted to wear something completely different than the ball gown: something that looked expensive but sexy at the same time.

It had seemed like a Christmas miracle. Just as she sent Ian a text, he called her phone. They both laughed and then they were talking at once: Ian described his morning in the Plaza's vault and Sabrina said she spent the afternoon reading the Eloise books in her suite. Technically she had been transcribing Grayson's notes. But she did flip through *Eloise in Moscow* on the coffee table. She hadn't been lying; she just didn't tell him the whole truth.

Then he'd asked if she was busy tonight and she'd felt like a teenager being invited to her high school prom. It took all her willpower not to answer too quickly. Finally she said she had to work for a few hours and she could meet him for a late supper.

Had Ian been thinking about her all day, or did he just want some company? It didn't matter; just talking to him made her happy. And he seemed eager to see her. They both said at the same time that the other could choose the restaurant, and then they burst out laughing.

Now it was 4:00 P.M. and she had to go to Grayson's suite. First she wanted to pick out an outfit. The last thing she needed was to be debating whether she should wear the black cocktail dress that Grayson gave her or stick with Chloe's Theory jumpsuit when she was supposed to be listening to Grayson's story.

"Sabrina, please come in." Grayson ushered her into his suite.

The sun was setting and the view from the window was like a Christmas card. Skyscrapers were lit with twinkling lights and a fresh snow blanketed Central Park. Even Fifth Avenue seemed festive: taxis picked up shoppers carrying bright packages, and Sabrina could see long black limousines idling at the curb.

"There's no place like New York at Christmas." Grayson followed her gaze. "The summers are so humid, I always have to bring extra shirts. I would never visit in February: it's twenty-eight days of sleet and snow." He sat on the sofa. "But Christmas in New York is magical. Spending Christmas at the Plaza was one of the perks of being a butler. Everyone was in a good mood, and you should have seen the guests: Prince Rainier and Grace Kelly visiting her family in Philadelphia, and Marilyn Monroe and her husband that year, I think it was Arthur Miller. And of course, Sophia Loren." He paused. "God, that woman looked good in clothes. She could make a duffle coat and snow boots look glamorous." He smiled at Sabrina. "Times have changed. I had a meeting with a rapper who wants to start an art collection. I was afraid we wouldn't be allowed in the Palm Court: he wore baggy pants with holes in the knees and sneakers covered with graffiti. Then guests asked for his autograph. He's sold six million records and his name is Kendrick Lamar."

"I listen to his music." Sabrina nodded, opening her laptop.

"I'm too old to listen to new music," Grayson sighed. "Getting old is cruel. Every night I have insomnia and I can't trust my memory." He poured a cup of coffee. "Though I suppose there are good things about aging. When you're young, you're so busy looking ahead you don't notice the people around you," he said meditatively. "But when you're older you slow down and pay attention. Kay, for instance, could read people better than anyone I met. And she always wanted to help." He stirred cream into his cup. "She had a brusque exterior, but underneath was a heart of gold."

Plaza Hotel, December 1960

"There's nothing worse than birthdays." Kay sat hunched at the pink desk in the suite's living room. "Once you're too old to host birthday parties where there's a pony or a clown or whatever one has at a child's birthday, birthdays should stop altogether. You'll never see Eloise's mother celebrating her birthday in my books. Even Nanny's age remains as secret as the code for the atomic bomb."

"Is it your birthday?" Grayson asked. "It's not written on your card."

All the hotel guests filled out cards with their birthdays and anniversaries and graduations. Every year, Grayson sent Mrs.

Goodman in the Carnegie Suite flowers on their anniversary. He even wrote the card and signed it in her husband's name. Mr. Goodman loved his wife, but he was hopeless at remembering dates.

"That's because I don't divulge that kind of information," Kay huffed. "The last two years I've been on the West Coast; this is the first year I've stayed at the Plaza. And look what happened," she said to Grayson. "The general manager sent me this pink desk as a gift. Eloise has made the Plaza the most famous hotel in the world, and he wanted to give me something I could use every day. What I could really use is a magic potion to forget my birthdays."

"You look younger than the day we met," Grayson said diplomatically.

"That was only two years ago," Kay replied. "And even I've noticed I've aged. I should move to Paris like Eloise's mother. The French aren't obsessed with youth like Americans." She stopped and looked at Grayson curiously. "Are you feeling all right? You didn't refill the bowl of nuts, and your cuffs aren't buttoned."

Grayson glanced down at his shirt cuffs in horror.

"I hope you don't have a fever," Kay worried. "Christmas is the worst time of year to get sick, all the best doctors are in Florida."

"I feel fine." Grayson buttoned his cuffs.

"You look different." She studied him critically. "If you're not sick, it's something. . . ." She tapped her red fingernails on the desk. "I recognize that look! I wore it for six months when I worked with Frank Sinatra in an Arthur Freed musical. He barely noticed me but I followed him around like a puppy."

"I don't know what you're talking about." Grayson busied himself with the bowl of nuts.

"You're lovesick." She waved her hand at her typewriter. "Even Eloise would notice, and she's so busy splashing in *Eloise Takes a Bawth* she doesn't realize she's turning the Plaza's bathroom into an ocean."

Grayson couldn't hold it in any longer. Ever since Veronica had made him the ultimatum two days ago, he couldn't think of anything except finding her a suitable present.

"I did meet a girl, but she's completely out of my league," he confided.

He told her all about Veronica and her request.

"After I bought Christmas presents for my nieces, I have nine dollars and seventy-six cents left until my next paycheck," he finished.

"That's not going to buy you a bottle of eau de cologne," Kay agreed. "What kind of things does Veronica like?"

"It's hard to say, she's quite unusual," Grayson debated. "She's going to London to study art and she wants to be an art collector."

"Did you say art?" Kay perked up.

"Yes, the Royal Academy of Arts is one of the best in the world."

"That's it!" Kay said excitedly. "What time does your shift end?"

"After this I have to see Mrs. Smith in the Pulitzer Suite. Her grandchildren are coming on Christmas Eve and she needs help filling the stockings," Grayson thought out loud. "I should be done by midnight."

"Excellent. Meet me in the lobby," Kay said. "And wear black."

"Black?" Grayson questioned.

Kay's eyes twinkled and she looked ten years younger. "We're going to stage a heist."

The Plaza's lobby was almost deserted. A few couples in evening wear stood near the elevator, and now and then a blast of cold air shot through the revolving doors.

It was past midnight and Kay wasn't there. Grayson debated going home—it was already so late, it would take ages to reach the Bronx. But Kay was his last hope. If he didn't come up with a present for Veronica tonight, he might never see her again.

"There you are." A female voice.

He turned around and Kay stood before him. She was wearing black slacks and a black turtleneck sweater.

"I'm sorry I'm late. I couldn't find any black gloves." She held up her hands to display sheepskin gloves. "These will have to do."

"Why do you need gloves? Are we going outside?" Grayson asked.

His winter coat was hanging in his locker, and he'd freeze without it.

"So we don't leave fingerprints." Kay lowered her voice.

"What do you mean, fingerprints?" Grayson asked uneasily.

"Stop asking questions," Kay hissed. "And follow me."

They slipped through the hallway until they reached a small alcove. There was a fireplace hung with stockings, and above it was a portrait of Eloise. Eloise wore a black pleated skirt and black suspenders with a lace shirt. Weenie stood beside her, and behind her were a red velvet curtain and a red chair that resembled a throne.

"I never thought I'd say this, but Eloise is ruining my life." Kay studied the portrait. "I can't go anywhere without someone asking what's going to happen in the next Eloise book. If I knew, I wouldn't be sitting in front of the typewriter every night, chewing my fingernails," Kay grumbled out loud. "And God forbid, I act like Kay Thompson instead of Eloise's creator. Sometimes I never want to see the color pink again."

"What does that have to do with Veronica?" Grayson asked, puzzled.

"My illustrator, Hilary Knight, gave me this portrait for my birthday in 1956. The first Eloise book had been published a year earlier." Kay pulled herself back to the present. "I took the painting on a talk show. Jerry Lewis was the host and he joked that Eloise was the most famous girl in America, more famous than Gloria Vanderbilt in the 1930s. I didn't want to hang it in my suite. It was bad enough that every time the phone rang, someone inquired if there would be an Eloise movie and did Eloise eat the Plaza's cream cheese blintzes for breakfast every morning and could I send the recipe? I gifted the painting to the hotel and it's been hanging here ever since." She wiggled the frame. "Until tonight, when I'm giving it to you."

"To me?" Grayson said in surprise.

"So you can give it to Veronica." Kay tugged harder at the frame. "Hilary is quite famous; one day this could fetch a good sum. In the meantime, Veronica will own the only portrait of America's beloved Eloise and her dog, Weenie."

"You gave it to the Plaza," Grayson said frantically. "You can't take it off the wall, that would be stealing."

"Hardly stealing," Kay considered. "More like regifting."

"The Plaza will think it's stealing when it's gone," Grayson insisted. "They have their own private detective. If it's traced back to me, I'll get fired and go to jail!"

"No one's going to jail." Kay stepped back. "I didn't know about the private detective."

The doors to the Grand Ballroom opened and a group of young men in tuxedos stumbled out. Grayson could hear the band playing and wondered if Veronica was inside. But Veronica promised she had attended her last ball and was going to stay at home and paint until she left for London.

"I know!" Kay said when the young men had returned to the ballroom. "We'll say fraternity boys stole it. They'll do anything as a prank. I'll call Walter Cronkite and tell him myself, it will be all over the columns by tomorrow. It will be great publicity for Eloise, we'll sell more copies of *Eloise at Christmastime* than when it first came out."

Grayson considered this. After one debutante ball, he'd found a marble statue from the courtyard hidden in the men's bathroom. He still didn't know how the fraternity boys got it there without anyone noticing.

"I can't give Veronica stolen goods."

"There's that word again." Kay flinched. "I'll write a letter saying the painting belongs to you. You can keep it in case anyone ever questions it."

She opened her purse and took out a black cashmere scarf.

"Wrap it in this." She yanked the portrait off the wall. "And hurry. It would be embarrassing if we were caught red-handed."

It was almost 2:00 A.M. and Kay and Grayson were in Kay's suite. Kay finished wrapping the cardboard tube containing the portrait in Christmas paper and attached a red bow.

"You can carry it through the lobby and no one will suspect a thing." She handed it to Grayson.

Grayson suddenly felt all choked up. Veronica would love the painting and go out with him after all.

"How can I thank you?" Grayson asked.

"By making this girl fall in love with you." Kay sat at the pink desk. "Love can be as hard to find as one of those new Barbie dolls that are so popular at Christmas. And if you do find it, it can still make you as miserable as an actress on the opening night of her first flop." She blinked furiously and Grayson noticed tears in her eyes. "But when you're young, it's still the best thing out there. Now get going. Did you know that most writers suffer from insomnia?" She opened her typewriter. "This is the perfect time for me to write."

"Sabrina, is something wrong?" Grayson asked. "You seem distracted."

Sabrina looked up from her laptop. Grayson had been talking for ages and it was almost 6:00 P.M. She couldn't help sneaking glances at her phone. What if Ian texted and she missed it?

"Nothing's wrong." She hastily put away her phone. "Did Veronica like the present?"

"There's something different about you." Grayson studied her quizzically. "Did you get your hair done at the salon?"

"I wouldn't dream of doing that!" Sabrina said in alarm. "It must cost a fortune."

"You're right," Grayson chuckled. "Last time I was here, they sent up a barber and the tip alone could have paid for dinner for two. But there is something different about you. The one thing that hasn't changed with age is my eye. I've studied art for sixty years and I've learned to notice the smallest detail." He paused. "You said you went to the Snowflake Ball last night. Did you go with someone special?"

Sabrina busied herself by tapping on her laptop.

"Not exactly, just a friend I met at the hotel."

The suite's phone rang and Grayson got up to answer it. He spoke into the receiver and then turned to Sabrina.

"I told you my memory is slipping. I forgot I promised to have drinks with a client. We'll have to continue tomorrow."

"Of course." Sabrina tried to keep the relief out of her voice. She closed her laptop and hurried to the door.

"Have a good night, Sabrina," Grayson said kindly. "You've been working hard and it's Christmastime. Enjoy yourself."

This time Sabrina was the first to reach the lobby. All the anticipation and excitement she had felt earlier drained away and was replaced by nervousness. What if Ian didn't show up? Or worse, what if they didn't have a good time?

She studied her reflection in one of the lobby's gilt mirrors and wondered if the neckline of her blouse was too low. It would only take a minute to change into the black cocktail dress, and black was always the safest choice. She pressed the elevator button just as Ian stepped out of it. He looked handsome in a crisp white shirt and corduroy slacks.

"I hope you're not running away," he said with a smile.

"Of course not," she answered, relieved that he was here and embarrassed that she got caught. "I was going upstairs to change."

Ian's eyes traveled from her blouse to her wool slacks. An evening purse was slung over her arm and she wore the cashmere jacket that Grayson had delivered to her suite.

"Why would you do that?" he asked in surprise.

"I just thought . . ." Sabrina said awkwardly.

"That you're the most beautiful guest at the Plaza." Ian took her arm and led her away from the elevator. "Why don't we start with a cocktail, and then we can decide where to have supper."

They sat at the bar at the Rose Club and Ian ordered two brandy punches. Sabrina sipped hers and the tension ebbed away. Ian was warm and familiar and they enjoyed each other's company.

"I asked the concierge for restaurant suggestions. Some of the places need to be booked two months ahead, but he mentioned the Plaza and an opening appeared as if by magic."

Ian took out his phone and scrolled through the names.

"Ko is the place to go for the best Asian tasting menu, and Per Se is Thomas Keller's restaurant that is even better than his French Laundry in Napa." He looked up from his phone. "Not that I've been to Napa, but the concierge assured me the reviews were correct."

Ian kept talking and Sabrina sipped her cocktail. The brandy warmed her throat and suddenly she knew what she wanted to do.

"Would you do me a favor?" she said boldly.

"Would you like another drink?" He waved to the waiter. "I thought we'd wait until dinner, but we can order—"

"I don't want a cocktail, and I don't want to eat somewhere where it takes two months to get a reservation," she replied.

"There are other restaurants on here." He scrolled down. "Daniel is supposed to be—"

"What I'd really like is to go to the movies."

"I hadn't thought of that." Ian clicked to another screen. "There's a luxury theater in the Fulton Market. We can eat Buffalo wings and watch a movie at the same time."

For a moment she yearned to be herself, not some high-flying executive who washed her face with the Plaza's Jo Malone soaps and curled up in a monogrammed robe that cost more than her entire wardrobe.

"I'm not that hungry, and it's impossible to enjoy a movie when people are clinking wineglasses," she said slowly. "There's a cinema in the East Village that plays rom-coms. The guy in the ticket booth moonlights delivering pizza and he lets you smuggle in a couple of slices of pepperoni."

"Rom-coms?" Ian repeated.

"Romantic comedies," Sabrina prompted. "*Crazy Rich Asians* and *27 Dresses* and *Notting Hill*." She looked at Ian quizzically. "You have heard of a rom-com?"

Ian exhaled as if he just thought of something.

"Of course, you wouldn't be British if you hadn't heard of *Notting Hill* and *Bridget Jones's Diary*. I just thought it's Christmas week in New York and we should do something special."

Sabrina's confidence wavered, and she debated saying yes to Per Se. But the thought of sitting opposite Ian at some stuffy restaurant made made her feel deflated. Maybe she couldn't tell him that she couldn't afford a suite at the Plaza. But she had to find out if they enjoyed the same things.

She placed her glass on the counter and stood up.

"It's a double showing of classic rom-coms: *My Best Friend's Wedding* and *How to Lose a Guy in 10 Days*."

"All that and pepperoni pizza?" he asked, his smile as wide as Central Park. "How could we do anything else?"

They walked out of Cinema Village onto East Twelfth Street. The sidewalks were dusted with a light snow, and Christmas lights blinked in the store windows.

"You hated it," Sabrina said pensively. "You didn't laugh once, and you squirmed all the way through the last half hour of *My Best Friend's Wedding*."

"I was only squirming because the woman behind me dropped a Jujube down my back," he said.

"She didn't!" Sabrina said in horror.

"I think it was an accident, unless she could smell our pizza and got hungry," he said, smiling. "I loved the movies. Though I think Matthew McConaughey was kind of a jerk. I can't imagine behaving like that around women, but I guess that's the attraction."

"Not to all women." Sabrina gulped.

Suddenly she wanted him to know how she felt. She turned to him and stopped walking.

"Some women want a nice guy. A guy who doesn't mind seeing cheesy movies in a drafty theater at Christmas when he could be dining in a five-star restaurant where waiters push around silver bread carts. A guy who says she looks beautiful even though she's afraid she wore the wrong outfit and almost missed the whole date. A guy who—"

"Sabrina," Ian interrupted abruptly. "You don't have to apologize. I'm glad we tried something new."

Sabrina bit her lip. What was she thinking, taking Ian to a dingy theater in the Village and eating take-out pizza? And she had just admitted she was nervous about their date when he'd been assuming she was some ultraconfident corporate genius. She thought she could be herself, but she was wrong.

"You don't have to say anything," she said hurriedly. "Why don't we call a cab and go back to the Plaza."

"If you want to." He nodded. "But there's something I want to do first."

Sabrina waited for him to say he just wasn't the kind of guy who ate cold pizza, or he usually spent his evenings at the opera or the ballet instead of a movie theater. But instead he put his finger to Sabrina's lips. He held it there for a minute and then he reached down and kissed her.

His mouth was warm, and a thrill traveled down her spine.

"Now we better get that taxi," he said when they parted. "Someone must have spilled Coke on my coat, because the collar is damp."

The taxi let them out in front of the Plaza, but Sabrina didn't feel like entering the hotel. It was almost as if she was Cinderella in reverse. When she stepped through the door, she had to be the woman who tried on emerald and diamond pendants in the jewelry store and sent mysterious midnight faxes from the business center.

Ian's kiss was still fresh on her lips and she looked up at him.

"Would you like to keep walking?" she asked.

"Only on one condition," he said and his voice was serious.

Sabrina faltered. He was going to ask again what she did for a living. Or worse, he would want to know where she had traveled: Paris or Rome or Madrid. How could she explain she hadn't been farther than Florida to see her grandmother, and a few college ski trips to Vermont?

He took out his phone and flipped open a screen.

"You didn't like the concierge's suggestions for restaurants, but he did say that ice-skating in Central Park was a 'don't miss' in New York at Christmas," he said sheepishly.

"You want to go ice-skating now?" Sabrina asked.

"It sounds touristy, but I watched *Home Alone 2* on the plane. The scene set at the skating rink made it look like fun."

For some reason she felt happier than she could remember.

"You do like cheesy movies!" She started laughing.

"I watched it because it takes place in New York at Christmas," he said, his cheeks turning red. "But if you're too tired—"

"I'm a very good ice-skater, you know." She started walking. "I took figure skating lessons as a child."

"So am I." He took her hand and strode beside her. "We'll see who's faster around the rink."

Central Park was beautiful in the crisp night air. Pine trees were entwined with colored lights, and horse-drawn buggies were festooned with huge red ribbons. Sabrina watched couples skating in circles around the rink and thought it all looked so simple: holding hands with someone you liked and enjoying hot chocolate with marshmallows. Perhaps taking a horse-and-buggy ride through the park and snuggling under a wool blanket.

"I'm glad we came here," Sabrina said when they had been outfitted with skates. "Most people prefer Rockefeller Center, but it's always so crowded, you can't skate without worrying you'll knock someone over. And the music is so loud it's like being at a rock concert. Here, you're in the middle of a park." Sabrina inhaled the scent of pine needles. "It all feels magical."

"I agree." Ian stepped onto the ice. "In London, most people love skating at Somerset House because it has a giant Christmas tree and the best cinnamon buns in London. But if you pull on your gloves after you've eaten a bun, they get sticky, and the lights from the Christmas tree can be glaring on the ice. I prefer skating at Hampton Court Palace. Though I haven't been in a few years because we've spent the holidays at Sandringham."

"What's Sandringham?" Sabrina questioned.

"The Queen moves the royal household to the village of Sandringham the week before Christmas. It's only a couple of hours from London, but it feels like an English village from the eighteenth century. There are Christmas markets, and the royal family attends Christmas services at St. Mary Magdalene on Christmas morning. Then the Queen hosts a special luncheon."

"You celebrate Christmas with the Queen?" Sabrina asked in wonder.

The closeness she had felt with Ian—watching rom-coms together and eating greasy pizza—was erased as quickly as the lines her skates made on the ice. Even his kiss seemed forced: it had been so quick; he probably was being polite. Kissing on a date was expected, and he didn't want to hurt her feelings.

"I don't attend the lunch," Ian said awkwardly. "That's reserved for the immediate members of the royal family. But the Christmas services are lovely. The church has stained-glass windows and it's so small, you can hear the priest rustling his papers," Ian said with a smile. "He confided that no matter how many sermons he gives, standing up in front of the Queen always makes him anxious. He's even been known to take a small nip from his flask. I'm sure the Queen wouldn't mind, she often has a sip of sherry before noon."

"I see," Sabrina said stiffly. "I've never met anyone really famous. I did almost run into Beyoncé. We were both getting on the elevator at Bloomingdale's. I didn't ask for her autograph. I was afraid her bodyguard thought I did it on purpose and would have me escorted from the store."

"I waited for hours outside a charity function to get Daniel Radcliffe's autograph," Ian admitted. "And I tried jumping onstage at Wembley Stadium to get the autograph of a member of One Direction. A schoolmate dared me to do it. I almost got trampled by a bunch of teenage girls waving their knickers at the band."

Sabrina giggled at the image of Ian stuck in a swarm of gushing girls throwing their underwear onstage.

"I waited for hours to see Justin Timberlake backstage," she rejoined. "It was worth it. He's very polite and his smile is even more electric up close."

Ian looked closely at Sabrina. He leaned forward and pushed a strand of her hair from her cheeks.

"I've loved everything about this evening: the movies and the pizza and the cab drive to Central Park," he said slowly. "There's only one thing I would have done differently."

"One thing?" Sabrina repeated.

"Our kiss. I wanted our first kiss to be special. You looked so beautiful in the lamplight, I couldn't resist kissing you. But I'm British. The minute our lips touched, I could only think about the people watching."

Sabrina gulped. She glanced around the ice-skating rink.

"We could kiss now. The rink is almost empty and the couples are too preoccupied to notice."

Ian pulled her close and put his mouth on hers. Sabrina stood on tiptoe and kissed him back. This time the kiss was so long, she had to catch her breath.

"That was much better," Ian said when they parted.

He took her hand and headed to the middle of the rink.

"Come on. The rink will close soon, and we haven't raced yet."

The doors of the elevator opened on the fifteenth floor, and Sabrina and Ian stepped out. After they'd finished skating, they'd strolled past the Christmas windows at Bloomingdale's.

Now it was almost midnight and Sabrina was tired. She still wasn't ready to invite Ian into her suite, but she wondered whether he would kiss her again.

"Thank you, I had a wonderful time," she said when they reached her door.

"So did I," Ian agreed. "You are a very good skater; I may have to take lessons if we try it again. I wondered if . . ."

He was about to say something when his phone buzzed in his pocket. He took it out and frowned at the screen.

"If it's Tabitha, feel free to answer it," she said playfully.

Ian slipped it back in his pocket.

"Not Tabitha—Lady Violet," he replied in a worried tone.

"Lady Violet!" Sabrina couldn't keep the excitement out of her voice. "I know she's your mother, but she's also a duchess. I've seen pictures of her. She has something special: not beauty, exactly, but a grace and poise you rarely see."

"She is special." Ian rubbed his forehead. "It's very early in London, I wonder why she called."

Sabrina could tell that Ian was distracted.

"Why don't you go call her back," she prompted. "It's late and I should go to bed."

Ian looked up and nodded.

"I probably should." He leaned forward and kissed her briefly. "Good night, Sabrina. Thank you for a lovely evening."

Sabrina hung her cashmere jacket in the closet and slipped on a robe.

The night had been perfect, and then Ian's mother had called. Sabrina remembered the photos she had seen of Lady Violet in magazines: Lady Violet chatting with the Queen and Prince Philip at the christening of some royal nephew, Lady Violet shaking hands with Daniel Craig at the premiere of a new James Bond movie.

For a brief while when they had been talking about getting autographs of famous people, she believed she and Ian had more in common than she had thought. But Ian and his family moved in a world she could only imagine. He attended Christmas services with the Queen and the royal family! Did she really think he would be interested in her if he knew she was a struggling writer who couldn't afford the peanuts they gave away on a British Airways flight?

She turned down the covers and slipped into bed. She might be at the Plaza at Christmas, but that didn't mean everything would work out. Because right now, being with Ian seemed as unlikely as Santa Claus and his reindeer landing on the Plaza's slate roof.

Thirteen

It was 9:00 the next morning and Ian stared dejectedly at the platter of bacon and sausages the butler had set on the coffee table. He should be grateful. He didn't even have to put on slippers, let alone the wool jacket and muffler he always wore for the short walk from his flat in the village to Braxton Hall. At the Plaza, he could have breakfast and work without leaving the heated luxury of the Pulitzer Suite.

But the cranberry juice reminded him of the brandy punch he and Sabrina had drunk at the Rose Club. The sausages made him think of the pepperoni pizza at the movie theater, and the copy of *The Times* the butler had folded on the tray had a photo of a Christmas pageant that Lady Violet had attended.

What had he been thinking, blurting out that Lady Violet called? Sabrina had commented that she was Ian's mother and he hadn't corrected her.

And he was worried about the phone call itself. Why had Lady Violet called at 5:00 A.M. London time, and why hadn't he been able to reach her since?

Until that moment the night had been perfect. At first when

the concierge had given him the list of restaurants, his stomach had turned at the prices. But he was determined to show Sabrina the kind of evening she was used to. Instead, Sabrina suggested seeing a romantic comedy. He happily paid for the movie plus four slices of pizza, and two tickets to the ice-skating rink in Central Park.

There had been something different about Sabrina. She had looked beautiful and elegant in that pink cashmere jacket but she seemed so relaxed. They had been like children racing each other around the rink, and she'd wolfed down the pizza as if she ate takeout every night.

He had been about to say he had something to tell her when his cell phone rang. How could he admit now that he had lied and he wasn't Lord Braxton?

His phone buzzed and he noticed an unfamiliar number.

"Ian? It's Lady Violet," a female voice said.

"Lady Violet, is anything wrong?" He sat up straight. "You called at midnight and I haven't been able to reach you. . . ."

"Remind me never to get up so early again. I added a dozen wrinkles to my forehead," she groaned. "Spencer's grandmother fell and sprained her ankle and I had to come and stay with her."

"Is she all right?" Ian asked.

Lady Violet's mother lived alone in a cottage by the sea near Brighton. Once a year Lady Violet asked her to come and live at Braxton Hall, but she was fiercely independent.

"She's fine, but she won't admit her limits. If I weren't here, she'd be driving because she doesn't like to miss volunteering at the animal shelter. Every time I visit, I remember where Spencer gets his kind heart. I haven't been here for twenty-four hours and she's already found homes for three stray kittens and a puppy."

"She's lucky to have you."

"We're all fortunate to have family," Violet agreed. "The cell phone reception is terrible, so I thought I'd call and give you her number." She paused. "How is Spencer? I hope he's not getting engaged to some American girl. His grandmother gave me a fright in the middle of the night—I can't take any more surprises."

"Spencer is behaving quite responsibly," Ian said evasively.

"You mean he met someone, but he hasn't flashed the Braxton diamond?" Lady Violet said with a mix of laughter and concern. "What about you? Any holiday romance?"

"Me?" Ian asked in surprise.

"Sometimes I think I made a mistake. I shouldn't have asked you to be Spencer's personal secretary." Her tone was serious. "You're handsome and intelligent, girls should be falling all over you. But you're almost thirty—you can't spend all your time stopping Spencer's love affairs. At some point you have to find love yourself."

Lady Violet's question made him feel strangely off-balance. He pictured Sabrina leaning over and whispering to him in the movie theater and pushed the image out of his mind.

"I'm happy running the foundation. And Spencer still needs supervision." He tried to keep his voice light. "Fiancées aren't stray puppies. You wouldn't be happy if he brought home a complete stranger and installed her at Braxton Hall."

"I suppose you're right," she sighed. "Do you remember the time I found a family of ducks in the downstairs bath? Someone organized a shooting party, and Spencer wanted to keep them safe. Duck feathers were stuck to the tub for days."

"Are you sure you don't need us to come home early to help?" He tried to change the subject.

"Heavens no. Spencer's grandmother would have a fit if more people were here to look after her. You must stay for the opening of the collection." Her voice drifted. "I have to go. Give my love to Spencer, and think about what I said. You could at least allow yourself a holiday romance. I would try one, but the only single men here are fishermen. I don't like the smell of fish, I'd much rather find a nice farmer."

Ian hung up and placed his phone on the coffee table. The smell of the sausages and bacon made his stomach turn and he covered the plate with a silver dome.

Had he ever been in love? There was Annalise his freshman year at Oxford. That had been the uncomplicated first love, when every day was about discovering each other. But then Annalise didn't return, and he came down with a winter flu that lasted all semester.

He stared at the fire crackling in the suite's fireplace and tried to remember if there had been anyone else. There was Cherie, the sister of a girl named Aimee who Spencer had followed to the south of France. Aimee had told Spencer that she was related to the royal family of Monaco and invited Spencer and Ian to her family's villa in Monte Carlo.

When they arrived, Spencer learned that Aimee and her mother and sister worked as maids at one of the estates overlooking the Mediterranean. Aimee thought if she pretended she was French royalty, Spencer might propose and she could move her whole family to Braxton Hall.

Ian remembered sitting with Spencer on the horseshoe-shaped beach and Spencer sipping banana daiquiris and shaking his head. What Aimee hadn't realized was that Spencer would have had a relationship with her even if she was a maid. He might even have paid for her and her sister to go to school so they could get better jobs, and set her mother up in her own shop.

Ian and Cherie had enjoyed a fleeting relationship for five heady days on the Riviera, but it certainly wasn't love.

And what about Sabrina? Could that be love, or was it like the Christmas scenes in the department store windows: dazzling and intoxicating, but it would all be packed up and put away when the holidays ended?

His real life was about running the foundation. He recalled the Christmas a few years ago when he worried that he was doing the wrong thing and wasn't really helping children at all. A ten-year-old boy named Everett was stealing books from the library and selling them to a used bookshop.

Everett was one of the children that Ian was most proud of. His father wasn't around and his mother worked two jobs. Everett had scarcely read a book when he joined the club; he came for the biscuits and hot cocoa. But after the first few weeks, Ian noticed him flipping through the books and he even started taking some home.

Everett was bright and curious and Ian had felt an instant connection. How could he have abused Ian's trust and stolen the books?

Ian combed the village but he couldn't find Everett anywhere. Finally he entered the newsagent to buy a pack of lozenges. Everett was standing behind the counter. When he saw Ian he ducked into the back room.

"What are you doing here?" Ian tried to hide how furious he was. It wouldn't help to lose his temper in the shop.

"Mrs. Bowen needed help wrapping during the Christmas rush." Everett pointed to a table scattered with soaps and bottles of cologne.

"I need to talk to you," Ian said brusquely. "Come with me."

They stood on the sidewalk and Ian slipped his hands in his pockets. He couldn't help but notice that Everett's thin jacket was too small, and there were holes in the sleeves.

"You lied to your mother about attending the after-school club. And you stole the library books and sold them to the bookshop."

Everett's small forehead creased in a frown.

"It wasn't really stealing," he wavered. "I was going to buy the books back eventually. That's why I'm working at the newsagent."

"Why did you take them in the first place?"

Everett's brown eyes were round and frightened.

"I wanted to buy my mother something pretty for Christmas," he answered. "Even helping at the newsagent, it would take weeks to save the money, and Christmas would be over. Glenn said he wouldn't sell them. He was only keeping them until I could buy them back."

"I see." Ian nodded.

Taking the library books was still stealing. But how else could a ten-year-old boy without a father afford a Christmas present for his mother?

"Please don't tell my mother," he begged. "Every morning she looks at her reflection in the mirror and frowns. I thought if she wore something new she'd realize how pretty she is and be happy."

"I'll buy the books from the bookshop and return them to the library. You can pay me when you have the money."

"Are you sure? You won't send me to jail?"

"Perfectly sure," Ian said.

"That's a relief." Everett wiped his forehead. "I bet the jail is colder than my bedroom. Could I take *Charlie and the Choco-*

late Factory home after we get it back? I want to see how it ends."

"Maybe we'll read it together," Ian suggested. "I'll ask Lady Violet if you and your mother can come for dinner at Braxton Hall. There's the biggest fireplace you've ever seen, and the cook makes a delicious Yorkshire pudding."

Everett's smile was so wide Ian thought his face would crack.

"That's an excellent idea, but can we wait until after Christmas?" he asked solemnly. "Then my mother can wear her new blouse."

Ian poured a cup of tea and stirred in lemon and honey. Now Everett was a scholarship student at Harrow and he was a class prefect. Ian had changed his life by introducing him to books. How could anything compare with that?

But then he thought about last night with Sabrina. The way she pressed her cheek against the window of the cab so she didn't miss the decorations on Fifth Avenue. How soft her lips had been when he kissed her; the scent of her perfume.

The door to the suite opened and Spencer stepped inside.

"I didn't think you'd be awake." Spencer set a shopping bag on the coffee table. "You weren't home when I went to sleep. This morning you were snoring so loudly, it was worse than foghorns on the Thames."

"I had too many brandy punches," Ian admitted.

"That sounds promising." Spencer took the silver dome off the plate and picked up a slice of bacon. "How was your date with Sabrina?"

"We saw a movie and ate pizza and then went ice-skating."

"That's the best you could do in New York at Christmas?" Spencer raised his eyebrow. "First Tabitha and I saw the ginger-bread houses at William Poll on the Upper East Side. My favorite had Frosty the Snowman peeking through the window. Then we drank Bloody Marys at the King Cole Bar and visited the Christmas village at the St. Regis. They turn one of the ballrooms into a winter wonderland for children. We ended the evening with glasses of prosecco at a boutique hotel on West Fifty-Third Street called Baccarat." He pointed to the shopping bag. "I bought a few things from their gift shop. My mother will love their tea towels, and I got some jams for our cook."

Ian was about to say that the jams were probably imported from England and Braxton Hall had closets filled with tea towels. But his head pounded and he didn't have the energy to argue.

"Sabrina and I don't need to dine at five-star hotels and take in the sights of New York to enjoy ourselves," he said huffily. "We're happy watching rom-coms and drinking blue Icees."

Spencer stopped with his fork in midair and looked at Ian.

"You took a girl to see a rom-com?"

"Sabrina suggested it," Ian admitted. "But I had a great time."

Spencer leaned back on the sofa and whistled.

"You have fallen for her. You never go to the movies—you think they're a waste of time when you should be working. And I tried to get you to drink an Icee once but you said the blue dye would ruin your teeth."

"You're the one who said I can't work all the time," Ian retorted. "And the Icee wasn't too bad. I quite enjoyed it."

"All I'm saying is Sabrina has made an impression." Spencer went back to eating his sausage. "What are you going to do with her tonight?"

Ian's head throbbed and he groaned.

"I did something terrible. I don't know if I can see her again."

"You haven't done anything terrible your whole life," Spencer chuckled. "Unless you count when you put a tadpole down Louis Smith's back when we were fourteen. That was only because I made a bet that I could do it and chickened out. You didn't want me to lose thirty pounds."

"It was your whole term's allowance. Your mother would have been furious," he said. "This is serious. I did something and I don't know how to fix it."

"You can start by telling me what you did."

Spencer was Ian's best friend, but he couldn't tell him the truth. Ian was supposed to be levelheaded and responsible. How would Spencer feel if he learned that Sabrina thought Ian was Lord Braxton and Ian hadn't corrected her?

"It's too complicated." Ian shook his head.

"There's one simple solution," Spencer said easily. "Buy her a present."

"I'm not like you," Ian replied. "I can't buy John Lobb shoes or reserve the private salon at Tiffany's."

"It doesn't have to be expensive," Spencer said. "When I was nine, I fell in love with Rosie Addams. I ran over her pet turtle with my bicycle and almost crushed his shell. She was so upset, I went down to the chemist and emptied my piggy bank. All I could afford was one of those soaps shaped like a flower. She kept it in her bathroom but she didn't let anyone wash their hands with it."

A present was a good idea. With a little note saying he had a wonderful time and was looking forward to seeing her again.

"What would I get her? Everything in the Plaza's shops is overpriced."

"You're in New York at Christmas." Spencer finished his sausage. "You'll find something."

Ian walked to the closet. His throat was sore and he dreaded going outside. But it would be worth it if he could make Sabrina smile.

"Could you stop and get some cinnamon rolls from Zabar's?" Spencer looked up from his plate. "Tabitha and I had some yesterday and they're delicious."

Ian rubbed his hands together and trudged down Fifth Avenue. For the last two hours he had been wandering in and out of the stores searching for the perfect gift. Bergdorf Goodman had seemed promising. The window display was of two polar bears wearing snowshoes. Scarves were wrapped around their necks and they wore multicolored mittens.

Ian entered the store and approached the salesgirl in the accessory department. But the mittens were hand-stitched in Peru and the scarves were cashmere and both were out of Ian's price range. Ian asked if anything was on sale and the woman brought out a brass whistle that was perfect for hailing a cab. Ian pointed out that most people use their phone to call an Uber, and even on sale it was two hundred dollars.

Saks was just as disheartening. The window display was of Mrs. Claus baking cookies in the North Pole's kitchen. The elves wore red and green aprons, and there was an array of cooking utensils with the Saks logo. But the aprons were Christian Dior, and the Saks logo seemed to double the price of the simplest cookie cutter.

He walked down Fifth Avenue and stopped in front of Tiffany's. The exterior was painted eggshell blue, and the building was wrapped with a red ribbon. There wasn't a chance he'd find anything at Tiffany's but he couldn't help admiring the window. Miniature diamond skyscrapers touched the sapphire sky. A gold Statue of Liberty carried a ruby torch, and there was an emerald and diamond replica of the Brooklyn Bridge.

In the corner there was a selection of charms of different New York landmarks. Ian noticed a charm of the Empire State Building and one of a stately mansion. He looked more closely and recognized the gabled roof of the Plaza Hotel.

"I can as likely afford that as I can the Ferrari that's idling on the corner," he said out loud.

He was about to keep walking but changed his mind. He ducked into the store and approached the jewelry counter.

"Can I help you?" the saleswoman asked, and Ian immediately regretted his decision. Her hair was pulled back in a severe bun and she wore bright red lipstick.

"How much are the charms?" He pointed to the window. "I was interested in the charm of the Plaza Hotel."

"The charms are one hundred dollars on special until New Year's. But that's the only one we have in stock, and we can't sell pieces from the window displays."

Ian had to have it for Sabrina. It would be the perfect gift to make her remember their time together at the Plaza.

"Could you make an exception?" he pleaded. "I've been searching for hours, and it's just what I'm looking for."

"I'm afraid not." She took out a cloth and polished the glass case. "Our window artists take their work seriously. It would be like chipping off a piece of Michelangelo's *David*."

Ian almost said a Christmas window was hardly the same as a famous statue, but he didn't want to make the saleswoman angry.

"Have you ever met someone who makes you see the world differently?" Ian asked instead. "Someone who makes you question everything you've been doing?"

The woman put down her cloth and glanced around as if she was looking for a security guard.

"Ever since I was twenty-two, I thought if I did good deeds and tried to help people, I'd be happy. But then I met someone and realized there's more to life than that. There's a level of happiness I couldn't even imagine." He waved at the jewelry case. "Like discovering the most dazzling sapphire, when you thought there was only aquamarine."

"We don't sell aquamarines in this department," she said huffily.

"What I'm trying to say is, wouldn't you do anything not to lose that new feeling?" he hurried on. "Because it would be like the sun never coming out again."

"I suppose so," she said doubtfully.

"I met someone who makes me feel like that, and I want to give her something special. I can't afford a diamond-studded watch or those ruby teardrop earrings." He pointed at a pair of earrings. "But I can afford a silver charm of the Plaza Hotel and it would be the perfect gift."

"I could replace the charm of the Plaza Hotel with one of Times Square." She picked up a silver charm.

"Everyone pictures Times Square when they imagine New York," Ian agreed eagerly.

"You can have a Tiffany's box, but I can't wrap it," she said, and something in her expression had softened. The lines around her mouth relaxed and the creases in her forehead disappeared. "We only wrap if you spend over five hundred dollars."

"I don't need wrapping." Ian couldn't remember feeling so happy. "And I never use those sticky bows, they just fall off."

The saleswoman rang up the purchase and handed Ian the small blue box.

"Sabrina was right about Tiffany's," he said, slipping the box into his pocket.

"Who's Sabrina and what did she say?" the woman asked.

"Sabrina is the girl I met. She said that the first time she came to New York she stood in front of the window at Tiffany's and knew all her dreams could come true."

Ian entered the Plaza's lobby and approached the concierge's desk. The regular concierge was gone and an unfamiliar man stood behind the counter.

"Can I help you?" He glanced up from his computer.

"I'd like this to be delivered to the Fitzgerald Suite." Ian put the Tiffany's box on the counter.

"Certainly, sir, are you staying with us?" He tapped through his screen.

"I'm in the Pulitzer Suite," Ian replied.

He was about to say something when he noticed a young woman crossing the marble floor. She moved closer and he recognized Sabrina's dark hair.

He couldn't run into Sabrina here, it would spoil everything!

"I have to go." He turned toward the elevator.

"You can't leave," the concierge called after him. "Who is the box for and who is it from?"

Ian couldn't answer his questions. If he didn't get into the elevator, she'd run right into him.

"I'm sorry, it's an emergency," Ian called back. "I'm sure you'll figure it out."

Ian entered his suite and dropped his scarf on an armchair. The living room smelled of furniture polish and chrysanthemums. The curtains were drawn back and there was a tray of mini sandwiches on the sideboard.

His heart thudded with happiness and he loved everything about the suite: the silk robe that hung on a hook in the marble bathroom. The magazines that the butler replenished daily so there was always something new to read. The velvet slippers that sat by his bed at night, and the newspaper and fresh coffee that greeted him when he stepped into the hall in the morning.

He hadn't eaten breakfast and now he was starving. He selected a smoked salmon sandwich and added a puff pastry. It was only when he was wolfing down the pastry that he remembered he had been in such a hurry to get in the elevator, he hadn't written a card. He ate a bite of chicken wrapped in flaky crust and told himself there was nothing to worry about. Who else would send Sabrina a silver charm of the Plaza Hotel?

Sabrina would love the gift and he would admit the truth about himself and tell her he had feelings for her. Because if he lost her, he didn't know what he'd do.

Fourteen

Sabrina entered her suite and placed her shopping bags on the end table. It was early afternoon and the sun streamed through the living room windows. A crystal vase was filled with red and white chrysanthemums and the maids had left a coffeepot and a plate of vanilla truffles.

When she woke up, she had turned over in the king-sized bed and almost couldn't remember where she was. But then the night came back to her: going to the cinema in the East Village and ice-skating in Central Park. Passing the silver lights of the Pulitzer Fountain when they walked back to the hotel, and the scent of pine needles in the Plaza's lobby. And best of all, Ian's kisses. His kisses were warm and soft and she wanted to kiss him again.

Then Lady Violet had called and Sabrina remembered that Ian was a member of the British aristocracy. Fitting in to his world was as unlikely as being able to afford the Frette sheets she was sleeping on or the Turkish towels in the suite's bathroom.

But there was no point in dwelling on it and it, was a beautiful day. Grayson couldn't meet until after lunch, so she had decided to spend the morning buying presents for her parents and Chloe.

Even if she couldn't afford more than a bag of colored jelly beans at Dylan's Candy Bar it would be fun to play tourist for a few hours.

First she visited the Winter Village at Bryant Park and wished Ian were there. They could have played broomball or ridden the bumper cars or had their pictures taken at Santa's Corner. She browsed in the holiday kiosks that had sprung up in October and weren't taken down until New Year's. This year was the best she had seen: pottery from Jamaica and blankets the color of the African sun and wooden clocks made in Switzerland.

She bought a shawl from Belgium for her mother and a book about Mount Everest for her father. She would send them with a note saying she was sorry their presents were late, but she'd had to wait until she got a job. Then she selected a pair of espadrilles for Chloe. They weren't anything like the designer shoes Chloe owned and she couldn't wear them until summer, but they were bright and whimsical and caught Sabrina's eye.

She debated buying a gift for Ian but changed her mind. If she gave him something from a kiosk—a beer mug from Munich with MERRY CHRISTMAS written in German, or fuzzy earmuffs—he might wonder why she didn't buy a proper present: a leather wallet or the gold tie clip she saw every time she passed the men's store in the Plaza's lobby.

"Would you like a Yankees cap?" A man stood behind a booth cluttered with sports memorabilia. "I have one signed by Derek Jeter. It's only two hundred dollars."

Sabrina didn't follow baseball, but even she knew that Derek Jeter was one of the Yankees's most famous players.

"That sounds like a bargain. Is it really signed by Derek Jeter?"

"For a pretty girl like you, a hundred fifty," he said hopefully. "I'll even throw in Derek Jeter's sweatband."

"I'm sorry." She smiled. "I'm not a baseball fan."

"Your boyfriend must be. Every guy in New York is a Yankees fan. It's like knowing how to ride the subway or getting your first kiss at the foot of the Empire State Building."

"I don't really have a boyfriend, and the guy I'm seeing is British," she wavered. "He doesn't live in New York."

The man looked at her thoughtfully.

"Then he's losing out on both fronts. He's missing being with a beautiful woman and he's not living in the best city in the world."

Sabrina left Bryant Park and headed up Sixth Avenue toward the Plaza. Perhaps she would buy Ian a present. After all, he had kissed her. And his feelings for her couldn't all be based on the couture gown she wore to the Snowflake Ball or the fact that she could afford to buy an emerald and diamond pendant.

So what if Lady Violet shared an umbrella with the Duchess of Kent at the Christmas services at Sandringham? That didn't mean Ian couldn't date whomever he wanted. Ian said he had fun last night and they had eaten take-out pizza and watched romantic comedies.

She hurried along the sidewalk and stopped in front of a brick building with KINOKUNIYA BOOKSTORE written in black lettering. Kinokuniya had been one of her favorite stores when she graduated from college. She arrived in New York and decided a real writer needed a fountain pen and pretty notebooks. But then she saw the prices and decided she would stick with typing on her aging laptop and using the back of a college binder as a diary.

"Can I help you?" the man behind the counter asked. He wore black leather pants and his black hair was spiked on the top of his head.

"I'm looking for a gift."

"We just got in some Japanese comic books," he offered, pulling them from the rack.

She knew exactly what to get Ian. She moved to the stationery section and selected a box of cream-colored stationery. The envelopes were lined with gold and there was a box for the airmail stamp.

"Could you wrap this, please?" She handed it to him.

"Are you sure?" He held it gingerly. "No one writes letters these days."

Sabrina reached into her purse for her credit card and smiled.

"Perfectly sure. I couldn't give him anything else."

Sabrina took the wrapped parcel out of her shopping bag and wondered when she would give it to Ian. He hadn't called or texted and she would be working with Grayson all afternoon.

There was a knock at the door and she answered it.

"Good afternoon, Miss Post." The butler made a bow. "I have a delivery for you."

He handed her a small blue box and Sabrina turned it over in her hand.

"Can I do anything else?" he asked. "Would you like your coffeepot refilled or some sparkling water?"

"Who is it from?" she asked, reaching into her purse for a five-dollar bill. "I don't see a card."

"The concierge asked me to bring it up." The butler accepted the bill and smiled. "You never know at Christmas. You must have a secret Santa Claus."

The butler left and Sabrina opened the robin's-egg blue box. Inside was a silver charm of the Plaza Hotel.

"Oh, it's beautiful!" she breathed. She sifted through the box but there was nothing but tissue paper.

It had to be from Ian; who else would buy something from Tiffany's? But Grayson had given her the cashmere jacket and the black cocktail dress when she arrived. Perhaps he'd sent the charm as a thank-you. Or maybe it was a gift from the Plaza for spending Christmas at the hotel.

She picked up the house phone and pressed the button for the concierge.

"I received a blue Tiffany's box," she said when the man answered. "But there's no card."

"Ah, yes," the man said. "I helped the gentleman myself."

"Did he give his name?" she asked.

"He was in a bit of a hurry but he was staying in the Pulitzer Suite." He paused as if he was looking up something. "That would be Lord Braxton."

It was from Ian!

"Did he say anything else?" she wondered.

"I'm afraid not," the concierge said. "Is there a problem? Was the box damaged, or—"

"Not at all." She pressed the phone to her ear. "Everything is wonderful."

The light from the chandelier reflected on the charm and Sabrina felt a thrill of happiness. She wanted to call and thank

Ian but she didn't have time. Grayson was expecting her and she couldn't keep him waiting.

"Sabrina, come in." Grayson ushered her into his suite. "I'm sorry I couldn't meet this morning. I had lunch with a client who wants to donate her collection to a museum. It always makes me happy when people share their art with others. Did you know that New York has more art museums than any city in the world besides Amsterdam? There's the Met and the Guggenheim, of course. But there's also the Whitney and the Frick and the Museum of Modern Art."

"I didn't know that." Sabrina sat on the sofa and opened her laptop.

"That's one of the reasons I love New York," he said. "You can see the great masters for a small entrance fee. And that doesn't include the galleries. If you wander around SoHo, you might stumble across a Mark Rothko or a Jasper Johns without paying a dime."

"I never thought about it like that." Sabrina kept typing.

"Ever since I was a teenager and worked at the Plaza I thought Manhattan was the most exciting place to be." Grayson poured two cups of coffee and handed one to Sabrina. "I couldn't imagine why Veronica wanted to leave. England had the worst food at the time—the British existed on cauliflower cheese and soggy peas. And the weather! Veronica wrote letters about all the rain," he chuckled. "She had to ask her parents for a special shoe allowance because she ruined every pair."

"Did Veronica stay away long?" Sabrina stopped typing.

"She was only going to be gone for three months." He put

down his cup and his expression seemed far away. "But things didn't go as planned."

Plaza Hotel, January 1961

"Let's spend the afternoon at the Frick," Veronica said, flipping through *The New York Times*. It was a Sunday afternoon and they were sitting in the living room of her friend Becky's Park Avenue apartment. "There's an exhibit of Italian Renaissance painters: Botticelli and Tintoretto."

"I thought you were only interested in modern artists who think art is tying shoelaces together and covering them with paint," Grayson said gruffly. "That's why you're going to London."

"Many modern artists are inspired by classical painters." Veronica stood up and walked to where Grayson was sitting. "Afterward we can see the new Fellini movie, *La Dolce Vita*."

"I can't afford any more movies, and I don't want to use your father's charge card," Grayson grumbled.

"Why not? I've earned it by being a good daughter." She leaned down so he could smell her perfume. "And the cinema is a perfect place to kiss. I've been wanting to kiss you properly all day."

Grayson had given Veronica the portrait of Eloise two weeks ago and since then they had been inseparable. Veronica told her parents she wanted to visit all the museums before she left for London, and moved into the Park Avenue apartment owned by Becky's parents. Grayson stopped putting in extra shifts at the Plaza, and they spent his free time exploring the city.

They strolled through the quiet enclaves of the Upper East Side, past the doorman buildings on Riverside Drive. Veronica loved Greenwich Village with its mix of elegant ladies walking their dogs around Gramercy Park and a new influx of young people wearing knee-high boots and beads.

Every day was different and he had never experienced so many emotions at once. There was the heady excitement of being with Veronica, coupled with the knowledge that in a few weeks she'd be gone. Sometimes he longed for the time before he met her, when his days consisted of taking Mrs. Rosen's Pekinese for a walk and delivering Kay's dry cleaning. But then Veronica's lips would brush his cheek and he wanted to take her in his arms and hold her forever.

"All right, we'll go," he said. "But does it have to be a Fellini movie? I can't speak Italian, and my eyes get tired when I read subtitles."

Veronica flopped on a chair and picked up a magazine.

"I don't want everyone in London to think I'm an uncultured American." She looked up at Ian. "And we should invite Kay to dinner tomorrow night."

"You want to invite Kay Thompson to dinner?" Grayson asked incredulously.

"Taking her own portrait and pretending it was stolen by a fraternity boy is the most daring thing I've ever heard." Veronica flipped the pages. "I want to thank her. Plus she'll get to see Eloise hanging on the wall."

Grayson had debated not telling Veronica how he got the portrait, but he wasn't good at keeping secrets. And Veronica thought the caper was as thrilling as the gift itself.

"I doubt that she'll come," Grayson said. "Kay has dozens of famous friends. Last week she got an invitation to dine at the White House."

"You're the one who says she sits alone, eating peanut butter and jelly sandwiches and tapping on her typewriter," Veronica countered. "She'll be thrilled. Becky is bringing her mother's pork roast."

"I'd love to come to dinner," Kay said, eating a spoonful of muesli.

It was the next morning and Grayson was fixing Kay's breakfast of Swiss muesli and goat's milk. Kay was afraid of losing her memory, and she had read that the Swiss had the most alert minds.

"But you have all these invitations." Grayson waved at the stack on the side table. "The maharaja is visiting from India and asked you to dine at the Carlyle. And the president of Disney booked a table at the Four Seasons."

"The maharaja wants a signed copy of *Eloise* for his niece at boarding school, and the president of Disney wants me to write a book where Eloise meets Mickey Mouse. I love Mickey Mouse, but he's not the kind of guest one finds at the Plaza." Kay chewed the muesli loudly.

"In that case, we'd love to have you to dinner," Grayson said, trying not to worry. Veronica and Kay were both strong personalities and he hoped they would get along.

"Stop looking so frightened." Kay noticed his expression. "I won't say anything to embarrass you."

"It's not that, it's . . ." He couldn't put it into words.

Kay studied him. "You're in love, and you're afraid to upset it. But love can't exist in a vacuum forever. At some point you have to pop the bubble and expose it to real life."

Was Veronica part of his real life? In ten days she would be on a plane to London. Would they write to each other like Veronica promised, or would their time together turn into a sweet holiday memory? Like last week when they saw *Bye Bye Birdie* on Broadway. Veronica loved it so much; she wanted to see it again. But by the time they got home, she'd forgotten all about it and bought tickets to *West Side Story* instead.

None of that mattered now. Veronica had invited Kay to dinner and Kay had accepted. His stomach clenched and he wondered if he should buy some Alka-Seltzer. Somehow he thought he would need it.

"What a fabulous apartment," Kay said, stepping into the mirrored entry. "When I arrived in New York I shared a studio with three other girls. My bedroom was the closet." She handed a bouquet of flowers to Veronica. "It wasn't so bad. I used the coats on the coatrack as a blanket."

Veronica placed the flowers on the dining room table. The whole apartment was done in white. There was a step-down living room with white carpet and a hallway leading to all-white bedrooms.

"That sounds like fun," Veronica said enviously. "My parents wouldn't let me live in New York unless it was in a doorman building."

Veronica had dressed carefully for Kay's visit, and Grayson felt a swell of pride. Her dark hair was styled around her shoulders and she wore a belted red dress.

"My mother bribed the doorman to tell her what time I come

home every night. I had to pay him double to fib." Veronica smiled. "I'll be twenty-one in April, but my parents treat me like a schoolgirl."

"My mother kept my bedroom in St. Louis the same for twenty years." Kay followed Veronica into the living room. "Then she turned it into a nursery in case I got married and brought home my family. I finally told her that the only little girl in my life is Eloise, and she wouldn't be caught dead in St. Louis."

Veronica's mouth dropped open.

"You didn't say that to your mother."

"Not really." Kay took out a packet of cigarettes and offered one to Veronica. "But I'm tempted to."

"I'm too young to get married." Veronica accepted a cigarette. "That's why I'm going to London. I want to do something thrilling before I spend my days warming baby bottles and driving a station wagon."

Grayson shifted uncomfortably on the sofa. He wanted to say that there was nothing wrong with marriage; his sister got married when she was nineteen and she was perfectly happy. But he didn't want to spoil the dinner party.

"Talking about marriage makes me break out in hives." Kay took a drag on her cigarette. "Why doesn't Grayson fix us drinks? This is a Park Avenue apartment. There's probably a bottle of Cinzano or a decent scotch in the minibar."

They moved to the dining room and Veronica brought out the first course. She had picked up a pumpkin soup to go with Becky's mother's pork roast, and there was sautéed asparagus.

After dinner they sat in the living room and Grayson poured three glasses of sherry. Veronica served cheesecake and told Kay about art school in London.

"Why would you want to leave a five-room apartment with free booze and weekly maid service for a bedsit in London?" Kay asked, eating a small sliver of cheesecake.

"That's the point. I've been comfortable my whole life," Veronica replied. "I'll die of boredom if I attend another debutante ball or sit in another college class where the girls flash their engagement rings and pick out pieces for their trousseau. I want to meet new people and experience new things."

Kay put down her fork and eyed Veronica thoughtfully.

"Most girls your age only want to see the bridal suite at the Plaza before their honeymoon. I like your style." She waved at the portrait above the fireplace. "Eloise ended up in the right place."

Veronica leaned forward and her mouth wobbled. For a moment her confidence dropped away and she was a young girl about to jet across the Atlantic.

"Then you don't think I'm crazy for wanting to go to art school?" she asked.

"If I had stayed in St. Louis, I'd be wearing house slippers instead of six-hundred-dollar designer shoes," Kay said. "The most satisfying thing I'd have done was entering a watermelon in the county fair. Instead, I've visited a dozen countries and made a movie with Fred Astaire. There's nothing worse than being comfortable. It's one step closer to being dead."

Veronica turned to Grayson and her eyes had a new sparkle. "You see, I am doing the right thing. Who knows what will happen in London!"

Grayson tried to stop the choking sensation in the back of his throat.

"Let's talk about something else." Kay turned to Grayson. "Why don't you put on a record? I feel like listening to Elvis."

It was the next morning and Grayson was slicing bananas for Kay's muesli. He didn't know what he was most upset about: that Veronica was thrilled about leaving, or that Kay had encouraged her. But Kay was a guest at the Plaza. If he showed his feelings, he might lose his job.

"What's the matter?" Kay folded her newspaper. "You look like Nanny when she discovered Eloise was running a poker game for the guests on the fourteenth floor."

Grayson couldn't keep it in any longer.

"You practically told Veronica she was better off in London." He sprinkled nuts on the muesli. "And you made marriage sound as tempting as a visit to the dentist during a snowstorm."

"That girl shouldn't get married." Kay shuddered. "Her asparagus was overcooked and the soup was cold. Her husband would need an iron stomach."

"I don't care if I eat white bread sandwiches my whole life." Grayson sliced the bananas vigorously. "I'm in love with Veronica and I want to marry her."

"Do you really want Veronica to come back to New York because she promised her parents?"

"I don't understand." Grayson frowned.

"You'll always wonder if she loves you or if she's doing what is expected of her." Kay paused. "You want her to come back because she can't live without you."

"But what if she doesn't love me? She's never said the words—" he stumbled. "What if she stays in London and I never find out?"

"Veronica is in love with you. She can't see it yet." Kay pointed to her glasses. "It's like forgetting you're wearing glasses because they're sitting on the tip of your nose. Let Veronica go to London. She'll be back before the end of the January sales."

Grayson stretched his legs and picked up his coffee cup.

"It's hard to believe that was sixty years ago. Sometimes I still feel like I'm twenty."

"Kay sounds fascinating." Sabrina stopped typing.

She was so caught up in his story, she felt like Kay was in the same room.

"Kay believed that life was a paint box and it was your duty to use all the colors," he chuckled. "I guess that's why she got so upset that everything about Eloise was pink."

"Did Veronica stay in England?" she asked.

"We'll get to that." Grayson checked his watch. "I've got a conference call with a collector in Tokyo. Why don't we continue this evening?"

Sabrina gulped. She had hoped to see Ian tonight.

"Of course." She nodded.

"We can order room service and I'll try to talk faster." Grayson grinned and suddenly he looked younger. "We only have four more days, and I have a lot to cover."

Sabrina entered her suite and placed her laptop on the end table. The sun had set and the lights of the skyline twinkled.

A text glimmered on her screen and she read it quickly.

Wondering if you were free for dinner. Fighting a sore throat so was hoping we could stay at the Plaza. I'll make reservations at the Rose Club or we can order in pizza. Don't worry; I wouldn't assume that I'm invited into your suite or that you want to come to mine. I'm happy eating in the hallway. I'll even ask the butler for cushions and silverware. Ian

Sabrina read it again and tried not to laugh.

Rose Club is fine but I have to work through dinner, she tapped on her phone. *Could we do early drinks instead?*

She pressed Send and waited anxiously for the reply.

Pizza two nights in a row is probably bad for my cholesterol anyway, and there's nothing better for a sore throat than heated brandy. Five o'clock?

She had one hour and she had to take a bath and decide what to wear. She raced into the bathroom and turned on the faucet. The marble bath filled with steam and she gazed at her reflection in the mirror. Ian had given her the charm, and now she was meeting him at the Rose Club. Christmas week at the Plaza kept getting better.

"Sabrina." Ian greeted her when she entered the Rose Club. "It's wonderful to see you."

Ian looked handsome in a turtleneck and slacks. Sabrina remembered the first time she saw him, asleep on the sofa beside the fireplace. His dark hair had been rumpled and he had been wearing an expensive-looking gray suit.

"You look far away," he said when the hostess seated them at a table.

"I was thinking about when we met," she answered. "I was hungry and everything was closed. You offered to share your caviar and lobster rolls."

"It was the least I could do. If you hadn't woken me up, my neck would have been killing me by morning."

Sabrina was about to thank him for the silver charm but Ian was still talking.

"Why don't you choose our cocktails," he suggested. "You know the menu better than I do."

"I do?" Sabrina blurted out before she could stop herself.

"You're working through dinner, you must eat at the Plaza all the time." He picked up his menu.

For a moment, Sabrina had forgotten that Ian thought she was a high-powered executive who could afford the Rose Club's thirty-dollar cocktails.

"Of course." She glanced at her menu. "Why don't we get the Mary Queen of Scots?"

"Bowmore scotch blended with vermouth and Poire Williams brandy," he read from his menu. "I'm a fan of Poire Williams brandy, it's distilled in Switzerland," he said approvingly. "But isn't it an after-dinner drink?"

Sabrina scanned the description. Of course, Ian would know his cocktails. Sabrina had never even heard of Poire Williams brandy.

"Well, yes." She tried to sound confident. "But since we aren't having dinner, I thought we could try it now."

"An excellent idea." He placed his menu on the table and glanced at Sabrina. "You're wearing the charm."

She had fastened it to a silver bracelet and it dangled on her wrist.

"It's beautiful. There wasn't any card, so I wasn't sure who it was from," she said awkwardly. "But I called the concierge and he said it was from Lord Braxton."

"The concierge said that?" Ian looked surprised.

"Well, yes." Sabrina held up her wrist. "It's beautiful. There's nothing I would have liked more."

She reached into her purse and took out a parcel.

"I got you something too."

Ian unwrapped the paper and opened the box.

"Stationery." He turned it over curiously. "How thoughtful."

Sabrina's cheeks flushed and she tried to hide her embarrassment. What had she been thinking? Ian probably had boxes of stationery engraved with the family crest.

"You can exchange it," she said hurriedly. "The gift receipt is in the bag."

"Why would I exchange it?"

"I didn't mean you had to write to me," she went on. "I just thought . . ."

Ian put the box on the table. He didn't talk for a few moments and then he glanced at Sabrina.

"You're right, I don't want to write to you."

Sabrina tried to hide her disappointment. The charm was a goodbye gift to thank her for a lovely time. Maybe Ian did that with girls he met in different cities: a charm of the Eiffel Tower after a romantic weekend in Paris, a charm of the Colosseum after a getaway in Rome. But she studied his brown eyes and thought that wasn't like him at all.

"You don't?" she managed to say.

"I don't mind writing letters. I write dozens of letters for the foundation." He fiddled with the glass. "With you I'd like to do something different."

"Different?" she repeated.

"Stay in New York longer to get to know you, or . . ." He stopped.

"Go on," she prompted.

"I don't really know," he said, perplexed. He leaned back in his chair and sighed. "Maybe writing letters is a good idea for now."

Sabrina sipped her drink. It was rich and sweet and she'd never tasted anything better.

"I had a pen pal in the sixth grade and we exchanged letters every week." Her eyes danced. "If you write, I promise I'll write you back."

Sabrina entered the elevator and pressed the button for Grayson's floor. Cocktails at the Rose Club had been wonderful. Ian ordered a plate of crudités and they talked about the foundation. When she stood up to leave, he kissed her and she could tell he wanted to kiss her longer.

Could they have a future together? Ian seemed so sincere when he said he wished he could stay in New York. She remembered Grayson saying that Veronica had promised to write but things got in the way. What happened and where was Veronica now?

The elevator doors opened and she stepped out. There were only two days until New Year's, and they had to finish the memoir. She knocked on the door of Grayson's suite. She was about to find out.

Fifteen

Ian paced around the Pulitzer Suite and tried to stop his pulse from racing. The night skyline sparkled with Christmas lights but he barely noticed the skyscrapers or the tops of the trees in Central Park. All he could see was Sabrina's expression when he said he didn't want to write to her and explained why.

He hadn't meant to say anything. But she gave him the stationery and he imagined never seeing her again and the words spilled out before he could stop them. And the smile on her face—open and bright after she had been disappointed—was so glorious he would say them all again.

Could they have a future together? Even he could see how many things stood in the way. They hardly knew each other at all; they'd only shared a couple of kisses! Ian was tied to the foundation and to Spencer; he couldn't hop on a plane anytime he wanted. And he was terribly busy. He barely had time to FaceTime his parents and his sister's family during the holidays, let alone set aside hours in the day for a long-distance romance.

He wasn't even considering the biggest obstacle of all, the one that loomed larger than the Christmas tree in Piccadilly Circus. Sabrina thought he was Lord Braxton, and when she found out he had lied, she may never want to see him again.

He stared dejectedly at the bottles lined up in the minibar. Another brandy would help his throat, but he'd already had two cocktails at the Rose Club and he wouldn't be able to think clearly. A better idea would be to order a bowl of soup and a pot of hot tea. But then he would have to admit to himself that he was actually sick and that wouldn't help his mood.

There was an open bottle of cognac and he poured a small shot. If only he had included a card with Sabrina's gift. Then the butler wouldn't have told Sabrina that the silver charm was from Lord Braxton. The more he tried to get out of this mess and tell Sabrina the truth, the deeper he seemed to sink.

He waved the cognac under his nose and groaned. It was usually Spencer who got into trouble and Ian's job to bail him out. He remembered the Christmas at Sandringham when Spencer had wanted to invite a girl he met at the Christmas markets to Princess Beatrice's holiday lunch.

Ian loved spending Christmas at Sandringham. The village was as picturesque as any postcard. Thatched cottages were covered in snow and there was a castle with a proper turret. Ian's favorite event was the Sandringham Christmas Craft Food & Gift Fair. It took up the whole square and there was entertainment and booths selling crafts and photography. That year, Santa Claus had sat on an ice sculpture of a sled and Ian laughed that his red suit must be cold and wet.

But the whole reason they were there was to keep Spencer away from a girl he met at the Dorchester whom he had promised to take on a world cruise. Instead, Spencer disappeared with a brunette who sold a delicious marinade. Ian remembered pacing up and down for hours, waiting for Spencer to return.

"Where were you last night? You weren't home when I went to bed," Ian said when Spencer appeared in the morning. "Don't tell me you were with that girl selling marinade."

"I didn't sleep with her, if that's what you're asking. I was helping her package marinade," Spencer said huffily. "We went to dinner after drinks and I asked her to join me at Princess Beatrice's lunch." He glanced at his watch. "I'm picking her up in two hours."

Ian bumped his coffee cup and liquid spilled on the white tablecloth.

"You invited a shopgirl you met at the Christmas markets to a lunch given by the Queen's granddaughter?" he asked incredulously.

"Her name is Samantha, and she's not just a shopgirl. Her father is some big American businessman, and he's sponsoring her marinade business. One of the supermarket chains in America is about to take it on."

"And you believe her?" Ian scoffed. "What would she be doing with a stall in the British countryside?"

"Her mother is British and she set up a stall because she wants her marinades to be authentic. Here, look at her Instagram. These are some of her investors." He scrolled through his phone. "There's a photo of her with Ashton Kutcher and one with that guy, Mark Cuban, who owns an NBA basketball team."

Ian took the phone. Samantha was pretty. She wore tight pants and a white sweater and her skin had a golden glow.

"You haven't even known her for twenty-four hours." He handed back the phone. "Do you really think you should take her to a royal lunch?"

"At least it will be someone new." Spencer wolfed down his eggs. "Princess Beatrice invites the same people to all her parties. I've known them since we were in nappies."

"How was it?" Ian asked. "Did you and Samantha have a good time?"

The lunch had been for the young members of the royal family, so Lady Violet hadn't attended. Spencer said Ian was welcome to join him and Samantha, but Ian had decided to stay at the cottage.

Spencer walked straight to the sideboard and poured a cup of tea. His cheeks were pale and there was a dusting of snow on his collar.

"It didn't quite go as I hoped." He took off his coat and folded it over a chair.

"Don't tell me Samantha started flirting with Prince Harry," Ian said, smiling. "All the Americans love him. They think he's the most accessible royal, even though he's married."

"She didn't flirt with anyone." Spencer fiddled with his teacup. "She did try to sell them marinade."

"What are you talking about?" Ian put down his pen.

"It turns out her father isn't a successful businessman. She doesn't have a father; he left before she was born. And the photos on her Instagram page are at some celebrity event she worked as a caterer in Los Angeles."

"A lot of Americans work when they're in college," Ian replied. "They could still be sponsoring her marinade."

"It's not even *her* marinade," Spencer sighed. "She was minding a booth for a friend. She thought if she could get members of the royal family to try the marinade, her friend would give her a permanent job."

"She wanted the guests to sample her marinade?" Ian said in horror.

"She went out to the car while I was getting our drinks and brought in a platter of pork chops and little pots of marinade," Spencer said miserably.

Spencer's skin had turned a ghostly white and there were deep lines on his forehead.

"Oh God," Ian groaned.

Ian tried to imagine the drawing room at Sandringham House with its portraits of King George V and the Queen Mother on the wall. There was a library filled with books over a hundred years old, and the dining room had candelabras given to Queen Elizabeth by Winston Churchill.

"You don't understand," Spencer continued. "Princess Beatrice is on a health kick. It was a vegan lunch. The cook spent days putting together a plant-based meal everyone would enjoy: macaroni and cheese made with tofu and vegan linguine and a cauliflower steak you'd have to blindfold me to eat," Spencer said, and Ian had never seen him look so guilty. "Samantha stood in the middle of the drawing room passing around the most heavenly smelling pork. Princess Beatrice had to ask her to leave—she didn't have a choice."

Ian's stomach turned and he cringed. Lady Violet wouldn't be happy. The event would feed the royal gossip mill for weeks.

"Did you find out the secret ingredient?" Ian asked finally.

"It was molasses. I should have known Samantha and I weren't meant to be together when she told me," Spencer grunted. "I hate molasses. When I was a child my mother made me drink molasses with milk and I always poured it down the drain."

Ian sipped his cognac and walked to the window. The stars were silver confetti against the night sky and Fifth Avenue was bright with cars. If only Sabrina weren't working, they could take a horse-and-buggy ride in Central Park or have dinner at some intimate restaurant.

Spencer was always falling for women; he was a puppy who couldn't live without love. Ian was different; he had never felt like this before. And he was positive Sabrina felt the same. But he didn't stand a chance unless he came clean about everything, and what if she didn't understand?

Sabrina thought he was Lord Braxton! She probably imagined their lives together would consist of eating at swanky restaurants in Chelsea and having front-row theater tickets at Covent Garden. He did those things with Spencer, but what if he quit the foundation and started something of his own? Then all the perks—the occasional suit Spencer bought for Ian when he visited his tailor on Savile Row, the holidays in Spain and Portugal—would disappear.

Of course, they'd be invited to Braxton Hall for special occasions; Lady Violet and Spencer were like family. But they'd have to live in a tiny flat and they wouldn't be able to afford holidays and expensive dinners. Sabrina would never go for that. She was used to staying at the Plaza Hotel and dining at the Palm Court.

His throat was scratchy and he wondered if he was coming down with a fever. He put the cognac on the table and grabbed his coat. He'd go to Duane Reade and buy cough syrup and some paperback spy novels. He had to do something to soothe his throat and stop thinking about Sabrina. If he didn't, he didn't know what he'd do.

Ian stepped off the elevator and ran straight into Tabitha's father's new wife. Her hair smelled of hairspray and she wore an evening dress.

"Trina! What are you doing at the Plaza?" Ian exclaimed. "I thought you and Tabitha's father went back to Milwaukee."

"Ian!" Trina beamed. "This is a pleasant surprise. I wanted to thank you for recommending Fortnum and Mason's orange marmalade. I bought a jar in the food hall at Macy's and Scott and I think it's delicious."

"You came to the Plaza to thank me for recommending marmalade?" Ian said, puzzled.

"No, I'm here to pick up theater tickets from the concierge," she corrected. "We decided to stay in New York for a few days, there's no better place for a honeymoon. Spencer left us tickets to see *Anastasia* on Broadway tonight since he couldn't use them."

"Why not?" Ian asked. "He had the evening all planned."

"Tabitha told him she'd worked as an usher and saw the production a dozen times. Spencer immediately said they'd do something else." She leaned forward conspiratorially. "She's meeting him at the Rainbow Room. He reserved the private dining room." Her face broke into a smile. "Christmas in New York is even better than I imagined. Scott and I had our wedding lunch at the Four Seasons, and now Tabitha has been invited to dinner at the most glamorous location in Manhattan." She patted her hair. "It really does make you believe in Christmas miracles!"

Or Spencer's endless allowance, Ian thought grimly.

A pain gripped his chest and his throat was so dry, he could barely swallow.

"How do you know Spencer reserved the private dining room?" he asked.

"I heard Tabitha on the phone. She was worried she didn't have anything to wear, and Spencer said it didn't matter because they'd be dining alone. Then he offered to send her a dress from Bloomingdale's but she declined." Trina tipped her head. "Tabitha isn't that kind of girl. She doesn't like to accept presents from men."

"Where is Tabitha now?" Ian said wildly.

"Getting ready," Trina said. "Spencer had to run some errands so he's sending a car for her. I lent her my Chanel perfume. Scott bought it for me from the duty-free store when we went on a cruise. Perfume is very important—"

"I really have to go," Ian interrupted. "It was nice seeing you."

"Don't forget to visit us in Milwaukee," Trina called after him. "We'll have so many memories to share, I feel like we're old friends."

Ian waited while the valet summoned a taxi. Spencer hadn't said anything about a change of plans. And what was he doing at the Rainbow Room! Ian had read about it on the Plaza's list of New York's most romantic venues. It was on the sixty-fifth floor of Rockefeller Center with walls of windows and 360-degree views. The menu changed daily and there was some world-renowned chef with better credentials than the chefs at Buckingham Palace.

A sick feeling formed in Ian's stomach. Spencer had sworn to Ian he wouldn't spend more money on Tabitha, and now he was taking her to one of the most expensive restaurants in New York. Not to mention that heights made Spencer dizzy. There was only one reason he would pick the Rainbow Room, and that's because he planned on getting down on one knee and turning over his great-grandmother's engagement ring.

But the engagement ring was in the safe at the Plaza along with all the Braxton jewels. Trina said that Spencer was doing errands before he met Tabitha. He could easily run in to Van Cleef & Arpels and pick up one of the diamond rings that glittered in the window. Knowing Spencer, he'd buy something to match: diamond teardrop earrings, or a tiara the salesgirl convinced him the future Lady Braxton must have on her engagement.

The cab pulled up in front of the Plaza and Ian hopped inside.

"The Rainbow Room," he said to the driver. "And please hurry, I have to stop an international incident."

The taxi let him out in front of Rockefeller Center and Ian stepped out. A line of brightly lit fir trees and gold angels wrapped in lights surrounded the giant Christmas tree. Ian had to crane his neck to take it all in. Every branch held an ornament or a colored light and the top was adorned with a silver star.

Rockefeller Center was filled with couples holding hands and Ian wished he were meeting Sabrina. They could go ice-skating and drink hot chocolate at one of the little tables facing the rink. But there was no time to think about that. He had to get to the elevator before it was too late.

"Can I help you?" a guard asked when he entered the lobby.

"I'm going to the Rainbow Room," Ian said.

"The main restaurant is closed for a holiday function," the guard answered.

"I'm not eating at the restaurant." Ian tried to hide his impatience. "I'm going to the private dining room. The reservation is under the name Lord Braxton."

"Can I have your name please?" the guard asked.

"It's Ian Westing," Ian said.

"I'm sorry, the only person on the list besides Lord Braxton is a young lady." The guard glanced up from his computer.

"What's the young lady's name?" Ian moved closer.

"Lord Braxton didn't give her name."

"What do you mean, he didn't give her name?" Ian said, frustration bubbling up inside him.

"Many of our clients want to be discreet. Once the private dining room was booked completely anonymously," he said and for a moment he seemed almost approachable. "It turned out to be the whole cast of *Friends*."

Ian took out his phone. "I'll call Lord Braxton and tell him I'm here."

"Cell phone usage isn't allowed in Rockefeller Center." The scowl returned to his face. "You'll have to turn that off or give it to me."

Ian counted to ten the way he learned when he was at Harrow. Most things could be solved if he just took a moment to figure them out.

"Then you call Lord Braxton." He handed him his phone.

"I can't use a private individual's phone." The guard appraised Ian warily. "But if you give me Lord Braxton's number, I can call him on the security line."

Ian gave him Spencer's number and waited while the guard talked into his phone.

"You can go up." The guard pointed to the elevator. "Next time have Lord Braxton put you on the guest list. We take the security of our guests very seriously."

"Ian, what are you doing here?" Spencer said when Ian flung open the door of the private dining room.

It had taken Ian twenty minutes to find his way through the maze of rooms on the sixty-fifth floor. The private dining room was tucked into a corner at the end of a mirrored hallway. Double oak doors led into an entryway with plush red carpeting and gold wallpaper.

"What am I doing? Why are you here?" Ian demanded, and for a moment his eyes were drawn to the view. The Empire State Building was directly in front of them and the Brooklyn Bridge loomed in the distance. The tops of skyscrapers seemed close enough to touch, and the cars below were tiny Matchbox figures.

Spencer sat at the end of a long table with two place settings. Glass chandeliers dangled from the ceiling and candles flickered on the sideboard. There was a fireplace with a crackling fire and a small Christmas tree decorated with silver and gold lights.

"I ran into Trina at the Plaza and she told me everything," Ian continued without waiting for Spencer to answer. "You booked the private dining room and you sent a car to pick up Tabitha because first you had to run some important errands." Ian felt himself growing angry all over again. "Really, Spencer, you promised you weren't going to do anything impulsive. And the Rainbow Room! It's on every list of top places to propose in New York."

"You think I asked Tabitha to dinner to propose?" Spencer raised his eyebrows.

"I haven't looked at your recent charges. I hope you didn't buy up Van Cleef and Arpels."

"I haven't been near a jewelry store," Spencer returned. "I did invite Tabitha to dinner to ask her a question. But it wasn't whether she'd marry me."

Ian glanced at Spencer to see if he was joking, but he looked perfectly serious.

"What kind of question?" Ian wanted to know.

"The concierge told me about a New Year's Ball at the Rainbow Room. It's black tie and dinner is six courses and there's a twelve-piece band." Spencer fiddled with his tie. "But then I got a call asking if I'd attend a New Year's Eve fundraiser for the Animal Haven Shelter. They rescue animals from overseas." His voice was tight. "Last year they saved fifty dogs. The event is at some club in SoHo and there's Mexican food and a DJ, but you know how I feel about animal rights. I couldn't say no."

"What does that have to do with Tabitha?"

"I already asked Tabitha to the ball at the Rainbow Room," Spencer explained. "I worried she'd be upset if I told her we were attending the fundraiser instead. If we had dinner at the Rainbow Room tonight, she might not be angry about missing the ball."

"You did all this just to ask her to a different party?" Ian waved at the crystal water glasses and white tablecloth set with fine china.

"I'm not the kind of guy who breaks his word," Spencer answered. "Anyway, it doesn't matter. Tabitha isn't coming."

"Of course she's coming," Ian responded. "Trina said she was getting ready."

"I got a message from the security guard." Spencer shook his head. "Tabitha's brother, Stephen, hurt his wrist ice-skating and they're on their way to urgent care. She probably won't make it at all."

"Oh, I see." Ian pulled out a chair and sat opposite Spencer.

The room really did look beautiful. Urns were filled with white and red roses and there was a grand piano. Pinpoint lighting illuminated framed paintings, and the floor was a sleek mahogany.

"You think I'm crazy to put so much effort into a date. But I'm more like you than you think." Spencer took a roll from the silver bread basket. "Doing things for other people makes me happy. And planning something special for someone I care about is the best feeling in the world."

Ian was quiet for a while.

"I don't think you're crazy," Ian said. "I know exactly what you mean."

"You can't." Spencer buttered the roll. "You've never come close to falling in love: the feeling of anticipation when you wake up in the morning that's better than a jolt of caffeine. When you're together everything is exciting: hearing a song in an Uber and discovering you like the same music, eating warm pretzels from a stand and finding out you both like them with ketchup instead of mustard." His eyes traveled to the window. "Watching the New York skyline change from pink to black and never wanting the moment to end." He turned back to Ian. "One day the right woman will come along, and I'll know in an instant I want to spend the rest of my life with her just like my parents did. But for now there's nothing better than sharing things with a pretty girl and trying to make her happy at the same time."

"I know exactly how you feel," Ian said darkly. "You meet someone completely out of the blue and you don't even think about love. But you keep running into her and you're taken by her beauty and charm. You go to bed each night hoping the feeling will pass because anything else would make life impossible. But the next morning it's even stronger and all you can do is hope that every mistake you've made can be washed away like the slush on the sidewalk." Ian's throat was dry and he took a sip of water. "Because you have to be together or you'll never be happy again."

Spencer looked at Ian curiously.

"What are you talking about?" he asked.

"I think I'm falling in love with Sabrina," Ian said, admitting it to himself for the first time. "But I've lied to her about everything, and when she finds out she'll never want to see me again."

"You don't know how to lie," Spencer chuckled. "It's as foreign to you as speaking Chinese or learning to deep-sea dive."

Ian told Spencer about meeting Sabrina at the Rose Club after midnight on the night they'd arrived. He recounted running into her when he was having afternoon tea at the Palm Court with the woman from the Met. Sabrina had assumed that the Braxton collection belonged to Ian and that he was Lord Braxton.

He went over all the times he'd tried to tell her the truth: when they visited the Empire State Building and Ian had to dash out of the taxi because he was late to meet Spencer at Tiffany's. At the Snowflake Ball when he had been about to tell her everything and Ed Sheeran appeared onstage. Watching rom-coms in the East Village and ice-skating in Central Park and the urgent call from Lady Violet. Forgetting to include a card with the gift, and the concierge telling Sabrina it was from Lord Braxton.

"It's like the plot of that Mark Twain novel we read at Harrow," Spencer said when Ian finished. "*The Prince and the Pauper.*"

"You're not a prince, and as you keep pointing out I'm not exactly a pauper." Ian loosened his collar.

"If you ever need money, my mother would be happy to lend it to you—or the foundation could give you a loan," Spencer said seriously.

"My salary is perfectly adequate." Ian shook his head. "But Sabrina is used to staying at the Plaza and eating caviar and lobster rolls. She thinks I can buy two pairs of John Lobb shoes at a time and I've got a collection of priceless jewels in the family vault."

"I haven't met Sabrina, but I've known you since we were fourteen. You would never fall for a girl who was only interested in the size of your bank account or the fancy prefix before your name."

"Even if Sabrina didn't care that I'm not going to inherit one of the great houses in England, she'll care very much that I lied," Ian said earnestly. "I told her I want to keep seeing her after I leave. But once she finds out the truth, she'll delete my email and block my number on her phone."

"You *have* gotten yourself into a situation," Spencer agreed. "We have to figure a way out."

"But how?" Ian asked.

There was a knock at the door and a waiter appeared in the doorway.

"Would you like me to serve the first course?" the waiter asked.

A silver cart was rolled into the dining room. There were dishes covered with domes and salads arranged artfully in bowls.

"Do you remember when we were at Harrow and we begged the cook for extra desserts? She smuggled a whole tray of sweets into our dorm," Spencer said to Ian.

"She was afraid you were too thin and wanted to fatten you up," Ian recalled, smiling.

The cook had delivered two dozen jam roly-polies, and Spencer shared them with all the other boys.

"We ate every one until we got stomachaches and talked about school and girls," Spencer said.

"What are you saying?" Ian asked.

"There's nothing that can't be solved over a thick steak and a pudding." Spencer waved at the table. "Tabitha isn't coming and I already paid for the meal. We may as well eat it."

Ian filled his plate with sweet potato and buttermilk puree.

"All right, why not?" he agreed, wishing Sabrina were beside him. "But don't let me see the bill. It will only give me heartburn."

Sixteen

Sabrina sat in the living room of Grayson's suite and waited for him to appear. He had still been on his conference call when she arrived, and she busied herself reading over her notes.

It was hard to concentrate when all she could think about was cocktails with Ian at the Rose Club. Whenever she pictured him saying he wanted to keep seeing her, she felt a delicious warmth. But then she wondered how that could work, and the warmth was replaced by an uneasy nervousness.

What if Ian invited her to a special event in London? She could barely afford subway fare and a breakfast bagel, let alone last-minute flights! It would be awkward to ask Ian to cover her expenses when he thought she was the kind of woman who racked up enough points to fly first class whenever she pleased.

It would be just as bad if Ian visited her in New York. Her job with Grayson would be over and she'd be back in Queens. She couldn't show him her apartment when he was used to staying at the Plaza and having afternoon tea at the Palm Court.

The prospect of not seeing him again was unthinkable. Even

now, sitting and waiting for Grayson, she had a heady sensation as if she was keeping some wonderful secret. Ian was kind and handsome and being with him made her happy.

"Sabrina, I'm sorry to keep you waiting." Grayson emerged from the bedroom. "The translator wasn't able to be on the call and my Japanese isn't very good. It took forever for Mr. Tanaka and I to understand each other."

"You speak Japanese?" Sabrina asked in surprise.

"I learned a lot of things when I was young. But if I don't use them, they become as rusty as an old bicycle," he chuckled.

He opened the room service menu and handed it to Sabrina.

"I promised you dinner—please order anything you like."

Sabrina took the menu and scanned it quickly.

"A bowl of soup and a salad would be fine." She handed it back.

"Is that charm new?" Grayson wondered. "I haven't seen it before."

Sabrina had forgotten to take off the charm bracelet! She didn't want to tell Grayson about Ian. Their relationship was too new and she didn't want to spoil it.

"It's pretty, isn't it?" She held it up. "It's the Plaza Hotel."

"It's lovely." Grayson admired it. His eyes traveled from the charm to Sabrina. "You look different from the first time I saw you. It's not your hair, it's something else."

"Who wouldn't look different staying at the Plaza?" Sabrina said lightly. "The bathroom is filled with face creams that don't have labels because they're so exclusive. Every time I enter the suite, there's a platter of chocolate truffles and a pot of coffee so fresh, I can imagine the beans being ground and roasted. Not to mention the butler whose job is to say, 'Good evening, Miss Post.

May I recommend the almond milk with vanilla and spices?'" she finished, smiling. "I'll never be the same person again."

"The butlers at the Plaza are terrific," Grayson agreed and Sabrina was relieved to change the subject. "When I was a butler I was so proud of knowing everything about the guests: the ages of their children and which television shows they watched." He sat back in his chair. "Except Kay, of course. I thought I knew Kay, but she kept parts of herself secret. When she told me the truth, I almost didn't believe her."

Plaza Hotel, April 1961

"You know what I envy about Eloise?" Kay said, turning the channel on the television. "That she's six years old and doesn't have to fall in love. Falling in love is worse than having the measles. At least when you have the measles, people see you're uncomfortable and offer sympathy. When you're in love you can be in so much pain you can't breathe, but others think you're perfectly happy."

"Love can be wonderful," Grayson countered, arranging melba toast and cottage cheese on a plate.

It was evening and Kay was watching her nightly programming: the six o'clock news followed by *Bonanza* and *The Ed Sullivan Show*.

"That's right, you and Veronica are still exchanging sappy letters." Kay picked up a piece of melba toast. "Is Veronica enjoying living in a bedsit in London and eating her meals in a communal dining room?"

"It's not a bedsit, it's a room in a large house on Grosvenor

Square." Grayson stirred Ovaltine into warm milk. "And it's not a communal dining room. She eats dinner with the family where she's staying."

Veronica had been in London for three months and at first Grayson missed her so much he barely got through his day. But then he began to receive her letters describing the art school that she loved, and the student quarters she couldn't stand. There was no heating, and on the first night a mouse ran across her bed.

Her parents set her up in the Belgravia mansion of a family friend. How could she refuse? She had her own bathroom and dinners were prepared by the family's cook. At the end of the third month, Veronica wrote and said she was going to stay longer; there was so much to explore. She had only visited the Victoria and Albert Museum once and she hadn't seen a play in the West End.

Grayson didn't mind. It gave him time to work extra shifts and save up for a diamond ring.

"I'm not drinking Ovaltine tonight." Kay shook her head. "Fix me a gin and tonic."

"You almost never drink in your suite," Grayson reminded her. "It makes you depressed."

Ed Sullivan bounded onto the television screen and Kay flinched as if she'd been struck.

"I'm going to be depressed anyway." She put out her hand. "I may as well be drunk."

Ed Sullivan finished his monologue and a fresh-faced man of about thirty sat on the couch opposite him. He had dark curly hair and wore tight slacks and a ribbed sweater.

"I made him a star." Kay lit a cigarette and stared at the television. "Andy Williams was a nineteen-year-old kid from Ohio and I hired him and his brothers to sing on movie soundtracks at MGM. Then I put them in my cabaret and we became the biggest hit in Las Vegas. We sold out shows for a year!

"His brothers decided to do their own thing, so I made Andy a solo star. Who do you think wrote his top-twenty hit, 'Promise Me, Love'?" She warmed to her theme. "What thanks do I get? Andy is going to spend his summer on a European tour so teenyboppers can throw wadded-up Kleenex at him. While I sit here like those god-awful prunes you serve with my breakfast," she sighed. "Love is worse than the measles and the mumps combined. I'm never letting Eloise grow up."

Grayson's jaw dropped open and he almost spilled the gin.

"Don't look so shocked." Kay glanced up at him. "If Andy was in his fifties and I was thirty, we'd be like all the other couples waltzing through the Plaza's lobby. I might not have platinum blond hair or the bust of a Marilyn Monroe, but Andy always said I had great legs."

"I'm just surprised." Grayson regained his composure. He filled the glass with ice and handed it to Kay.

"Why do you think I spent all that time abroad?" Kay accepted the drink. "It wasn't only to do research for Eloise in Paris and Moscow. Andy and I wanted to spend time together away from photographers. And the only reason I filmed *Funny Face* was because I decided I had to be mature and break it off." Her face crumpled and she turned back to the television. "But I couldn't find a good reason to break up. Andy's good-looking and talented and the sweetest person I ever met."

Grayson didn't know what to say. In the three years he had been Kay's butler, she'd hardly ever shared anything personal.

"Don't worry about me, that's why I have Eloise." She sipped her cocktail. "I'll write something new—how about *Eloise in Tahiti*? Eloise in a pink bathing suit and Nanny drinking pink daiquiris and Eloise's mother in a bikini like Sandra Dee in that Gidget movie."

"*Eloise in Tahiti* would be a bestseller," Grayson said encouragingly.

"If you ever take my advice, listen to me now." Kay wasn't paying attention. "Have something of your own, even if it's selling vacuum cleaners or life insurance. Because if you let love rule your life, you'll end up sitting in a hotel room drinking a gin and tonic with too much ice."

"I'm sorry, Miss Thompson," Grayson said. "Did I use too much ice?"

Kay handed him back the glass. "Pour out the ice. I need to make room for more gin."

It was almost midnight and Grayson unlocked the door of his apartment. After he finished his butler shift he'd polished silverware in the Plaza's kitchen. His back hurt from being on his feet all day and he never got enough sleep. But in a few weeks he'd be able to go into the Delage jewelry store and put a diamond ring on layaway.

The mailman had slipped the mail under his door and he grabbed the airmail envelope. Inside were three sheets of writing paper scribbled over in Veronica's flowery cursive.

Dear Grayson,
I wish I could picture you reading this but you never let me see your apartment. I'll take a stab at

it anyway: you're wearing your butler uniform and you're sitting at your kitchen table, drinking hot cocoa. You do keep fresh milk in your fridge, don't you? And some fruit and vegetables. It's important to eat well.

I'm rambling but I want to pretend we're having a chat the way we did when I was staying in Becky's apartment. We'd sit at the dining table and eat Becky's mother's cold cuts and talk about everything.

I don't know how to write what I have to say next. I won't be returning to New York anytime soon.

Grayson stopped and gripped the writing paper. He filled a glass with water and started reading again.

My father's business has gone bust. It was a combination of higher rents and poor sales and a little bad luck at the races. That's what my father wrote; my mother's letter put it differently. They had to sell the house and the furniture, and even my father's beloved Jaguar. They're moving in with my mother's sister in Kentucky until my father gets back on his feet.

Which leaves me. My parents decided I should stay here in London with the Magnussons. They've offered to keep me for free if I help look after their daughter, Lily. I'm teaching her to draw and she's showing me how to care for her pet rabbit.

I guess I won't be staying in art school and

returning to Vassar is impossible. But I didn't really know what I wanted to be. I just knew what I didn't want: which was to get married and start a family.

I can picture you now and you're looking for the brandy you have stashed in the kitchen. Don't do it, Grayson. Drinking late at night gives you a headache.

Please don't worry about me. This isn't a life sentence; it's a temporary setback. Isn't there some cliché about April showers bringing May flowers? I'm going to hang on to that because clichés are based on the truth.

All my love,
Veronica

Grayson found a piece of paper and sat down to reply. He would use the money he was saving for the ring to buy Veronica a plane ticket to New York. They didn't need a church wedding or a reception at the Plaza. A justice of the peace would marry them and they'd live in Grayson's apartment. Veronica could go to secretary school or train to be a nurse.

Before he wrote the first sentence, he knew it would never work. Veronica had lasted four days in the student lodgings in London. She'd be like a flower without sun in the Bronx. And could he imagine her eating a brown bag sandwich at a typist's desk while her friends lunched at the Four Seasons and shopped at Bendel's?

Veronica had agreed to stay in London because it was the only way to save her pride. Nothing he could say would dissuade her and it would only cause friction between them.

Grayson crumpled the paper and pictured Kay, drinking a gin and tonic and watching Andy Williams on *The Ed Sullivan Show*. Kay said he shouldn't let love rule his future, but what choice did he have? Veronica had burst into his life like a golden comet and he couldn't let her go.

He rummaged through the cabinet under the sink and found the bottle of brandy. Then he sat down at the kitchen table and reached for a glass.

The phone rang in the suite's living room and Grayson answered it.

"Excuse me," he said to Sabrina.

It was 9:00 P.M. and Sabrina wondered what Ian was doing. Was he still lingering in the Rose Club, listening to jazz and reading a book by the fireplace? Or had he decided to go out and see the Christmas windows on Fifth Avenue?

"That was my Japanese client, Mr. Tanaka." Grayson hung up the phone. "I'm sorry, I have to call him back. We'll have to continue tomorrow."

"That's all right," Sabrina said, hoping it wasn't too late to catch Ian. "Though I can't wait to find out what happened. Veronica doesn't seem like the kind of woman who would be down for long."

"Sabrina, I want to thank you," Grayson said when she walked to the door. "It's not often that an old man gets to recount his past to a good listener. I'm enjoying myself more than I thought."

"It's a wonderful story." Sabrina nodded.

He was about to say something and changed his mind.

"You really do look different," he said instead. "Staying at the

Plaza agrees with you. I'm glad you're getting something out of this too."

The elevator doors opened and Sabrina stepped into the lobby. Every time she saw the Christmas tree—tall and fragrant and decorated with colored ornaments—she wanted to pinch herself to prove she wasn't dreaming. She really was staying at the Plaza Hotel over Christmas.

Did she look different? Her hair was shiny because she was using the Plaza's shampoo and the lotions made her skin smooth and buttery. But it wasn't that. And it wasn't the pink cashmere jacket that Grayson gave her or the silver charm that tinkled on her wrist. If she was different, it was because she couldn't stop thinking about Ian. All she wanted was to see him again.

"Miss Post." The concierge stopped her. "What are you doing here?"

"I was going to the business center," she replied.

"Lord Braxton's reservation was at seven p.m." The concierge glanced at his watch. "That was two hours ago."

"But I had to work tonight," Sabrina said, perplexed.

"If you don't mind my saying, it's not the kind of reservation you want to miss." The concierge rubbed his forehead. "The private dining room at the Rainbow Room! And Lord Braxton hinted at the menu. . . ."

Sabrina tried to think. Had Ian been planning a special evening, and if so, why hadn't he said anything?

"I'll try calling him." Sabrina pressed Ian's number but it went straight to voice mail.

"I can have a house car take you," the concierge prompted.

Sabrina glanced down at her slacks and sweater. "But I'm not dressed."

"You look lovely, but it is the Rainbow Room." He studied her. "Why don't you run up and change. I'm sure Lord Braxton won't mind waiting a little longer."

"Do you think I should?" Sabrina hesitated. "What if he isn't there?"

"It's not every day that a beautiful woman joins a man for dinner at the most romantic restaurant in New York." The concierge returned to his desk. "If I were Lord Braxton, I'd wait as long as I had to."

Twenty minutes later Sabrina sat in the back of a white Rolls-Royce. Her hair curled around her shoulders and she wore lipstick and a floral perfume.

She had debated wearing the party dress she had owned since college. But at the last minute she slipped on Grayson's black cocktail dress. The neckline was lower than she was used to, and the skirt was a bit short. But she loved the silky fabric and the way it hugged her body.

"We're here, Miss Post." The driver stopped in front of Rockefeller Center. "Would you like me to wait?"

Would Ian still be there? What would she do if he weren't?

"No, thank you," she said with more confidence than she felt. "I'm going to be fine."

The lobby of the Rockefeller Center had a black marble floor and twin escalators. Giant wreaths lined the walls and there was a Christmas tree decorated with red and green tinsel.

"Can I help you?" the security guard asked.

"I'm meeting Lord Braxton in the Rainbow Room." She approached the podium.

"You must be the young lady." The security guard beamed. He pointed down a corridor. "The private elevator will take you to the sixty-fifth floor."

On the sixty-fifth floor, the coat check girl directed her down a winding hallway. She pushed open double doors and entered a small foyer with floor to ceiling windows. Ian sat at a table in the private dining room. A fire roared in the fireplace and there was the scent of candles and some kind of sweet dessert.

"Ian." She entered the room tentatively.

Ian looked up and Sabrina's heart skipped a beat. He looked so handsome. He wore a navy blazer and the corduroy slacks he had been wearing at the Rose Club.

"Sabrina." He jumped up. "What are you doing here?"

"I tried to call but your phone is off," she began. "I wasn't going to come at all. But the concierge insisted, and I thought . . ." She noticed his empty dessert plate. "It's late and you've already eaten. Maybe I should have stayed at the Plaza."

Ian was quiet as if he was taking it all in. He crossed the room and took her hand.

"I finished dinner but then the strangest thing happened," he said. "I took the elevator to the Rockefeller Center's lobby and realized I forgot the key to my suite."

"Your key?" Sabrina echoed.

"I must have taken it out of my pocket." Ian kept talking. "So I took the elevator back to the sixty-fifth floor."

"Did you find it?" Sabrina wondered.

"I asked in the kitchen but no one had seen it." He shook his head. "I was about to search under the table."

"So if it weren't for the key, you'd be driving back to the Plaza while I was in a car coming to the Rainbow Room?" she said slowly.

He put his arm around her and kissed her. She kissed him back and he pulled her closer.

"You know what's the best thing about the Plaza Hotel?" he whispered.

The imprint of his mouth was on her lips and she felt almost giddy.

"There are so many things, I can't think of just one," Sabrina answered.

"I can." He kissed her again. "That instead of replaceable key cards, they have those ridiculous old-fashioned keys that are too heavy to keep in your pocket."

Ian ordered another dessert and they ate pecan pie with bourbon and watched the lights twinkling on the Empire State Building.

"When I was ten, our teacher asked us to write our own version of a Christmas story," Sabrina said between bites. "Most kids wrote about Frosty the Snowman, but I chose *Eloise at Christmastime*. In my version it's Christmas morning and Eloise is opening her presents. The manager, Mr. Salomone, gave her nonskid pink slippers so she stops sliding through the lobby, and the valet gave her a silver whistle so she can call a taxi whenever she liked. Her mother sent dresses and tights from Paris because her flight was canceled and she couldn't be there for Christmas.

"Eloise put on a new dress and she and Nanny and Weenie and Skipperdoo went down to the Palm Court for Christmas brunch. The menu had Eloise's favorite dishes: macaroni and cheese, jelly and cream cheese sandwiches, and miniature cupcakes with pink icing.

"After lunch they went back up to their suite so Nanny could take a nap. Eloise played with her new things but she wasn't happy. She stuffed her presents into pillowcases and dragged them down to the lobby. Then she loaded them into a house car and instructed the driver to drive around the city.

"Eloise delivered toys to children at New York Presbyterian Hospital and dropped some off at an orphanage. She left a pile of books in front of the New York Public Library. When she came back to the Plaza, all she had left was Weenie's dog collar and some pink taffy.

"Then she went up to her suite and called her mother in Paris to thank her for her gift and said it was the best Christmas she ever had," Sabrina finished. "My teacher gave me a B plus. It was well written, but she doubted that any little girl would give away her Christmas presents," Sabrina said, laughing. "That's when I decided I wanted to be a writer when I grew up."

"You never said you wanted to be a writer." Ian looked up from his dessert.

It would be so easy to tell Ian the truth—that she was a struggling journalist—but she couldn't imagine doing anything else. One day she was going to write something that would make a difference in people's lives.

But the lights sparkled on the Christmas tree and Ian leaned forward and kissed her and the words dissolved like the whipped cream on top of the pecan pie.

"What did you want to be when you grew up?" she asked when they parted.

"Besides James Bond?" Ian grinned. "I guess what I'm doing now. I always wanted to help others."

She ate a bite of pecan pie and nodded. "You're lucky to do what you love."

"I have always felt lucky." He touched her hand. "But I've never felt luckier than I do tonight."

The elevator door opened on the fifteenth floor and Sabrina fumbled for her key.

The whole evening had been easy and relaxed. Driving back to the Plaza, they talked about everything. She wondered if she should invite Ian inside. So what if Ian noticed her beat-up running shoes or tattered laptop case? She could make up an excuse that she became attached to them in college and couldn't let them go.

"If you'd like to come in for a nightcap, I'm sure the maids left glasses of sherry," she said, trying to hide her nervousness.

"The last few times we stood here, something interrupted us." Ian chose his words carefully. "There was a phone call about Tabitha or you had to go to the business center, or I missed Lady Violet's call. Tonight there's nothing standing in our way and I can't think of anything I'd like more."

Ian stopped and Sabrina heard her own heart beating.

"But I won't."

"You won't?" she repeated, looking up at him.

"You're beautiful and bright and when we're together, I feel happy and alive. Is it all right if we wait and savor that feeling?"

"Of course." She nodded, not trusting herself to say more.

Ian leaned forward and kissed her. He tasted of pecan and cinnamon and she kissed him back.

"I was afraid you would think I'm a stodgy Brit who doesn't know how to have fun." He smiled. "But it's the opposite of that. I know when I've found something important, and I don't want to mess it up."

Sabrina pulled on a robe and slippers and padded into the suite's living room.

In three days it would be New Year's Day and the Christmas lights on the Pulitzer Fountain would be turned off. The Christmas tree in the Plaza's lobby would be carted away and all the tinsel and wreaths would be put in boxes.

But there was still so much to look forward to. Grayson had to finish his story, and Ian wanted to see her again, and who knew what would happen on New Year's Eve.

She pulled her robe tighter and walked to the bedroom. It was Christmas week and she was staying in a suite at the Plaza Hotel. Anything could happen; all she had to do was believe.

Seventeen

Ian entered his suite and pulled off his jacket. God, what a night! First he'd accused Spencer of planning to propose to Tabitha, and then he'd admitted to Spencer everything that had happened with Sabrina. And just as he told himself there was no hope of things working out, Sabrina had appeared in the private dining room like some magnificent mirage.

It was late and he was so tired. His head throbbed and his throat was dry and he wanted to take a bath and go to bed. But they were leaving in four days and he and Spencer hadn't figured out how to tell Sabrina the truth.

Sabrina hadn't said anything about coming to London. What if she thought Ian was merely a charming diversion while she was staying at the Plaza? She didn't have time to flit across the Atlantic to see a man she had known for four days.

Lady Violet had encouraged him to have a holiday romance. But what he felt for Sabrina was so much more. His stomach churned and he wondered if Sabrina felt differently. He remembered when Annalise didn't return to Oxford and he couldn't get her out of his mind. He'd spent the spring holidays at Braxton Hall reading spy novels until one morning Lady Violet entered the library and found him sitting by the window.

"You've been reading the same book for three days, and you're the fastest reader I know." Lady Violet joined him on the window seat.

"I like this book." Ian closed the book he was reading. "It's an old James Bond I found on the bookshelf."

"I didn't come here to talk about books or about Spencer." Violet sipped her tea. "I came to talk about Annalise."

"There's nothing to talk about." Ian stiffened. "She's not returning to Oxford."

"Spencer told me all about it." Violet nodded. "You've been as much fun to live with as our dog, Millie, after she gave birth to eleven puppies."

"Spencer can get another roommate," Ian said sharply.

"He wouldn't dream of it. You're his best friend." Violet's voice was soft. "He's worried about you. He asked me to help."

"That's very kind, but there's nothing you can do."

"Do you know what I miss most about Peter?" Lady Violet reflected. "It's having someone to share things with. You're nineteen, Ian. I'm not saying you should look for the girl you're going to marry, but you should find someone to have fun with."

"I don't know any other girls," Ian said. "And if I did, they wouldn't be interested in a scholarship student. Oxford is crawling with guys whose fathers are big shots in London financial circles or have three titles before their name."

"I don't believe you." Lady Violet put down her teacup. "You're afraid."

"Afraid?" Ian repeated.

"You're not like Spencer. A girl could break his heart and by the following week it would be completely mended. You're too serious. You're worried that if you fall for a girl and get rejected, you'll never be happy again."

Lady Violet was right. It had been two months since he'd received Annalise's letter, and he couldn't stop thinking about her.

"I don't need to fall in love." Ian opened his book. "I'm happy the way I am."

"You can't read spy thrillers all day, and you can't ignore the way you feel." Lady Violet stood up and walked to the door. "We have hearts so we can use them. Don't miss out on the best part of life."

Ian tried to follow Lady Violet's advice. He went on a double date with Spencer and invited a pretty blonde in his history seminar to the Commonwealth Ball. But his date only wanted to talk about her summer internship at an investment firm, and Ian had to feign interest in coffee futures. By the next term he gave up and spent his free time volunteering at the Cherwell School near Oxford.

Ian sat at the desk in his suite and tried to think. It would have been easy to accept Sabrina's invitation for a nightcap. But he couldn't let things progress while she thought he was Lord Braxton. He had to find a way to tell her the truth.

The door opened and Spencer entered the suite. He wore a navy overcoat and his scarf was wrapped around his neck.

"It's freezing out there." Spencer pulled off his gloves. "Next Christmas we should loan the Braxton collection to a museum somewhere warm: Bermuda or the Virgin Islands."

"How is Tabitha's brother?" Ian asked.

Spencer had left the Rainbow Room and gone to join Tabitha at urgent care.

"Miserable, his wrist is sprained," Spencer replied. "He's watching Netflix at Tabitha's apartment." He studied Ian's pale cheeks. "What's wrong with you? You look as bad as Stephen, and he's loaded up on painkillers."

Ian told Spencer about Sabrina appearing in the private dining room.

"That sounds like a Christmas miracle." Spencer whistled when Ian finished his story. "But why did you say no when she invited you into her suite? Don't tell me you've sworn off sex."

"That wasn't implied." Ian bristled. "We just didn't want the evening to end."

"You're both single and attracted to each other." Spencer unraveled his scarf and grinned. "Unless you're saving yourself for marriage. In that case, you better learn to take cold showers."

"This isn't the time for jokes." Ian's eyes were dark. "How could I do anything like that while Sabrina thinks I'm Lord Braxton? She'd never forgive me, and I wouldn't blame her."

"I see your point," Spencer said thoughtfully. He walked to the minibar and poured a glass of water.

"Maybe it's better this way." Ian rested his elbows on the desk. "I need to focus on the Met exhibit. Tomorrow morning I'm meeting with the security guard who'll escort the jewels to the museum. One doesn't toss the Braxton tiara into the back of a taxi."

Spencer put down his water glass and his eyes lit up.

"That's it!" he said excitedly. "We'll tell Sabrina you pretended to be me to protect me from women who are only interested in my title. Celebrities do all sorts of things to avoid being recognized when they travel. Tom Cruise used to check in under the name of one of the seven dwarfs."

"No offense, Spencer, but you're not Justin Timberlake or Leonardo DiCaprio. You don't even have an Instagram account. No one knows who you are."

"I may not be famous, but the Braxton jewels are," Spencer said. "You just said you need a guard to take them across Manhattan."

Ian considered it. The Braxton exhibit at the Met had been written up in *The New York Times* and *The New Yorker*.

"I suppose it's possible," Ian said hesitantly. "But I'd be lying to Sabrina again."

"It's a little white lie. I'll join you and Sabrina for dinner and tell her myself," Spencer said. "Then you can invite Sabrina to be your guest at the exhibit opening gala. How could she pass up sitting at the head table and receiving a favor from Tiffany's?"

Ian had almost forgotten about the gala dinner. It was being catered by one of New York's top caterers and guests would receive replicas of jewels in the collection.

"What will Tabitha say?" Ian said, warming to the plan.

"Tabitha is going to be with Stephen all day, I won't see her until tomorrow night," Spencer replied. "I'll have plenty of time to meet Sabrina. Then I'll explain everything to Tabitha." He grinned. "She won't mind. She'll think it's a fascinating glimpse into the life of a modern royal."

"I suppose I don't have any other ideas—"

"You don't need any." Spencer cut him off. "It's all about your commitment to the foundation. It will show Sabrina how loyal you are. Trust me, women love that kind of thing."

Spencer went into the bedroom, and Ian finished composing some emails. He was about to take a bath when his phone buzzed.

"Lady Violet." He recognized her cell phone number. "How is your mother? Is everything all right?"

"Lady Braxton is fine." Lady Violet's voice came down the line. "We're in London."

"Not at a hospital?" Ian asked anxiously.

"Definitely not a hospital." Her laugh tinkled. "In the first-class lounge at Heathrow about to board a flight to New York."

"What did you say?" Ian wondered if he had a fever and was imagining things.

"My mother gets so restless in the winter, and spraining her ankle made it worse," Lady Violet said. "I told her about the Met exhibit, and she decided we should attend the opening—"

"I thought she could barely walk," Ian interrupted.

"She's much better. Her doctor said as long as she uses a wheelchair on the plane, she'll be fine. She's very excited. She made us stop at Harrods and buy new dresses."

Ian's mind raced and he tried to maintain his composure.

"What time does your flight land? Spencer and I will pick you up."

"You don't need to drive all the way to JFK. I was going to have the Plaza send a car but Lady Braxton insisted we take an Uber." Lady Violet laughed. "She wants to experience the true flavor of New York."

Sabrina thought Lady Violet was his mother! What if Sabrina ran into Lady Violet before he told her the truth?

"You're staying at the Plaza?" Ian gulped.

"I already called and reserved a suite." Lady Violet's voice was dreamy. "I'm looking forward to central heating and a king-sized bed."

"I'll tell Spencer," Ian said. "We can't wait to see you."

"Why don't you make reservations for the champagne brunch at the Palm Court?" she suggested. "My mother adores champagne. She believes it's the only cure for her arthritis."

Ian hung up and tried not to panic. Sabrina was working all day. But what if she ran into Lady Violet and her mother in the lobby?

He had to keep Lady Violet and Lady Braxton busy. After brunch, he'd show them some tourist sights: the World Trade Center memorial and the Statue of Liberty. They'd go up to their suite to take a nap and freshen up while he and Spencer met Sabrina for dinner.

It was past midnight and Ian stifled a yawn. He remembered Sabrina standing outside her suite in her black cocktail dress. Her kiss had been warm and sweet, and all he had wanted was to follow her inside.

If only he'd told Sabrina the truth in the beginning . . . but it was too late to think about that. He had to go through with Spencer's plan; it was the only way Sabrina might forgive him. If she didn't, his heart would be like the tinsel that fell off the Plaza's Christmas tree: crushed and never able to be used again.

Eighteen

It was the day before New Year's Eve and Sabrina thought the New York skyline had never looked so beautiful. It had snowed overnight and Central Park was crisp and white underneath a blue sky. Even the cars on Fifth Avenue seemed as if they had been washed and polished.

Sabrina woke up with so much energy she couldn't stay in bed. She raced down to the gym and did thirty minutes on the elliptical machine, followed by fifty laps in the indoor pool. Then she spent an hour in the spa sampling Guerlain perfumes. Champs-Élysées smelled like lilacs and mimosas and Chamade was heavy and dramatic and Jardins de Bagatelle reminded her of the Conservatory Garden in Central Park in the spring. Finally she treated herself to a small bottle of L'Instant eau de parfum. It came in a gold bottle and she could wear it tonight for dinner with Ian.

At first she was disappointed when Ian declined her offer to come into her suite for a nightcap. But then he explained he had feelings for her and he wanted to take things slowly. They were going to have an early dinner and she was nervous and excited. Would tonight be different, and where would it lead?

First she was going to spend the day with Grayson. There was still so much more to his story, and they were running out of time.

"Sabrina, please come in." Grayson ushered her into the suite. The table was set with an array of plates, and the air smelled of sausages and cinnamon buns.

"We have so much to accomplish, I thought we'd start with a good breakfast." Grayson followed her gaze. "The coffee is Arabian Mocha-Java. The butler promised it's the strongest the Plaza serves."

"A cup of coffee and a muffin sounds wonderful," Sabrina said, noticing a framed painting leaning against the wall.

"What a gorgeous painting." She moved closer. "Is that a Bouguereau?"

"You have a good eye. William-Adolphe Bouguereau was a painter with the French academy in the nineteenth century. Not many people have heard of him."

"I had a print of *The Broken Pitcher* in my college dorm," Sabrina replied. "My former roommate left it behind but I got attached to it. It's hanging in my apartment."

"That's the wonderful thing about art, it becomes part of your family," Grayson agreed. "I picked this up for a client to give to his wife for their thirtieth anniversary. Edward was one of my first clients; he and his wife met at a Sotheby's auction. They both wanted the same painting and were afraid neither of them would get it. I suggested they pool their resources and buy the painting together. They took turns keeping it and once a month they would meet to exchange it." He poured two cups of coffee and handed one to Sabrina. "By the end of the first year they were married and the painting took up a permanent place in their new home." He smiled. "Every anniversary, Edward gives his wife a painting to remind them how they met."

"What a wonderful story." Sabrina sat down and opened her laptop.

"My favorite clients aren't the ones with the fattest bank accounts or the biggest houses. They're the clients who buy art because they're in love," Grayson reflected.

"I thought you didn't believe in love," Sabrina said lightly. "Kay said you had to build something of your own."

"Even Kay didn't always follow her own advice." Grayson settled back in his chair. "When she let down her guard, she became as giddy as a new bride about to leave on her honeymoon."

Plaza Hotel, June 1961

"What do you think of this bathing suit?" Kay asked Grayson, holding up a striped two-piece swimsuit. "It's a bikini, and it's all the rage in the south of France. I've never worn one but I don't want to look like an uptight New Yorker."

"You're going to the south of France?" Grayson finished pouring a cup of coffee. He added cream and two sugars and handed it to Kay.

"I can't drink this." She handed it back. "From now on I only want black coffee. And skip the muesli at breakfast. I don't know how the Swiss maintain their figures, starting their day with dried fruits and nuts. Lunch will be a piece of chicken, and for dinner you can bring me a bowl of clear soup. It's bad enough I have flabby arms, I'm not going to sit on the beach in Cannes with rolls on my stomach."

"You're as thin as a bird," Grayson said. "You didn't tell me you were going to Cannes."

"That's because I just found out!" Kay pointed at a letter and her eyes shone like a schoolgirl. "Andy is on tour on the Riviera and invited me to join him. He wanted to stay at some quaint bed-and-breakfast, but I'm not going to have a pretty French girl flutter her eyelashes while she pours his café au lait. I booked a week at the Hotel Carlton in Cannes. The service is as good as the Plaza, and the suites overlook the Mediterranean."

"But you have two television talk shows next week, and you told your publisher *Eloise Takes a Bawth* will be done by July."

"Television shows have bookers, they can get other guests. Sammy Davis Junior always gets a laugh and everyone loves Natalie Wood." Kay shrugged. "And the world can live without another Eloise book for a while. *Eloise in Moscow* is still selling copies."

Grayson was quiet and Kay looked up from the blouses and skirts spread out on the bed.

"I know what you're thinking," she commented. "How can I ignore my professional commitments to run after some thirty-year-old crooner?"

"I would never tell you what to do." Grayson colored. "It's just that—"

"I told you to stop spending all your time writing to Veronica and get a life of your own." Kay finished his sentence. "But that's the thing about love. It's like a cancer doctor I knew. Dr. Shapiro could diagnose the most elusive cancer by listening to a patient's symptoms. But then he got a lump on his throat and refused to acknowledge it until two weeks before it killed him."

"Love isn't deadly." Grayson grinned.

Kay straightened up and walked to the sideboard. She inspected the platter of mini sandwiches and selected cucumber on melba toast.

"Love can make you give up all the things you enjoy: butter and red meat and the chocolates the maids leave on the pillow at night." She stood at the window. "And then it can take you away from the places you adore: the Four Seasons for its Baked Alaska and the nail salon on Seventh Avenue because Miss Lee gives the best manicures."

She turned to Grayson and her eyes were as bright and shiny as her diamond earrings.

"You even toss Eloise and Nanny and Weenie to the side when they've been your loyal friends for almost a decade. Because turning your back on love—tearing up the airline ticket and canceling the hotel reservation—is as unthinkable as Eloise wearing blue instead of pink."

"You invented Eloise, you can dress her in whatever color you like."

Kay put down the uneaten sandwich.

"That's the thing. I'm a fifty-two-year-old woman in control of every part of my life except for the most important thing: my own heart."

Grayson was quiet. He stirred a packet of saccharin into the coffee and handed her the cup.

"I like the green bikini better than the striped one," he said kindly. "The green brings out the color of your eyes."

Grayson strode down Park Avenue and nodded at the doormen in their gold uniforms. Veronica's friend, Becky, had some of Veronica's things and had asked him to pick them up.

In the last month, Veronica's letters had become sporadic. One week he received long letters filled with humorous descriptions of walking Lily's bunny in Hyde Park. The next week his mailbox was empty, and yesterday he received a postcard with no message at all except Veronica's scrawled signature.

The last few times he tried calling her, she'd been out. When she called him back she said she couldn't talk because phone calls cost a fortune. He was almost tempted to buy a plane ticket and go to London, but what would that accomplish? He'd use up his savings, and begging Veronica to come home wouldn't help. She'd come back when she was ready.

"Grayson," Becky greeted him when he rang the doorbell. "Come in and sit down. Would you like a cup of coffee?"

Grayson followed Becky into the living room. His eyes traveled to the portrait of Eloise hanging over the fireplace. Veronica had decided not to take it to England and had left it with Becky for safekeeping.

"No, thank you." Grayson shook his head. "It's late and I've got to get all the way up to the Bronx."

"Let me go into the den and get the package," Becky said. "I'll be right back."

Grayson sat down and waited for Becky to return. Suddenly

he inhaled a familiar scent. He looked up and Veronica stood in the doorway. Her cheeks were pale and her hair was cut in a new style, but she looked the same.

"A girl travels all the way from England and you sit there like a statue." Veronica walked toward him. "Don't I get a hug or a kiss?"

Grayson jumped up and put his arms around her. She wore a striped sweater and multicolored pants and her lips were coated with red lipstick.

"Why didn't you tell me you were coming?" he demanded. "I would have picked you up at the airport."

"I can still afford cab fare." Her voice was throaty. "And I've always loved surprises."

"You didn't say anything in your letters—"

"It was a spur-of-the-moment decision." Veronica moved to the bar and poured a shot of scotch. "I packed a suitcase and took the first British Airways flight to New York. After all that British rain, a girl is allowed a vacation."

"Vacation?" Grayson echoed.

"My return ticket isn't until next Friday." Veronica filled the glass with ice. "And the weather report predicts sunshine. We can go to Coney Island or drive out to the Jersey Shore."

"You're going back to England?" Grayson's voice was tight.

"What else would I do? My parents are still in Kentucky. My father is working in my uncle's general store and my mother is a substitute teacher. I can't stay here, Becky got two new roommates."

"You'll stay with me," Grayson decided. "We'll go to city hall and get a marriage license. Kay will be a witness; she'll probably even spring for the wedding brunch. I'm getting a raise in July and we can afford a bigger apartment."

"I'm already getting married," Veronica said, avoiding Grayson's eyes. "The invitations haven't been sent out yet. Apparently there's only one stationer in London who suits Lady Miranda's tastes. But you are on the guest list. William wanted a June wedding; he likes to fish and thought we could go to Scotland on our honeymoon. But a bride needs time to buy a dress." She rolled her eyes theatrically. "Lady Miranda wanted me to wear her gown, but I'm quite sure it's from the Victorian era. I see myself in something floaty. Becky and I are going to the bridal salon at Saks."

Veronica finally stopped talking and Grayson cleared his throat.

"You're not marrying anyone but me."

"I considered that, I really did." She raised her glass to her lips. "I even wrote letters to a few art galleries on the Upper East Side. The pay isn't much, but you take clients to lunch and at least I wouldn't end up a hunchback like the typists you see walking down Madison Avenue." She gulped her drink. "But then a few things happened. The people I'm staying with are moving to Spain for a year, and I wasn't invited. And I got a letter from my mother." She looked up at Grayson and her face was as luminous as an angel. "My father got into more trouble at the race track, and some unpleasant types are breathing down his neck. They'll need quite a bit of cash, and William's family is loaded." She paused. "So, you see, there's nothing to discuss."

"There has to be another way," Grayson said. "A loan from a bank . . ."

"If a bank would loan my father money, he wouldn't be in this mess." She set her glass on the table. "I don't want to talk about it tonight. Why don't I treat us to a burger and shake at Sardi's? The only good thing about getting married in England is no one is forcing me to diet. The British believe girls with bigger thighs are better at producing heirs."

It was the last night before Veronica left for London and they were sitting in the living room in Becky's apartment.

Grayson took all his vacation days and they rode the Ferris wheel at Coney Island and took the ferry to the Statue of Liberty. Kay insisted on renting them a car and Grayson drove out to Long Island. Besides a few chaste kisses, Veronica refused to cheat on her future husband and Grayson agreed with her. They walked on the beach and ate crab cakes and watched the sun set.

"Lady Miranda called and said the invitations are ready." Veronica fixed two gin and tonics. "Would you like yours mailed to the Plaza or to your apartment?"

"I don't need an invitation," Grayson said gruffly. "I'm not coming to your wedding."

"I didn't think you would." Veronica sucked on an olive. "You wouldn't like it anyway. There are so many names to remember, and you have to address everyone by their title. William is an honorable, and when his father dies he'll be a lord or maybe an earl." She handed Grayson his glass. "I'll be Lady Veronica, which sounds like a character in a book." She gazed up at the portrait. "That reminds me, you can keep the portrait of Eloise."

Grayson remembered Kay in her black slacks and turtleneck, pulling the painting off the wall.

"It was a present," he said stiffly. "It belongs to you."

"Eloise wouldn't be comfortable in England. The people are stuffy, and it's difficult to make friends." Veronica grinned impishly. "Can you see Eloise traipsing through the White's club on

St. James's? They don't even allow women." She rolled her eyes. "And I thought London was so progressive. But William's family have been members of the club since the eighteenth century and they have the best wine cellar in London."

Suddenly it was the most important thing in the world that Veronica take the portrait.

"Eloise belongs with you," Grayson said stubbornly.

"Don't worry, Eloise doesn't need to keep an eye on me. I'll be fine." She sat next to Grayson on the sofa. "One day, I'll come to New York again on holiday. I'll have two children by then: a boy who loves cricket and a girl who is mad about Beatrix Potter. We'll meet in the city for lunch and you'll tell me about your life. You'll have some pretty wife and a beautiful little girl with your eyes. You'll be a big shot executive with a Cadillac and we'll laugh about how you helped me find the key to my father's Jaguar."

Her eyes glimmered and a tear fell on the white upholstery.

"How can it not work out for both of us? We're young and we deserve to be happy."

Grayson stopped talking and Sabrina glanced up from her laptop.

"Did Veronica get married?" she asked. "What happened to the portrait of Eloise?"

A message blinked on Grayson's cell phone and he tapped a reply.

"My client, Edward, is downstairs," Grayson said. "Would you mind taking him the painting?"

"You want me to deliver the Bouguereau to your client?" Sabrina asked in surprise.

"I would call a butler, but Edward is in a hurry," Grayson said.

"It will only take a minute and then we can continue." He smiled wanly. "It will give me a chance to collect myself. All that reminiscing is tiring."

"Of course." She stood up. "I'd be happy to do it."

Grayson draped the painting in a cloth and Sabrina took the elevator to the lobby. She passed the Palm Court and gasped. Ian was sitting at a table across from an older woman. The woman wore a cashmere dress and long suede gloves.

It wasn't the woman from the Met; that woman had grayish hair and was slightly frumpy. This woman had blond hair that had been styled in a salon and even from this distance, Sabrina could tell she had a refined beauty.

Why hadn't Ian told her he was meeting someone for lunch? There wasn't time to think about it now. She had to deliver the painting.

An older man in a gray suit collected the painting and Sabrina walked back toward the Palm Court. Ian had his back to her and the woman in the booth was telling a story and laughing.

She looked familiar, and Sabrina wondered where she had seen her before. Suddenly she froze. She knew exactly where she had seen her: on a royal website talking about the Braxton Foundation!

What was Lady Violet doing in New York, and why hadn't Ian told Sabrina she was coming?

Sabrina ducked behind a column and tried to control her breathing. Why shouldn't Lady Violet be here? She had probably come to attend the opening of the Braxton exhibit.

But if that had been the plan, Ian would have said something. What if Ian told Lady Violet about Sabrina and she flew to New York to stop Ian from seeing her?

She hurried across the lobby to the elevator. The doors opened and she pressed the button for the fourteenth floor. Lady Violet appearing in New York was as surprising as Santa Claus and his reindeer landing on the Plaza's roof. But there was nothing she could do about it. All she could do was listen to the rest of Grayson's story and hope Ian's mother wouldn't spoil Ian and Sabrina's romantic dinner.

Nineteen

Ian opened the door of the Pulitzer Suite and entered the living room. Spencer's jacket was draped across an armchair and the buzz of an electric shaver came from the bathroom.

"What on earth are you doing?" Ian stood at the bathroom door. "Lady Violet and I waited for you for ages at the Palm Court. I've had enough scones and jam to last until next Christmas."

Spencer switched off the razor and turned to face Ian.

"I'm sorry I didn't make it. I got held up."

"Your mother and grandmother arrived from England and you weren't there to greet them," Ian fumed. "You're lucky Lady Braxton went up to their suite to take a nap, she's not as forgiving as Lady Violet."

Ian wondered why he was so frustrated. Was it because Spencer hadn't shown up, or was it because Lady Violet was in New York and Sabrina still thought she was Ian's mother? The possibility of them running into each other before Ian told Sabrina the truth made his head throb.

"I did call my mother and apologize," Spencer reminded him.

"Tabitha's brother had a bad night and she asked me to pick up some pain pills. Once I got to her apartment, it was hard to leave. They needed a third player for Monopoly."

"Lady Violet didn't know anything about Tabitha," Ian grunted. "I had to explain why helping a girl you met five days ago was more important than having tea with your mother. It doesn't matter, you're back now."

Spencer glanced at the clock in the bedroom.

"Actually, I have to leave. I only came back to shower and change."

"What do you mean?" Ian demanded. "You weren't going to see Tabitha all day, and you already spent the morning with her. We're having dinner with Sabrina at six p.m. and you need to be there."

"Of course I'll be there," Spencer assured him. "Tabitha got tickets to a Broadway matinee. She thought it would be a great way to distract Stephen from the pain and asked me to join them."

Ian opened his mouth and closed it. There was no reason for Spencer to stay at the hotel.

"Everyone is busy this afternoon," Ian said sulkily. "I offered to take Lady Violet and Lady Braxton sightseeing, but they're going to see *The Nutcracker*. Lady Braxton has an app on her phone and bought tickets while they were on the plane." He smiled gently. "Lady Violet doesn't know whether to be perplexed or pleased that her mother knows all the latest technology."

"My grandmother was always ahead of her time." Spencer patted his cheeks with cologne. "She was the first person in the village to get an electric scooter. Everyone else rode bicycles and she whizzed around wearing a pink helmet."

"If you're so fond of her, you could have been here to say hello," Ian snapped.

"You're in a terrible mood." Spencer put down the cologne bottle. "It's the day before New Year's Eve and we're in New York. Try to cheer up."

"Of course I'm in a bad mood!" Ian said and anxiety welled up inside him. "Your mother's suite is directly above Sabrina's. If Sabrina finds out I'm not Lord Braxton before I tell her myself, she'll never speak to me again."

"Relax, my mother isn't going to tap dance on the parquet floor or hang her stockings out the window. Besides, they've never met. They could bump into each other in the elevator and it wouldn't make a difference."

"Everyone reads those royal blogs. They're as popular in America as Cadbury chocolate." Ian wasn't convinced. "I'll feel better after dinner. You'll tell Sabrina this was your idea and she'll forgive me."

"You see, you just said it will all work out," Spencer said, striding into the bedroom and pulling on a sweater. "You only have to keep yourself busy for five hours. You could watch a movie or do the *New York Times* crossword puzzle. You were always the fastest at doing crossword puzzles at Oxford."

Ian was too restless to stay at the Plaza and he had the whole afternoon to himself. It would be a good opportunity to go to the Met and make sure everything was perfect for the exhibit opening.

Ian had spent many days at the National Gallery and the British Museum in London, but the beauty and the grandeur of the Met was still very impressive. Its stone façade stood on the corner of

Fifth Avenue and Eighty-Second Street and its wide columns were wrapped in red satin ribbons. A red carpet led up to the entrance and through the glass doors he could see a Christmas tree.

The lobby was filled with priceless works of art and there was a sign leading to the gift shop and restaurant. A marble staircase led to the upper floors and there were rooms of Egyptian artifacts and medieval tapestries. Ian passed an exhibit of musical instruments from the court of Louis XVI and pottery made in A.D. 1000 by a tribe in the Sahara Desert. His favorite was a room filled with reindeer. There were paintings of reindeers and a life-size reindeer made entirely of semiprecious stones. Ian hoped to show it to Sabrina after the exhibit opening.

"Ian, it's a pleasure to see you again," the assistant head of the Met greeted him. "The collection just arrived and we're in a bit of a rush. It's not often we plan an exhibit opening and a gala dinner at the same time. But it's a wonderful way to start the new year."

It had been Lady Violet's idea to hold a dinner after the exhibit opening. Photos would appear on all the websites and it would draw interest to the Braxton collection.

"I'm sure it will go smoothly," Ian assured her. "The Met has hosted more important collections than the Braxton jewels."

"They're very special." The woman led him into a room with huge skylights. "Many of the pieces are so romantic. I feel like I'm peeking into the private boudoir of some elegant courtesan."

"I assure you there were no mistresses in the Braxton family tree," Ian said shortly.

"I only meant that each piece is so personal." The woman's cheeks flushed. "And your catalog copy is perfect. It's a shame that Lady Violet decided not to include the Ceylon sapphire and the Primrose brooch."

"What did you say?" Ian looked up from a glass case holding a black-and-white onyx ring from Madagascar.

"I love your description of the Primrose brooch," the woman sighed dreamily. "It was given to a girl named Primrose by young James Braxton in the late nineteenth century. They were madly in love but Primrose was a suffragette and believed marriage turned women into slaves. James thought he could convince her by giving her a diamond brooch instead of an engagement ring. But Primrose refused, and he married a woman he didn't love and drank himself to death."

Ian flinched. James Braxton had been a gambler and a philanderer. Lady Violet and Ian had debated including the brooch in the exhibit.

"And the story behind the Ceylon sapphire is so romantic I needed a handkerchief." The woman blinked. "Graham Braxton fell in love with a young duchess named Susanna in the eighteenth century. She was the prettiest girl in the county and had three other marriage proposals. But Graham wouldn't be rushed. First, he wanted to find a sapphire the exact color of Susanna's eyes. He traveled from Burma to Kashmir and finally found the perfect sapphire in Ceylon. He returned and proposed days before she was supposed to marry some stodgy landowner. Their marriage lasted fifty years and they had four daughters with Susanna's blue eyes."

"What do you mean, the pieces aren't here?" Ian's palms were sweaty. "The security guard came to the Plaza this morning. I sent the entire collection with him."

"They weren't in any of the jewelry cases." She shook her head. "Lady Violet must have changed her mind."

"I brought the jewels from England. The sapphire and brooch

were part of the collection!" Ian's voice rose dangerously. "Are you sure someone at the Met didn't misplace them?"

The woman stood up straight.

"We take the security of traveling exhibits very seriously," she said in a clipped tone. "Three assistants check in every piece and they are photographed and documented. If you'd like to talk to each of them individually—"

"That won't be necessary," Ian said distractedly. Perhaps the pieces had been left in the safe at the Plaza.

"I have to go." He turned to the door. "Thank you for showing me the collection."

"Is everything all right?" the woman called after him. "We don't want Lady Violet to be unhappy, and . . ."

Ian didn't hear the rest of what she said. He tore down the museum steps and raised his hand for a taxi.

"The Plaza Hotel," he said to the driver when he climbed in.

"Fifth Avenue is blocked, we may sit here for a while." The driver turned to the back seat. "Some Knicks player is giving away signed basketball shoes."

"I don't care if you have to teleport over the buildings." Ian clutched the headrest. "Get me to the Plaza as fast as you can."

Ian combed every inch of the safe, but the missing jewels were gone. He took the elevator to his suite and walked to the minibar. It was only midafternoon, but he'd do anything for a scotch. But he needed a clear head to think. He replaced the bottle and entered the bedroom.

He rifled through the drawers in the walk-in closet, but all he could find was Spencer's balled-up socks and boxer shorts. But something looked different. Spencer's heavy down jacket was gone and his snow boots were missing.

The sky was blue and the snow had been shoveled off the sidewalks. Why would Spencer need a ski jacket and boots to see a matinee on Broadway? Ian scanned the bedroom and noticed a sheet of paper on the bedside table.

Royal Inn Road, Rhinebeck was scribbled in Spencer's handwriting.

What if Spencer hadn't gone to a Broadway show? What if he had taken Tabitha to some quaint inn instead? The kind with canopied beds and roaring fireplaces and decanters of honey-colored brandy.

Spencer had promised that he'd join Ian and Sabrina for dinner and he wouldn't break his word. But Ian recalled other crazy things Spencer had done when he was in love. He hired the Boys' Choir to sing "Happy Birthday" to Anna in his geography seminar at Oxford. He parachuted out of a plane because Zena was an ex–Israeli soldier and he wanted to show his love for her was greater than his fear of heights. He flew to two cities in one day because Sally's Instagram posts said she was in Paris when actually she was in Rome. Sally was hiding from an ex-boyfriend and posted the photos to throw him off her trail.

Ian had to find Spencer or he might pull out the Ceylon sapphire over warm chocolate cake and by tomorrow he and Tabitha would be engaged.

He picked up the house phone and dialed the concierge's number.

"This is Ian Westing in the Pulitzer Suite," he said. "I was wondering if Lord Braxton called a car recently."

"I only came on the floor half an hour ago," the concierge replied. "But there's nothing in the books."

Ian breathed a sigh of relief. Perhaps he was wrong and at this moment Spencer was enjoying a Broadway musical. But then why were his boots missing?

He picked up the piece of paper. "Can you tell me anything about Rhinebeck?"

"It's two hours by train," the concierge said perkily. "It's perfect for a romantic getaway and has the most inns of any village in the Hudson Valley. I recommend the Beekman Arms. It was built in 1766 and each suite has a private bath. If you'd like me to make a reservation—"

"Not at the moment, thank you." Ian hung up the phone.

Spencer and Tabitha could have gone to Rhinebeck by train. He called Spencer's number, but it went straight to voice mail. He was about to try again when Lady Violet's number appeared on his phone.

"Ian," she said when he answered. "I'm glad I caught you."

"I thought you were at *The Nutcracker*," Ian replied.

"It's the first intermission," Lady Violet explained. "I stepped out to buy a box of malted milk balls. The Metropolitan Opera House serves all sorts of crudités, but my mother has a terrible sweet tooth."

"I'm glad you're enjoying yourselves," Ian said distractedly.

"I called because some young influencer is selling handbags at Saks and Lady Braxton wants to take a peek after the ballet. I didn't think you and Spencer would be interested, so I wondered if we could meet for a late supper."

"Yes, that's a good idea." Ian paced in front of the window.

"We're only in New York for a few days, and Lady Braxton

wants to pack in as much as possible," Lady Violet laughed. "I can't imagine what she would have arranged if she didn't have a sprained ankle."

Ian hung up the phone and glanced at the minibar. He really did need that scotch. Without Spencer, he couldn't go through with their plan to tell Sabrina why he pretended to be Lord Braxton. Lady Violet was expecting Spencer and Ian to join them for supper and Spencer might be anywhere between Manhattan and the Hudson Valley. Not to mention that two pieces of the Braxton collection were missing and it was Ian's fault.

The phone rang and he hoped it was Spencer.

"Good afternoon," a male voice said. "I'm confirming your six p.m. reservation at the Rose Club. Is there anything special we can prepare? A bottle of wine from our cellar or an appetizer that isn't on the menu?"

If Ian canceled the reservation, he could take a train to Rhinebeck and find Spencer. They'd be back in time to meet Lady Violet and Lady Braxton for supper and no one would know the Braxton jewels had been missing.

But how would he explain missing dinner to Sabrina, and what if she was hurt and didn't want to see him again?

Lady Violet once said Ian had to stop running after Spencer and find love. Was this love? And didn't the foundation come first, after all Lady Violet had done for him? And what about Spencer? Spencer was his best friend and he was about to make a terrible mistake.

"It's a busy night and we do have a waiting list," the male voice prompted. "If you want to cancel the reservation. . . ."

"No, I won't be canceling," Ian said firmly. "Six p.m. at the Rose Club."

The afternoon sun gleamed on the tips of the skyscrapers and the Manhattan skyline was a muted wonderland. He was at the Plaza Hotel at Christmas and he might never get the chance to be with Sabrina again.

"Could you serve lobster rolls as an appetizer?" He remembered the night he and Sabrina met. "And some of that delicious caviar."

"It will be our pleasure," the man replied. "We'll see you in a few hours."

Twenty

Sabrina paused in front of Grayson's suite. Her hand went to the door and she wished she had time to compose herself. But she could hardly explain to Grayson that she had seen Ian with his mother at the Palm Court when Grayson didn't know Ian existed. And she wasn't at the Plaza to fall in love; she was here to ghostwrite Grayson's memoir.

"Sabrina, I thought I heard footsteps." Grayson opened the door. "Please come in. Did Edward pick up the painting?"

"Yes, he said to thank you." Sabrina followed Grayson inside. "He was on his way to meet his wife at the King Cole Bar at the St. Regis."

"The King Cole Bar is one of their favorite places. I've listened to Edward serenade his wife on the piano many times." He smiled. "Love is a wonderful thing when it lasts a lifetime. They're a lucky couple."

Grayson moved to the minibar and poured a glass of sparkling water.

"Do you ever wonder why some people are lucky in love and for others it never works out?" he asked.

"What do you mean?" Sabrina glanced up from her laptop.

"When I was young, I believed getting married and having a family was a guarantee—like having acne as a teenager or learning to drive a car," he laughed. "Not in the same way, of course, but you understand."

"I suppose so," Sabrina said, wondering what he was trying to say.

"But then I became an adult and discovered it wasn't true. Many guests at the Plaza had everything except a partner: Kitty Parsons in the Fifth Avenue Suite was a model and every man who saw her fell in love with her. But she left behind her high school sweetheart for a career, and by the time she returned to her hometown he was married.

"And Raymond Phillips in the Penthouse Suite had so much money, I'd find hundred-dollar bills stuffed in his pillowcase. But he worked night and day and women got tired of saying yes to dinner and then waiting for him at the Palm Court."

"I see what you mean," she said slowly.

"Everything important in life has to be nurtured: if your car engine won't turn over, you get a new one, and if there's a hole in the roof of your house you patch it up. But people ignore love and think it will be there when they're ready for it."

"You told Veronica how you felt about her," Sabrina said boldly. "It wasn't your fault that she stayed in England."

Grayson gazed at Sabrina and his eyes flickered.

"At the time, I thought I did. But I always wondered if I could have tried harder." He sat on the sofa. "If I had taken Kay's advice earlier to make something of myself, maybe it would have turned out differently."

"Well, that's it." Kay clicked the lock on the steamer trunk. "The Plaza will store three trunks in their storeroom and the rest will be sent to the Hotel Danieli in Venice." She straightened up. "Though God knows if I'll ever need these things. I'll be perfectly happy if I never wear a pink suit again, and I'm quite comfortable living without my collection of French perfumes. Sometimes I don't know why we buy things in the first place. Who needs ten types of perfume? I only have two wrists and one neck."

"I can't believe you're checking out of the Plaza for good," Grayson said. "Are you sure this is the right thing to do?"

Kay had returned from Europe a month earlier. She never mentioned Andy Williams, and at first Grayson wondered whether Andy had jilted her and she was too upset to talk about it. But Kay had never been in a better mood. Her writing flowed easily and at night she danced around the suite to the Chubby Checker records she asked Grayson to play on the phonograph.

"If you think I'm going somewhere new to recover from a broken heart, you're mistaken." Kay checked her lipstick in the mirror. "It was wonderful being with Andy. We sipped martinis on the promenade in Cannes and danced in the moonlight in Monte Carlo. But every time one of his brothers sent photos of their children, Andy started clucking like a chicken. Even if I wasn't too old to have children, you know how I feel about them. They're noisy and messy and the only little girl I can stand is Eloise. One evening we ran into a family in a bistro. Andy mooned over the ten-month-old baby the way other men drool over supermodels. I left him a letter telling him how I'll always care about him and slipped out in the middle of the night."

"Then why are you going back to Europe?" Grayson asked.

"The point of living at the Plaza is so I wouldn't be tied down." Kay slipped on her pumps. "Why shouldn't I stay in different hotels? The Danieli in Venice makes the best Bellinis and the Villa d'Este in Lake Como is so peaceful and when I get to Mallorca in May I may stop writing and spend every day swimming in the ocean."

"It feels so sudden. . . ."

"I'm stagnant here, even Eloise can't get out of the bath. I need a new adventure." She looked pointedly at Grayson. "You should consider moving on too."

"Why would I quit the Plaza?" Grayson asked. "I do have other guests, and——"

"You'll never learn anything from them like you have from me." Kay waved her hand. "We've had this discussion a dozen times. How are you going to make something of yourself if you spend your time folding other people's clothes?"

"I make a decent salary, and I don't need much now that . . ." His voice trailed off and he remembered the last time he saw Veronica.

"Now that Veronica is married to that British earl?" Kay prompted. "That's exactly why you need to do something new. I have a friend who's an art dealer in Los Angeles. I bumped into Byron in the south of France and he's looking for an assistant. You could work for him for a couple of years and then go out on your own. There's a fortune to be made. All those movie stars want to buy important art but they don't have any taste."

"I don't know anything about art," Grayson protested.

"You and Veronica used to visit museums, and Byron would train you in what you don't know. All you need is to be able to listen to people, and you've been doing that at the Plaza for years."

"I couldn't move to Los Angeles, I've always lived in New York."

Grayson didn't say what he was really thinking. What if Veronica's marriage didn't work out and she returned to New York?

"That's exactly why you should move." Kay dropped her lipstick into her handbag. "How many times have I said that you have to grab an opportunity? Well, sometimes you have to create the opportunity yourself. At the Plaza you're comfortable: you eat in the hotel cafeteria and get a decent Christmas bonus and you don't even dry clean your own uniform." Her voice was sharp. "But really, Grayson, you're too smart to spend your life ironing someone's cashmere socks."

"A butler's job can be very stimulating," Grayson said hotly. "I juggle a dozen different requests and I—"

Kay put her hand on Grayson's arm.

"I'm sorry, that came out wrong. Do you know why I chose the Danieli in Venice instead of the Gritti or the Hotel Cipriani?" Her voice softened. "Because the Danieli has the best butlers, and the thing I'm going to miss most about the Plaza is you. I care about you, Grayson, but it's time you and I and even Eloise grew up."

Grayson imagined not making Kay's Ovaltine at night and his chest tightened.

"I'll miss you too, Miss Thompson."

Kay blinked and Grayson could swear she wiped a tear from her eyes.

"Here, take Byron's card." She handed him a business card. "The worst that will happen is you'll go to Los Angeles and see a palm tree. Who knows? In ten years I might visit your Bel Air mansion and you'll have a pretty wife and two blond children and a kidney-shaped swimming pool."

Grayson walked up Park Avenue to Becky's apartment. He hadn't heard from Veronica since her wedding and he didn't expect to. They'd agreed it wouldn't be right if they corresponded once she was married. But Veronica still wrote to Becky, and he stopped by now and then. He didn't know what he hoped to hear: that Veronica's new husband was impossible to live with and she was filing for divorce, or that her parents had regained their fortunes and she was coming home. But it was nice to be with someone who knew Veronica.

"Grayson, this is a pleasant surprise," Becky said when the doorman buzzed him up to her apartment.

"I was in the neighborhood." He entered the foyer.

"You're often in the neighborhood for a guy who lives in the Bronx," she teased him.

Grayson flushed and followed her into the living room. Boxes were scattered around the floor and most of the furniture was gone.

"Are you moving?" he asked.

"I'm getting married." She held out her hand to display a large diamond ring. "Gordon is a junior partner at a law firm with a five-room apartment on Riverside Drive. I'm moving back in with my parents until the wedding in June."

"You're getting married in June?" Grayson repeated.

Surely Veronica would return to New York for her best friend's wedding.

"It's going to be at the Plaza, my mother reserved the date the moment the ring came out of the box," Becky laughed. "I asked Veronica to be the matron of honor, but she can't. She's pregnant, in June she'll be the size of an elephant."

"Pregnant?" Grayson felt like he couldn't breathe.

"Are you going to repeat everything I say?" Becky raised her eyebrows. "It was practically a honeymoon baby. Veronica said it's a pity she's going to get fat. She's throwing up so much, she finally has the figure she always dreamed of."

"That sounds like Veronica." Grayson tried to smile.

He glanced above the fireplace and noticed the portrait of Eloise was missing.

"Where's the painting?" he asked.

"Veronica left it behind and you didn't want it. So I put it in the trash." Becky went back to filling a box with magazines.

"You put the portrait of Eloise in the trash?" Grayson's cheeks turned pale and his voice rose.

"I have to clear out everything." Becky shrugged. "My parents want the place back the way it was."

It wasn't Becky's fault. Grayson could have taken the portrait to his apartment. But it reminded him too much of Veronica. This way he could come and admire it whenever he liked.

"When does your trashman come?" he asked.

"Usually this morning, but I haven't checked," she answered.

"I have to go." Grayson jumped up from the chair.

"You just got here," Becky protested. "You could help me pack a couple of boxes."

"Another time." Grayson moved to the door. "Congratulations on your wedding."

Grayson searched through the trash, but the portrait wasn't there. He shuffled down Park Avenue, but his feet were leaden and he could barely make it to the subway.

Kay was right. Veronica was in England and Kay was moving to Venice and even Eloise was gone from his life.

He reached for a subway token and drew out Byron's business card. Then he entered a phone booth and dialed the number.

Grayson stopped talking and Sabrina glanced up from her laptop.

"Do you mind if we take a short break?" Grayson asked, and Sabrina thought he looked tired. His skin was ashen and there were deep lines in his forehead. "I could order room service for dinner."

Dinner! It was almost six o'clock and Sabrina was supposed to meet Ian at the Rose Club. She had been so flustered about seeing Ian with Lady Violet she'd forgotten to ask Grayson if they would be working this evening.

Grayson noticed Sabrina's expression and frowned.

"I didn't ask if you already had dinner plans," he said.

"I should have asked if that's all right," she apologized. "I can cancel. . . ."

"Tomorrow is New Year's Eve, and it's the last day we can work," he pondered. "I'm leaving on January second, and I've got back-to-back meetings on the first."

Ian would be waiting for her in a booth. But the memoir was almost done, and she couldn't cut short their meeting.

"I have an idea," Grayson said as if he was reading her thoughts. "I'll order room service for myself and you go have a quick dinner. We'll meet here again at seven."

Sabrina calculated in her head. It wouldn't be long enough to sip the Rose Club's specialty cocktails and listen to jazz, but she could see Ian and explain.

"Are you sure?" She gathered her laptop.

"I keep telling you to have a little fun," he said with a smile. "I'll be fine, I'll order a brandy and a bowl of soup. I might even see if I can find some old Chubby Checker songs on Spotify."

Sabrina called Ian's cell phone as soon as she entered her suite.

"I was afraid I wouldn't reach you," she said when Ian answered. "My meeting is running long and I can only take an hour for dinner."

"An hour?" Ian's voice came down the line. "The Rose Club is notoriously slow, we won't even get our appetizers."

"You're right." Sabrina tried to keep the disappointment from her voice. "We should probably cancel."

"That's not what I was thinking," Ian said. "How about if we have room service in my suite? I'll order a couple of steaks and salads, they'll be ready by the time you get here."

"In your suite?" Sabrina repeated and felt happy and nervous at the same time.

"I promise to be on my best behavior," he said lightly. "We can ask the butler to chaperone if you like."

"I did invite you into my suite last night, and it is only six p.m.," she teased back. "I think I'll be perfectly safe."

There was a pause and Sabrina wondered if they got disconnected.

"I'll see you at six p.m.," Ian said and his voice was low. "And there's no dress code like at the Rose Club. You'll look beautiful in whatever you choose."

Sabrina wished she could run down to the hotel's boutique and pick out something new to wear: a pair of silk pajamas like characters wore in romantic movies when they entertained a man at home. But there wasn't time and anything in the boutique would be too expensive. She settled on the Vince sweater she'd borrowed from Chloe and a straight skirt. She dabbed on her new Guerlaine perfume and slipped the silver charm bracelet around her wrist.

"Sabrina, you look lovely." Ian opened the door of his suite. "Please come in."

Sabrina entered the living room and glanced around. The suite was twice the size of hers and she wondered why Ian needed so much room. Gilt mirrors stood against the wall and parquet floors were covered with plush rugs. There was a velvet sofa and gold-patterned wallpaper and a Christmas tree decorated with silver and gold lights.

"It's beautiful," she gasped. "It must be the best suite at the Plaza."

"That would be the Royal Suite on the eighteenth floor," Ian said, smiling. "The Royal Suite has a dining room that seats twelve people and its own library."

Sabrina wondered if Ian had been in the Royal Suite; perhaps his mother was staying there. Her shoulders deflated and she felt like Cinderella before the stroke of midnight. In two days she'd be back at her apartment in Queens and Ian would return to a thirty-room estate in Sussex and a London flat at some smart address.

"I don't want to talk about the Plaza, I want to talk about you," he said, touching her arm. "You must be doing something terribly important to only take an hour's dinner break."

Sabrina brought her thoughts back to the present.

"It's time sensitive," she said quickly.

She suddenly longed to tell Ian the truth. But then she thought about Lady Violet with her designer handbag and dress that was probably couture. Ian hadn't mentioned his mother and Sabrina still didn't know why she was in New York. Now wasn't the time to blurt out what she was really doing at the Plaza.

"Then we should enjoy the time we have." Ian waved at the dining table. "The butler delivered the steaks. Let's eat before it gets cold."

A bottle of red wine stood on the table and there were candles and a silver bread basket. They ate French onion soup and prime rib and golden mashed potatoes.

"I requested lobster rolls like on the night we met, but there was a snowstorm in Maine and the lobsters didn't make it." He grinned between mouthfuls of steak.

Sabrina was touched that Ian remembered. Everything he had done was so thoughtful: the Christmas music playing over the speakers, the drapes drawn back so they could see the lights of the Pulitzer Fountain. Ian was a British lord; he could date almost any woman he liked. His feelings for her must be real. They wouldn't disappear when he learned that she only had one credit card and the last time she traveled it had been such a cheap flight, she had to pay extra to plug in her headphones.

"You'll have to ask the Plaza to send some lobster to England," she said in a playful tone.

"I have a better idea," Ian answered. "I can come back to New York."

Sabrina gulped. There was an awkward silence and she wondered if this was the time to tell him she was a struggling writer.

"When did you stop believing in Santa Claus?" Ian filled the silence.

"Santa Claus?" Sabrina said in surprise. She ate a spoonful of mashed potatoes and was glad to talk about something else.

"In the fifth grade. I sat next to Roger Hazelton in English. He had green eyes and blond hair and I loved the way he chewed the top of his pencil. He asked to see my Christmas list and I was flattered because he never noticed me before.

"My list had the usual things: a My Little Pony doll and Nancy Drew books and a Razor scooter that was all the rage. Then I asked to see his and he said he didn't have one because Santa Claus wasn't real. He went to the toy store and picked out what he wanted for under the tree." She grimaced at the memory.

"You should have told the teacher." Ian smiled. "Roger could have gotten in serious trouble."

"What about you? When did you stop believing in Santa Claus?"

Ian fiddled with his fork. He glanced up at Sabrina and he had never looked so handsome.

"I haven't actually," he began. "I suppose I was doubtful for a while. But a few years ago I met a little girl named Mallory. She joined the after-school club at the library and her mother asked me to tea to thank me. Her family lived above a shop in the village—Mallory and three sisters shared the bedroom and her mother and baby brother slept in the living room. They didn't have a Christmas tree and the only thing her mother served with the tea was stale biscuits that she bought for half price.

"I couldn't enjoy Christmas at Braxton Hall with the platters of baked ham and stockings filled with chocolates. I asked the cook to bake an extra ham and I bundled up one of Lady Violet's fruitcakes. Then I bought a Christmas tree and Lady Violet helped me wrap presents. On Christmas morning Mallory and her family woke up to a Christmas tree and presents and a proper Christmas lunch.

"I saw Mallory at church and she told me Santa Claus visited during the night and it was a Christmas miracle." He paused. "That's when I realized that Santa Claus was really about the spirit of Christmas. Making someone happy was a miracle, so how could I stop believing in Santa Claus?"

"That's a wonderful story," Sabrina said, reaching over to refill her wineglass.

"Sabrina, I need to tell you . . ." Ian began.

Sabrina's charm bracelet caught the edge of her glass and red wine spilled on the tablecloth. She tried to mop it up but it trickled on the rug.

"Oh, I'm sorry." She jumped up. "I'll get a towel."

She grabbed a towel from the cabinet in the bathroom and a velvet box fell to the floor. She was about to put it on the counter but the clasp opened and revealed a sapphire ring.

There were footsteps and Ian stood in the doorway.

"I was looking for a towel and this fell out." She realized she was holding the jewelry box. She looked up and her eyes met Ian's.

There was a long silence and Sabrina searched Ian's face to see if he was angry. He probably thought she was snooping through his things. She tried to think of something to say, but no words came out.

"It's beautiful, isn't it?" Ian said as if he could sense her embarrassment. He took the box and held the sapphire ring to the light. "Graham Braxton bought it for a young duchess named Susanna in the eighteenth century. He almost lost Susanna to another suitor, but he wouldn't give her a ring until he found one that matched her eyes. He traveled across the globe and finally discovered this ring in Ceylon. It's called the Ceylon sapphire."

"What a thrilling story," Sabrina sighed with relief. Ian didn't sound upset after all. "It must be wonderful to have the same heirlooms in the family for centuries."

Ian rubbed the ring as if he was thinking about something.

"I suppose so. But Lady Violet always says jewelry doesn't do any good sitting in a safe. It should be worn and admired." He took Sabrina's hand. "I want you to have it."

Sabrina took a deep breath. Her eyes widened and she gasped.

"You want me to have the Ceylon sapphire?"

"You must wear it. The sapphire is the exact color of your eyes." He slid it onto her finger. He looked at her and there was something new in his expression. "That is, if you want to."

Sabrina stared at her finger and the ring blinked back up at her. She felt as giddy as when she was a child and discovered the diary and pink feather pen she desperately wanted under the Christmas tree.

"I can't think of anything I'd like more," she replied. "It's the most beautiful ring I've ever seen."

Ian leaned forward and kissed her. She kissed him back and his breath tasted of red wine.

"I'm glad." He took her hand. "Now let's go back and finish dinner. We haven't finished our wine, and I ordered the Plaza's Christmas bread pudding. It would be a shame for it to go to waste."

Sabrina smoothed her skirt and waited for Grayson to answer the door. The sapphire ring caught the light in the hallway and she took a deep breath. She still couldn't believe what happened: knocking over the wineglass and finding the jewelry box and Ian sliding the ring on her finger. It had been overwhelming and she forgot everything she wanted to talk about at dinner.

Sabrina had promised to text Ian when she finished working, but what if it was after midnight? Ian might be asleep and it would have to wait until tomorrow.

"Sabrina, you're here." Grayson opened the door. "I was just finishing a slice of cheesecake. My cholesterol will go through the roof, but no one makes better cheesecake than the Plaza."

Sabrina followed Grayson into the living room but she barely heard him. All she could think about was Ian kissing her. It felt different than their kiss last night—it was deep and meaningful and she never wanted it to stop.

Sabrina opened her laptop and straightened her shoulders. She had to put Ian out of her mind. She was a writer on an important assignment, not some lovesick teenager.

"Tell me what happened after you called the art dealer in Los Angeles." She scrolled through her notes. "Is that where you started your career?"

Grayson was about to answer when something caught his eye.

"What an unusual ring." He leaned closer.

Sabrina felt a blush creeping across her cheeks. She was still wearing the ring!

"It was a present," she said quickly. "I think it's from Ian's family's collection."

"Your mystery man must be from an important family." He whistled. "I haven't seen such a clear sapphire in years."

Sabrina gulped. Grayson was obviously waiting for her to tell him the story. There was no reason to hide anything. Grayson had encouraged her to meet someone.

"I should have told you," she began awkwardly. "He's a British lord, actually, we met the first night I was here. His family owns the Braxton jewels—the exhibit is going to be on loan at the Met."

Grayson dropped his dessert fork.

"Did you say the Braxton jewels?" he asked. "That's one of the most important collections in England. A piece was auctioned a decade ago. It was just one tiara but the bidding set a record."

Of course Grayson would have heard of the Braxton jewels. Grayson attended Sotheby's auctions all the time.

"I'm sure the ring is nothing like that," she said quickly. "We've only known each other a few days."

"I'd like to meet him," he announced.

"You'd like to meet Lord Braxton?" she repeated incredulously.

"If you don't mind," he said and smiled. "After all, I feel responsible. It's because of me that you met. How about breakfast in the Palm Court tomorrow?"

Sabrina couldn't think of a reason to say no.

"Of course." She nodded.

"I'm glad that's settled." Grayson seemed to relax. He ate the last bite of cheesecake and settled back in his chair.

"Now we were talking about Los Angeles," he said. "Let me tell you what happened after I left New York."

Sabrina closed the door of her suite and placed her laptop on the table. It was almost 1:00 A.M. and a few embers glowed in the fireplace. She had texted Ian when she left Grayson but he hadn't answered.

A soft snow fell outside the window and it was completely quiet. Fifth Avenue was deserted and even the Plaza's valets in their red-and-gold uniforms had gone inside.

The sapphire ring glinted on her finger and she thought her heart might burst and break at the same time. She couldn't help it, she was falling in love. But Ian was leaving in three days and everything would be different.

She was too tired to think about it. She walked into the bedroom and turned down the bed. At least she would always have Christmas week at the Plaza Hotel. Every day had been a miracle and she didn't know what would happen next.

Twenty-One

Ian checked his phone and covered his face with a pillow. It was only ten minutes since the last time he'd checked. But he couldn't fall back to sleep, and getting up and facing the day seemed more than he could handle.

He yanked off the sheets and stepped into a pair of slippers. Spencer wouldn't call just because he was staring at the phone and he had to shave and shower for breakfast with Sabrina.

Breakfast with Sabrina at the Palm Court! It filled him with anticipation and dread at the same time. Anticipation because he wanted to see her more than anything in the world. But there was so much to worry about. Spencer still hadn't returned, and he couldn't put off telling Sabrina that he wasn't Lord Braxton. And now Sabrina was wearing the Ceylon sapphire. How would he explain it didn't belong to him and she would have to give it back?

He relived the moment she found it in the linen closet and groaned. What had possessed him to give it to Sabrina? He could easily have said it was part of the collection and put the jewelry box back on the shelf. But he had been a bit drunk from the wine and she had looked intoxicating in that sweater and skirt. Suddenly he wanted to give her the kind of present a woman who stayed in a suite at the Plaza Hotel would never forget. But he must have been mad. He'd have to tell Sabrina that Lady Violet insisted the ring be returned to the family. Then he'd transfer money from his savings account and buy her something else: a pearl brooch from Tiffany's. It would be more than he could afford, but it would be better than telling Lady Violet what he'd done.

He thought about Lady Violet and a deep pit formed in his stomach. She'd called last night and said they spent forever at Saks and jet lag finally caught up with them. They were going to have dinner in their suite and would see Ian and Spencer for brunch. What if she discovered the ring was missing before he could return it? It wasn't going to be easy to explain that Spencer had spent the night with Tabitha at some romantic inn and Ian had given the sapphire ring to a woman Lady Violet never met.

The door to the suite opened and Spencer walked in. He wore a bright scarf and his jacket was folded over his arm.

"It's nice of you to show up," Ian snapped, entering the living room. "Where have you been and why didn't you call or text? You were supposed to be seeing a Broadway musical and you disappeared."

"I did call." Spencer dropped his jacket on a chair. "Your phone was off and then mine ran out of battery."

"You called?" Ian tried to think. He'd turned off his phone when Sabrina came for dinner, but that had only been for an hour.

"Yesterday evening," Spencer said. "Then I called my mother but her phone went straight to voice mail. She called me back this morning; we're meeting for brunch at the Palm Court." He pulled back the curtains. "You really should open the drapes. It snowed last night but it's a beautiful day. Why don't we go for a walk and get coffee and bagels?"

Ian's blood boiled and he was tempted to take out his frustration on Spencer.

"Did you forget you were supposed to meet me and Sabrina for dinner?" he fumed. "You took Tabitha to a romantic inn to propose. Though you forgot the Ceylon sapphire. Did you buy a ring at some drugstore in Rhinebeck and promise Tabitha you'd replace it with a proper engagement ring when you returned to New York?"

Spencer stared at Ian as if he was babbling.

"I didn't go to Rhinebeck to propose to Tabitha. And I don't have any jewels in the Braxton collection."

"Two of them are missing. The Primrose brooch and the Ceylon sapphire. Except now Sabrina is wearing the sapphire because she found it in the linen closet. I got so wound up, I gave the ring to Sabrina!"

Spencer sat on the sofa and looked at Ian.

"I'd suggest a scotch, but it's nine o'clock in the morning. Why don't you sit down and tell me what you're talking about."

Ian told Spencer about the missing jewels and finding Spencer's note on the bedside table.

"I'm supposed to meet Sabrina for breakfast and I still haven't told her I'm not Lord Braxton," he finished. "And what did you say to your mother? I couldn't sleep because I worried what she'd do when she discovered you ran off with a girl."

"I told her the truth," Spencer said pleasantly. "Tabitha and I went to save puppies from a puppy mill."

"A puppy mill?" Ian repeated.

"Tabitha's neighbor bought a puppy for Christmas and it

wouldn't stop barking. The poor dog was sick and the neighbor admitted he bought it from a puppy mill. I called the Animal Haven Shelter but they couldn't shut it down without proof. We decided to take the train and save the puppies ourselves."

"You went to Rhinebeck to rescue puppies?"

"I thought we'd be back in time for dinner. But it took ages to find the puppy farm and some of the puppies were so small, we had to keep them warm overnight. We stayed in a motel and the puppies slept in one bed. I dropped them off at the shelter this morning. They'll make sure they're healthy and find proper homes."

"What about the jewels from the Braxton collection?" Ian inquired.

"I took them out of the safe a few days ago to show Tabitha. She's going to use them as part of her doctoral dissertation," he replied. "The Primrose brooch is probably still in the linen closet. I'm sorry, I must have forgotten to put them back."

"I'm responsible for every piece." Ian's anger returned. "You almost gave me a heart attack."

"At least I didn't give them to a woman I just met," Spencer said cheerfully. "Sabrina must have been surprised when you slipped the ring on her finger."

"I don't know what came over me. The wine affected me more than I thought and she looked so beautiful. I must have been mad." Ian flinched. "I'm meeting Sabrina at the Palm Court and I'm going to tell her the truth."

"I'll change and come with you." Spencer stood up. "We'll say you hid the ring so I wouldn't use it to propose to Tabitha. You were so flustered when Sabrina found it, you didn't know what to say."

Ian remembered the warmth of Sabrina's mouth. God, he had wanted to keep kissing her.

"I'm going alone," he said suddenly.

"I have to tell Sabrina this was my idea," Spencer reminded him. "It will only take a minute, I'll throw on some clean slacks."

"I'm going alone and I'm going to tell her everything: that I was afraid her feelings might change if she knew I wasn't a member of the British aristocracy, and I can barely afford my own bedsit, let alone a suite at the Plaza."

"You're going to say you lied about being Lord Braxton and you lied about Lady Violet being your mother and you even lied about the ring belonging to you?" Spencer asked incredulously.

"I didn't mean to lie, it was a snowball that picked up speed," Ian corrected. "I'll say I'm sorry and I'll do anything to make it up to her."

"You're making a big mistake," Spencer warned him. "Women hate it when you lie. It's the surefire way to make Sabrina not see you again."

"If I go ahead with your plan I'll always know I didn't tell her the whole truth," Ian said stubbornly. "I have to be completely honest or what's the point."

"You do have it bad." Spencer whistled. "I'll get us both coffee and bagels. I have a feeling once you tell Sabrina, breakfast is going to be over."

Ian entered the Palm Court and glanced around the room. If he were in a better mood he would appreciate the architecture. The domed ceiling was made of stained glass and there were potted palm trees and marble columns wrapped in Christmas lights.

"Ian." Sabrina waved from a table near the window. She wore a pink sweater and wool slacks.

"I'd like you to meet someone," she said. "This is Grayson Prescott. Grayson, this is Lord Braxton."

An older man stood up and shook Ian's hand. He must have been at least eighty, with white hair and wide shoulders like a football player.

"I didn't know anyone would be joining us," Ian stumbled.

"I suppose I didn't tell you." Sabrina colored. "It was so late when I texted you, it would have been difficult to explain."

"It's my fault, I hope you don't mind," Grayson cut in with a smile. "I've followed the Braxton collection for years. When Sabrina mentioned you, I couldn't pass up the opportunity."

"Sabrina mentioned me?" Ian gulped, wishing he had taken his own advice and stayed in bed.

"Why don't we have breakfast and I'll explain." Grayson handed Ian the menu. "It's my treat. Can I suggest the buttermilk pancakes? I've spent enough time in London to know it's hard to get decent pancakes in England."

Ian tried to compose himself while Grayson ordered pancakes and something called New York hash, which Grayson explained was eggs sunny-side up and pulled pastrami with whatever the chef had in the kitchen.

"Grayson is an art dealer," Sabrina said when the waiter served their dishes. "His career spans sixty years and he's the most respected person in his field."

An art dealer! Ian felt a twinge of relief, like when his fingers were numb with cold and he warmed them in front of the fire. Maybe Grayson wanted to meet because he was interested in the jewels, not because he knew Ian was an imposter. It didn't matter; he had to tell Sabrina the truth. But how could he do that in front of a complete stranger?

"I've been lucky enough to work with Sabrina all week," Grayson was saying. "It's funny, when we started I thought I'd want all the credit for myself. But the more time we spent together, the more I realized that was wrong. It wouldn't be half the book it's going to be with another ghostwriter."

"Ghostwriter?" Ian glanced from Grayson to Sabrina.

"The contract insists that it's kept confidential. But I'll be proud to have Sabrina's name on the cover," Grayson went on. "She's a wonderful listener; I've learned things about myself that I didn't know."

"You're a writer." Ian turned to Sabrina and somehow the knowledge made him incredibly happy. "No wonder you understand the importance of books."

"Ian runs his family's foundation," Sabrina explained to Grayson. "The Braxton Foundation builds libraries and funds afterschool activities for children who have nowhere to go."

"I met your mother, Lady Violet, years ago at a charity event." Grayson took a bite of his pancake. "Will she be joining you in New York for the opening?"

Ian put down his fork. The noise of the Palm Court—the bright clinking of glasses, the pleasant chatter of guests—faded, and all he could hear was his heart pounding in his chest.

Sabrina looked so beautiful with her dark hair curled around her shoulders. He wondered if he'd ever see those blue eyes looking at him in the same way again.

"Lady Violet is in New York," Ian confirmed. "She arrived

with her mother, Lady Braxton, yesterday." He turned to Sabrina. "But Lady Violet isn't my mother and I'm not Lord Braxton. I'm Spencer's personal secretary."

"I don't understand." Sabrina frowned.

"Spencer has been my best friend since we were fourteen. I was a scholarship student at Harrow and he took me in to his family. My parents divorced when I was young and my mother moved away. I spent holidays at Braxton Hall and we were roommates at Oxford. When I graduated, Lady Violet asked me to be Spencer's personal secretary and run the foundation."

"Why would you lie?" Sabrina was puzzled.

"The first night we ate caviar and lobster rolls and you were staying in the suite across the hall. It seemed too complicated to explain when I might not see you again," Ian began. "Then you saw me having tea with the assistant head of the Met and assumed I was Lord Braxton." He took a breath. "We had drinks at that cheesy bar and visited the Empire State Building, and I'd never had a better time. The more we were together, the more I didn't want to stop seeing you. I thought you might not be interested in me if I was only a personal secretary."

"You lied about everything." Sabrina's voice trembled. "You lied about the jewels belonging to you and about Lady Violet being your mother and you even lied about reserving the private dining room at the Rainbow Room."

"I should go." Grayson put his napkin on the plate. "You have a lot to talk about."

Ian pushed back his chair.

"I'll go. Thank you for breakfast." Ian glanced from Grayson to Sabrina. "Sometimes you meet someone and you realize that before you met, you were just existing. Even if you can't keep that person in your life, everything—the foods you eat, the colors that you see—are richer because of her. You're lucky to have Sabrina as a ghostwriter. I'll be the first one in line to buy the book."

Ian crossed 59th Street and entered Central Park. How could he have expected Sabrina to act differently? He had ruined her trust and she may never forgive him.

He couldn't go back to the Plaza; he needed to collect his thoughts. He did a loop around the lake and watched children sledding on Pilgrim Hill. He stopped in front of the carousel but a couple was kissing and he turned away. He browsed in the gift shop but everyone important in his life was in New York. There was no one he could give an *I Love NY* T-shirt to or a snow globe of the Statue of Liberty.

Finally he returned to the Plaza and took the elevator to his suite. It was almost noon and he didn't want to be late for brunch with Lady Violet and Lady Braxton.

The scent of perfume greeted him and he had a surge of happiness. The butler had let Sabrina in and she wanted to talk to him!

"Ian." A woman stood at the window. "I hope you don't mind. Spencer said I could wait here."

"Lady Violet!" Ian exclaimed. "Is everything all right? Is Lady Braxton not feeling well?"

"My mother feels so at home, you'd think she stays at the Plaza all the time," Lady Violet smiled. "The butler drew her bath and she asked the maids to iron her stockings. I've never worn ironed stockings in my life! And she adores the heated floors; she thinks I should install them in Braxton Hall. I told her that would use up every penny of Spencer's inheritance."

"I'm glad she's enjoying herself," Ian said. "Where is Spencer?"

"He had to run some errands." Lady Violet pointed to the coffee table. "This came for you a while ago, the butler delivered it."

A velvet jewelry box sat on the table next to an envelope. His stomach dropped—Sabrina had sent back the ring. He opened the envelope and read the card.

Please return this to whom it belongs. I don't think we should see each other again. Sabrina.

The card dropped onto the floor and Ian bent down to pick it up.

"Spencer told me everything that happened," Lady Violet said.

Lady Violet would be furious and he couldn't blame her. He impersonated her heir and almost gave away a family heirloom.

"I didn't mean for any of it to happen." Ian's voice was filled with anguish. "Sabrina and I met the first night we were here. Then she saw me with the lady from the Met and assumed I was Lord Braxton. I tried to tell her the truth but something kept getting in the way." He hung his head. "I understand if you want to fire me. I'll pay for my own flight to London."

Lady Violet inspected a loose thread on her jacket.

"You think I came here to let you go?"

"Why else would you be waiting in the suite?" Ian was puzzled.

"I'm here because you're like a son to me." Lady Violet folded her gloves. "Even when you were fourteen you had the clearest mind I'd known. You were an arrow pointed toward doing good. Do you remember the year you gave your Christmas presents to a boy whose mother was in the hospital with pneumonia? And I stopped giving you books as gifts because you always gave them to a girl or boy you met at church." Her expression was serious. "Spencer wouldn't have passed his exams if you didn't make him study, and when Peter died he would have dropped out of Oxford if you hadn't been there to comfort him.

"The only thing I've wanted for you is what Spencer finds so easily and what I was fortunate to have for so long." She looked at Ian. "The heady joy of being in love."

"I made a complete mess of it," Ian cut in.

"It wouldn't be love if it was any other way," Lady Violet assured him. "How many times was I afraid that Peter would find out I put castor oil in his porridge because his doctor said it was good for his heart? And when Spencer was a boy I told him his puppy missed its mother so much, it went back to live with her when in fact the puppy died."

"Those were little white lies to protect them," Ian said stiffly.

"I'm not saying you should have lied to Sabrina, but you didn't do it to hurt her," Lady Violet acknowledged. "You discovered something so precious, you were afraid of losing it."

"I *have* lost it." Ian pointed at the jewelry box. "Sabrina returned the ring and never wants to see me again."

"She was surprised and shocked," Lady Violet agreed. "But you're not going to let that stop you."

"What do you mean?"

"From everything that Spencer said, you're falling in love with her," Lady Violet replied. "You can't let her get away, you have to fight for her."

"Do you think she might say yes?" Ian asked. Suddenly he felt better, like a sunny day in England after weeks of rain. The grass is green and flowers bloom and all the cold, wet days are forgotten.

"You won't find out if you don't try," Lady Violet prompted.

"I can't go now." Ian remembered brunch. "We're supposed to meet Spencer and Lady Braxton at the Palm Court."

"I'll handle my mother," Lady Violet said with a smile. "She loves a great romance. When I was a girl she made me read the classics while she reread *Gone with the Wind*."

"Do you know what's the bright spot in this mess?" Ian wondered. "That you think of me as a son. You've been the greatest influence on me and I'm very lucky."

"We're the lucky ones," Lady Violet said. "Can you imagine how many times Spencer would have gotten engaged if wasn't for you? And I'd have to take up mahjong to keep busy instead of helping all those children. Go tell Sabrina how you feel. It's Christmas, it's the time for miracles."

Ian knocked on Sabrina's door but there was no answer. He called her phone but it went straight to voice mail. The elevator opened and a butler stepped out.

"Have you seen Miss Post in the Fitzgerald Suite?" Ian inquired.

"She was checking out," the butler replied. "I offered to help pack her suitcase."

"Checking out today? It's New Year's Eve."

The butler shrugged. "Perhaps she wanted to celebrate it with someone special."

"Are you sure she left?" he asked.

"I don't know, you could ask the concierge." The butler straightened his shoulders. "Though the Plaza doesn't divulge information about its guests. We take their privacy very seriously."

"That's a good idea, thank you."

Ian stepped into the elevator. Sabrina couldn't have left. He didn't have her address; he didn't even know her email. His heart thudded and it was hard to swallow. He had to find Sabrina; any chance of being happy depended on it.

Twenty-Two

It was early afternoon on New Year's Eve and Sabrina stood at the window of her suite. She stood in the same spot so often all week and the view always delighted her. But she barely noticed the freshly washed blue sky and the icicles hanging from the Pulitzer Fountain. Even the giant Christmas tree in front of the Plaza was a blur. All she could see was Ian sitting across from her at the Palm Court and admitting it had all been a lie.

She had gone over it endlessly since she and Grayson finished breakfast: sharing caviar with Ian on the first night and discovering they were staying in suites on the same floor. Running into Ian and the woman from the Met at the Palm Court and hearing about the Braxton collection. Ian could have told her he wasn't Lord Braxton so many times: when they were standing on the observation deck at the Empire State Building or inching up Fifth Avenue in the taxi. Strolling through the East Village after the movies or eating dinner in the private dining room of the Rainbow Room.

He hadn't told the truth because he didn't want to lose her, but there was never a good reason to lie. How could she trust him when he had concealed everything about himself? It was impossible to think about.

Then she remembered all the fun they'd had: dancing at the Snowflake Ball and feeling like a princess, looking at the Christmas window at Macy's and ice-skating in Central Park. And Ian's kisses! They were warm and soft and she wanted to keep kissing him.

Her head felt heavy and she wondered if she was coming down with the flu. It didn't matter; she didn't have any New Year's Eve plans or new assignments. She could go back to her apartment and stay in bed for days.

She clicked shut the suitcase and gathered her laptop. First she had to see Grayson and make sure he didn't have anything more to tell her.

"Sabrina, please come in." Grayson opened the door. "I was sending some Happy New Year's email. It's already New Year's Day in some parts of the world. I leave for Dubai on Sunday and then I'm going to South Africa."

"I finished packing but I wanted to make sure I got everything you wanted to say." Sabrina perched on a chair.

"You're checking out today?" Grayson was puzzled. "Your suite is booked through New Year's Day."

"I don't have a reason to stay," Sabrina said evasively.

It was bad enough that Grayson witnessed what had happened between her and Ian at breakfast. She had to behave professionally.

"There's no better place to be than the Plaza on New Year's Eve," Grayson commented. "Are you sure you don't want to stay a couple more days?"

"I'm positive. I'm going to be busy transcribing my notes." She shook her head. "And if I leave the heat off in my apartment for too long, it won't turn back on."

"You could transcribe your notes here." He handed her an invitation. "I bought two tickets to the Braxton gala tomorrow night; I thought you might like to attend."

"You're going to the opening of the Braxton collection?" Sabrina asked in surprise.

"I have meetings during the day, but I'll attend the gala. It's for a good cause, the proceeds go to charity," he said.

Ian would be at the gala with Lady Violet and Lady Braxton and Spencer. She pictured Ian looking handsome in his tuxedo with a crisp white shirt and gold cuff links.

Her chest tightened and she handed back the invitation.

"Thank you, but I'm not feeling well. I might be coming down with a fever." She changed the subject. "You never told me what happened to Kay. Did she come back to the Plaza?"

"Kay stayed in Europe for years. I'd get postcards from Italy and Spain. She returned to New York much later and lived with her goddaughter, Liza Minnelli."

"She never married?" Sabrina inquired.

"Kay grew bored too easily to be married," Grayson said thoughtfully. "Even Eloise started to bore her. *Eloise Takes a Bawth* was the last book she wrote, and it wasn't published until after she died." He fiddled with the invitation.

"Kay was unique. Even if she didn't always follow her own advice, she understood people better than anyone I met." He looked at Sabrina. "Do you know what was the wisest thing she ever said? Life isn't about being lucky, most of us are lucky: we wake up in a warm bed and step into a hot shower and eat cereal or toast for breakfast. Real luck is being able to look inside yourself and know the one thing that will make you happy. Because without that, life can be fun and entertaining but it will never touch you here." He pointed to his heart.

"I don't know what you mean." Sabrina studied her laptop.

"I saw the way you and Ian looked at each other at breakfast," Grayson said. "It reminded me of myself and Veronica. Don't make the same mistakes I did."

"Ian lied to me about everything." Sabrina let down her guard and all the feelings rushed back. "And you couldn't stop Veronica from leaving, it was out of your control."

"Nothing is out of our control if we want it badly enough," he disagreed. "I could have taken the first flight to England and interrupted the wedding ceremony, like in those romantic movies they show on the plane." He grinned. "Ian shouldn't have lied to you, but that doesn't mean he isn't falling in love with you. Life can be a game of poker. True love beats everything, it's having a handful of aces."

"I've never played poker." Sabrina was doubtful.

"Stay in your suite for one more night and give Ian a chance to explain," Grayson suggested. "If you still feel it couldn't work, at least you tried."

"My roommate is away, but I could ask my neighbor to turn on my heat," Sabrina wavered. "And a long bath might be what I need for the fever."

"You can't go wrong being at the Plaza Hotel on New Year's Eve," Grayson said, and there was a twinkle in his eye. "It's the best address in New York."

Sabrina zipped up her laptop and walked to the door.

"Thank you for an amazing week." She turned around. "I promise I'll do a good job on the memoir."

"Kay would say it was no accident that you turned up at my suite," Grayson mused. "She believed certain people had a lot to give each other."

Sabrina browsed in the Eloise shop in the Plaza's lobby. She wasn't ready to talk to Ian; she needed time to think. And it was the perfect opportunity to buy herself a small souvenir.

The salesgirl tried to convince her to buy a set of pink Eloise sheets, but they were out of her price range. She considered an Eloise journal with a list of New Year's resolutions on the inside cover, but she was terrible at keeping a diary. Finally she settled on a pair of Eloise socks and took her purchase to the cash register. The salesgirl dropped it into a pink bag and Sabrina turned and bumped straight into a man.

"Ian!" she said, when she recovered. "What are you doing here?"

"I saw you through the store window," Ian said. His cheeks were haggard and there were lines on his forehead. "I need to talk to you."

She was suddenly nervous. Maybe Grayson was wrong and this was a bad idea. "I don't know what you would say. You told me everything at breakfast."

"Please." Ian touched her arm. "Give me half an hour. If you still feel the same, I'll leave you alone."

"We can't talk in here." She glanced at the little girls pulling Eloise dolls off the shelves.

"We'll sit at the Rose Club," Ian urged. "It will be empty at this time of day."

Ten minutes later, they sat in a booth at the Rose Club and Sabrina fiddled with the pink Eloise bag.

"Pretending I was Lord Braxton was the worst thing I've ever done," Ian began. "Every time I saw you I wanted to tell you the truth but I didn't know how. The more we were together, the harder it became. I was afraid you'd be furious and never want to see me again."

"You already said that this morning," Sabrina said stiffly. This wasn't going to work. Ian had lied to her and she could never trust him.

Ian sat forward and drummed his fingers on the table.

"The first time we met was like hitting the jackpot. You were beautiful and poised but you had a playfulness about you," he tried again. "But you were staying in a suite that you paid for yourself while I was rooming with Spencer. And then you wore that couture gown and diamond and emerald pendant to the Snowflake Ball. I wondered if you'd be happy living the kind of life I can afford."

"That's why you didn't tell me you weren't Lord Braxton?" Sabrina's eyes widened.

"It was one of the reasons." He nodded. "You're used to a personal butler and afternoon tea at the Palm Court. One day I'll leave the foundation and start my own nonprofit. There won't be money for fancy holidays or expensive lunches."

"Grayson paid for my suite, it was part of my contract as a ghostwriter," she explained. "And the gown and the necklace for the Snowflake Ball were borrowed. I returned them after the ball."

"You can't afford to stay at the Plaza?" Ian asked, puzzled.

"I'm a journalist, I take any writing job to survive," Sabrina said. "When Grayson hired me, I could barely afford the hot dog I bought at the subway station."

Ian sat back in the booth as though he was thinking.

"So we're both staying in suites we can't afford and doing things we'd never dream of paying for ourselves."

"I suppose so," Sabrina said and something lit inside her, like a damp match that finally caught. But then she remembered Ian saying Lady Violet was his mother and the Braxton collection belonged to him. "But I never lied to you. How could I ever trust you?"

"Haven't you ever done something to protect the most important thing in the world?" His eyes flickered. "I'm falling in love with you. If you give me another chance, I'll do anything to show you made the right decision."

Ian was falling in love with her! Sabrina remembered Grayson saying being lucky was knowing when you find the one thing that will make you happy.

"We could try," she said cautiously.

Ian leaned forward and kissed her. She kissed him back and he put his arms around her.

"Tomorrow is the Braxton gala, and I wondered if you'd be my date," he said when they parted. "Spencer and Lady Violet and Lady Braxton will be there and they'd love to meet you."

"Thank you, I'd love to." Sabrina nodded and thought of something. "Would you like to do something tonight for New Year's Eve?"

Ian flushed and pulled at his collar. "I can't afford tickets to the Plaza's New Year's Eve Ball, and most events in New York cost a fortune."

Sabrina took the pair of Eloise socks out of the pink bag.

"I wasn't thinking of attending a ball. I have my suite until tomorrow, we could have dinner and watch rom-coms." She smiled mischievously. "It will give me a chance to wear my new socks."

"That's an excellent idea," Ian said and kissed her again. "I'll go and get a pizza."

"I don't think the Plaza allows you to bring in pizza," she said between kisses.

"It's the Plaza. They're used to any requests."

Sabrina gazed at his brown eyes and happiness curled up inside her.

"Please get some Junior Mints too. You can't enjoy a rom-com without a box of Junior Mints."

Twenty-Three

The Braxton collection gala was in full swing and Ian couldn't be more pleased. The lobby of the Metropolitan Museum had been transformed into some fabulous jewelry box. Purple velvet draped the walls and the marble floor was covered in thick white carpet. There were arrangements of flowers in all the colors of precious jewels: ruby-colored roses and emerald-green chrysanthemums and delphiniums the blue of sapphires.

The turnout for the opening of the collection exceeded Ian's expectations and the assistant head of the Met was pleased. Lady Violet complimented him on the catalog copy and even Lady Braxton, slim and elegant in a Halston gown and sapphire earrings, was impressed.

The best moment was when Ian entered the gala with Sabrina on his arm. She was effortlessly beautiful in a white evening gown borrowed from the storeroom at the Plaza. At first she laughed and said she couldn't play Cinderella again and borrow another gown. But then she changed her mind, and Ian was glad she did. The chiffon fabric made her seem like she was floating and the gold embroidery gave her skin a warm glow.

"Where is Sabrina?" Spencer asked. The dancing had begun and Ian and Spencer stood on a corner of the dance floor.

"She's saying hello to Grayson—he just arrived." Ian pointed across the room.

"I have to hand it to you. Not only do you find one of the prettiest girls in New York, she's fun and intelligent too," Spencer said. "And it's more than that. I've never had a woman look at me the way Sabrina looks at you. It's as if you've known each other for years."

"That's how I feel, like I found something I didn't know I was looking for," Ian said earnestly. "I apologize for thinking you were going to run off and propose to Tabitha."

"I told you I wasn't in love with her." Spencer shrugged. "And it would never work, she's intent on her studies. It got me thinking, I'm going to do some traveling."

"Traveling?" Ian gulped. He didn't want to spend the winter trailing after Spencer. "You'll have to buy new skis. You gave yours to the guy who worked at the ski lodge at the end of the season."

"I'm not going skiing—I'm not going on holiday at all."

"What are you going to do?" Ian wondered.

"I could never work for the foundation, I'd get bored arranging events and sucking up to committees," Spencer mused. "The Animal Haven Shelter asked me to speak at their upcoming winter gala, and I said yes. I'd like to become a spokesman for various charities." He grinned. "British royalty is in right now, we're more popular than pop stars."

"That's a wonderful idea," Ian agreed. "Any charity would be lucky to have you."

"And I'll meet some fascinating people," Spencer said casually. "The woman at the Animal Haven Shelter grew up in Santa

Monica. Her name is Ashley and puppy mills are a big problem in California."

Spencer wandered off and Lady Violet approached Ian. She looked regal in a blue satin evening gown and diamond earrings.

"You look wonderful tonight," Ian commented.

"My mother insisted we buy new gowns, we couldn't be upstaged by our own jewels." Lady Violet smiled. "She tried on every ball gown at Saks; the saleswoman was exhausted."

"The gala is going very well." Ian glanced at couples spinning around the dance floor.

"We've raised more money for the Braxton Foundation than we did last year," Lady Violet said approvingly. "I'm glad to have met Sabrina. She's perfect for you."

"She loved meeting you too," Ian commented.

"I was talking to some of the guests." Lady Violet gazed at the dance floor. "Did you know that last year the libraries in New York City had an eleven-million-dollar budget cut? Can you imagine how that affects the children?"

"What are you saying?" Ian wondered.

"Perhaps we could open a branch of the Braxton Foundation here," she suggested. "You could run it part of the time and I'd pop over. I love New York."

"What about Spencer?" Ian asked. "I'm his personal secretary."

"Spencer is almost thirty years old, he doesn't need a babysitter." Lady Violet frowned. "Think of how much you could accomplish with more time."

"That is a good idea." Ian beamed.

"And there's something I want to ask Sabrina with your permission," Lady Violet finished. "I'd like to put together a written history of Braxton Hall, it's important for future generations. Do you think she'd be interested?"

"It sounds intriguing," Ian said with a smile. "She's walking over now."

Sabrina and Grayson crossed the room. Grayson wore a black tuxedo and his white hair gleamed under the chandeliers.

"Lady Violet, this is Grayson Prescott," Sabrina introduced them.

"You may not remember, but we met years ago." Grayson made a small bow. "It was at a garden party for the British Red Cross."

"I do remember. It rained and all the meringues were ruined," Lady Violet laughed. "Let me introduce you to my mother."

Lady Violet turned, but Lady Braxton wasn't in her chair. Ian looked more closely and saw her kneeling on the floor.

"Are you looking for this?" Grayson crouched beside her and picked up a sapphire earring.

Lady Braxton straightened and her eyes met Grayson's.

"Hello, Veronica," Grayson said softly. "It's nice to see you after all these years."

Sabrina gasped and squeezed Ian's arm.

"You know each other?" Ian asked, puzzled.

"We met sixty years ago at a Christmas ball at the Plaza," Grayson explained. "I was working as a butler and Veronica was a debutante."

"I lost the keys to my father's Jaguar. I was under the table trying to find them." Lady Braxton took up the story. "Grayson climbed under the table and helped me."

A smile stretched across Grayson's face. "All I could see were her ankles, but they were the loveliest ankles I had ever known." He extended his elbow to Lady Braxton. "We have some catching up to do," Grayson said to her. "Would you like to dance?"

"My mother can't dance, she sprained her ankle," Lady Violet cut in.

Lady Braxton smoothed the folds of her gown. "That was only a few days ago." She took Grayson's arm. "I can manage a slow dance."

Grayson led Lady Braxton onto the dance floor. Ian moved to the bar and Lady Violet and Sabrina chatted in the corner.

"It's the most romantic thing I've ever seen." Sabrina joined him when she finished talking to Lady Violet. "One day I'll tell you all about it."

"Lady Braxton seemed ten years younger, they must have quite a history." Ian touched Sabrina's arm. "I'm glad you came. I'm having a wonderful time."

"I'm glad I came too. And Lady Violet told me about the writing position." Sabrina nodded. "I'd love to spend time at Braxton Hall."

"And it seems I'll be in Manhattan," Ian replied. "Lady Violet wants to open a branch of the foundation in New York."

"When I was a child, I hated when Christmas week was over," Sabrina said slowly. "The Christmas tree came down and the colored lights were put away and I had to wait three hundred and sixty-five days until it started again. But it's already January and it still feels magical."

The band played "Last Christmas" and Ian led Sabrina onto

the dance floor. He put his arm around her and she rested her head on his shoulder.

"I'm glad we met on our first night at the Plaza." He pulled her close and inhaled the scent of her perfume. "This has been the best Christmas I've ever had."

Twenty-Four

It was the morning after the Braxton collection gala and Sabrina made a final check of the suite's bedroom. When she agreed to attend the gala, Grayson insisted she keep her suite for another night. At first she protested; the suite cost a fortune, and the memoir was finished. But after last night—Lady Braxton searching for her earring and Grayson bending down and finding it—Sabrina was glad she accepted his offer. The memoir hadn't been finished, after all; Grayson meeting Veronica after all these years was the final chapter.

She wanted to ask him all about it, but he and Veronica disappeared. It had been the most wonderful night. The decorations at the Met were dazzling and Lady Violet was so welcoming and Ian was warm and attentive.

And Sabrina was going to Braxton Hall! She'd already texted Chloe, and Chloe texted back it was the best time to go to England: Sabrina could pick up a Tahari overcoat at the January sales and Chloe had some Hunter boots that would fit Sabrina perfectly.

There was a knock at the door and Sabrina opened it.

"Grayson." She ushered him inside. "Please sit down."

"I wanted to see you before I leave." He followed her into the living room. "My taxi is waiting downstairs, the flight to Dubai leaves in three hours."

"Last night was a fairy tale." Sabrina sat on the sofa. "How did you know that Veronica would be at the gala?"

"Veronica and I never corresponded, but she was often in the society section of *The Times*," Grayson said. "I knew that her husband was Lord William Braxton and they had a daughter named Violet. When you mentioned the Braxton collection and said Lady Braxton would be in New York, I had to see for myself."

"You must have known she was a widow." Sabrina frowned. "Why didn't you contact her before?"

"I did read about it; William died of cancer five years ago," Grayson acknowledged. "I'd lived so long without Veronica, I was afraid to change anything. Telling you the whole story made me realize how much I'd missed." His eyes glimmered. "Veronica hasn't changed, she's still beautiful and impetuous. We stayed up talking for hours, it was the best night I could remember."

"Will you see each other again?" Sabrina wondered.

"I have some business in London, and who knows how long I'll stay," he said with a smile. "I've always been a fan of Claridge's. Their suites have a view of Hyde Park and the butlers are every bit as good as at the Plaza."

"I'm glad for both of you," Sabrina said warmly.

"I wanted to give Veronica something, but she and Lady Violet are out." He took a package from under his arm. "I wonder if you'd deliver it for me."

Grayson pulled back the wrapping and revealed the portrait of Eloise. Eloise wore a black pleated skirt with suspenders, her flyaway hair tumbling over her shoulders.

"It's the portrait I gave to Veronica," Grayson said. "I want her to have it back."

"Where did you find it?" Sabrina gasped, recalling the story. "Veronica's friend, Becky, put it in the trash."

"I did a little research. Someone found it and sent it to Hilary Knight, the illustrator. Hilary sold it at auction at Sotheby's a few years ago. I contacted the buyer and made him an offer. It was delivered to my suite this morning."

Sabrina wondered how much Grayson had paid for the painting.

"Does Veronica know you have it?" Sabrina asked.

"It's a surprise," Grayson said with a smile. "I always thought the portrait belonged with Veronica. Kay would be pleased."

Grayson left and Sabrina finished packing. There was a knock and Ian appeared at the door. He wore a tan sweater and carried a bouquet of roses.

"These are for you," he said, kissing her.

"They're beautiful, thank you." She led him into the living room.

She clicked shut her suitcase and gazed out the window. Suddenly the thought of leaving all this—Fifth Avenue far below and Central Park across the street; Ian in the Pulitzer Suite and Grayson on the next floor—made her wobbly and she blinked back a tear.

"I have to deliver something to Lady Braxton but I'll come down to the lobby with you first." She gulped. "At least we can say goodbye before you head to the airport."

"I'd wait and take you all the way to Queens if my flight didn't leave soon." He took her hand. "Spencer is already waiting in the car. It's the first time he's ever been ready before me."

"I had a wonderful time last night." She gathered her coat.

"So did I. And everything is coming along perfectly." Ian

opened the door. "I'm looking for office space in Manhattan and the assistant head of the Met promised to make some introductions. And Lady Violet would like you to come to Braxton Hall in February. There's a winter ball attended by all the old families. It's a great opportunity to learn local history."

"I can't wait." Sabrina followed Ian to the elevator.

The elevator doors opened to the lobby and Sabrina and Ian stepped out. The Christmas tree had been replaced by huge potted palms and the air smelled of fresh flowers and scented candles. Crystal chandeliers glinted on tabletops and a fire crackled in the fireplace. Serena watched valets in gold-and-red uniforms carrying leather suitcases and guests smiling and sipping hot chocolate.

A week ago Sabrina had crossed the marble floor clutching her tattered laptop case. Now the portrait of Eloise was tucked under her arm and she was holding Ian's hand.

The concierge waved and she smiled. There was nothing like the Plaza Hotel in New York at Christmas.

Epilogue

December at Braxton Hall never failed to amaze Sabrina. It was something out of a Jane Austen novel: the great stone fireplace in the drawing room, the kitchen a constant hive of activity, the endless bedrooms made up with fresh linens and vases of flowers.

It was the third Christmas Sabrina had spent with Ian in England. Every time the flight attendant announced their arrival into Heathrow and she gazed down at Big Ben and the London Eye glittering below her, she had to pinch herself at how much life had changed.

On her first visit she was afraid things between them would be different. Perhaps it had been a holiday romance after all, and being a guest at Braxton Hall would be uncomfortable. But Ian met her at the airport and they spent the first day exploring the sights of London. He took her to the Tower of London and to see the Changing of the Guard. They held hands in Hyde Park and spent hours eating tea and scones in a booth at Harrods. By the time Ian turned the car onto the M3, her favorite songs playing on the stereo and his wrist grazing her knee, she felt as if they had never been apart.

Ever since her first sight of Braxton Hall—its long, stone buildings, the fields of snow that were pink and white in the evening light—Sabrina couldn't get over its beauty. All her childhood fantasies of great British houses had come to life. Lady Violet gave her the grand tour and Ian joked he knew why she came to England. It wasn't to see him, it was because she was in love with the house. Sabrina only smiled until they got back in the car and drove to his bedsit in the village. They hardly left it for two days until she convinced him that he was wrong, she had very much been looking forward to seeing him.

There was a knock and Lady Violet poked her head inside. Sabrina understood why Ian admired Lady Violet. She was so warm and welcoming. Sabrina had a wonderful time researching Braxton Hall, and Lady Violet always stopped to answer her questions. Once the phone rang and Lady Violet asked the caller to please hold while she finished giving Sabrina a quick history of the trophy room. It was only when Lady Violet said into the receiver, "I'm sorry to keep you waiting, Kate. I want to hear all about Charlotte's play at school," that Sabrina realized the Duchess of Cambridge was on the other end of the line.

"Where's Ian?" Lady Violet asked. "I can't find him anywhere."

"He's in the library writing his speech," Sabrina answered. "He's so nervous. You would think he's never spoken in public before."

"A wedding is different from a fundraiser." Lady Violet smiled. "No one cries at a charity event. Except for the moment they have to take out their checkbooks."

"I suppose you're right," Sabrina agreed. "Everything looks wonderful. Braxton Hall has never seemed so festive."

"I agree, the workmen have been preparing all month," Lady Violet said happily. "Braxton Hall has hosted many weddings over the centuries, but never a double wedding. There was almost a double wedding in the eighteenth century, but the second bride ran off with a footman on the way to the church." Her eyes sparkled. "I hired two carriages to get from the church to the house and the cook made two wedding cakes. One is chocolate and the other is strawberry shortcake." She paused. "I'm prattling on when you should be getting ready. You must be exhausted, you just arrived."

Sabrina's plane had been delayed, and then it had taken ages to get through customs.

"It's hard to be tired when I'm so excited." Sabrina took a deep breath. "I can't believe the day is finally here."

"It will be time for the ceremony and we'll all be in trouble if we're not dressed." Lady Violet checked her watch. "I wanted to check if you need anything. And to make sure you have the 'something borrowed, something blue.'"

"It's in my suitcase." Sabrina pointed to the bag the housekeeper had placed at the foot of the bed.

"Wonderful, I'm going to take a bath. I'll see you downstairs." She kissed Sabrina on the cheek. "Sometimes I can't believe Ian brought you into our lives only three years ago. So much has happened, and look where we are now!"

Lady Violet left and Sabrina opened her suitcase. Chloe had lent her the blue silk gloves. They were perfect for a winter wedding and the color matched the Ceylon sapphire. She closed the suitcase and entered the bathroom. Lady Violet was right. If she didn't hurry and take a bath, the ceremony might start without her.

The ceremony was over and guests were seated at tables in the Great Hall. Sabrina thought it all looked so romantic. The tables were covered with pale blue tablecloths, and blue and white lights were threaded around the fireplace. Candles flickered in silver candelabras and there was a white Christmas tree with blue and silver ornaments. Sabrina glanced at Ian, looking so handsome in his tuxedo, and couldn't believe he was beside her. How did she get from her cramped apartment in Queens to the dining room of one of the great houses in England?

"Ladies and gentlemen." Grayson stood up and tapped his champagne glass. "One usually waits until after dinner to give the speeches, but I'm over eighty." His eyes crinkled with humor. "You never know, I could keel over in the cream of potato soup."

Everyone laughed and Grayson's tone grew serious.

"First, I want to thank you for joining us." He gazed around the room. "Some of you are as old as I and Lady Braxton and it's not easy for you to travel. And for the younger generations, there are more exciting ways to spend Christmas week than seeing a couple of octogenarians get married." He blinked into the crowd. "That's one of the reasons I'm glad we decided on a double wedding. To share this moment with such a special couple makes it even more remarkable. But I'll let the other groom gush over his bride—I'm here to talk about Veronica. She may be Lady Braxton in Burke's Peerage, but to me she's the brash young debutante I met under a table at the Plaza Hotel.

"Veronica, it took me sixty years to propose and when I did, I used a ring that had been in your family for centuries. But when I heard the story of the Ceylon sapphire, I knew you had to wear it. Like its original owner, Susanna, you deserved a ring that your suitor traveled for months to find. But unlike Graham Braxton, my days of flitting around the world are behind me. It's not only because of my age." He paused. "It's because I finally had the courage to ask you to marry me. I don't want to be anywhere ever again without you beside me." He sipped his champagne. Sabrina noticed his eyes were damp with tears.

"The only drawback of a double wedding is other people need to speak, and I can't sing Veronica's praises all night. So please raise your glasses to my beautiful bride and the love of my life, the new Veronica Prescott."

Grayson sat next to Lady Braxton and everyone clapped. Ian stood up and took the microphone.

"Every day I marvel at how lucky I am to be part of this family," Ian began. "Lady Violet is the mother any boy would dream of and Spencer is more important to me than a brother. I didn't know anything about Lady Braxton and Grayson's history, but when I saw them together at the Braxton collection gala I knew they'd be together forever. The way they looked at each other felt like they were already two halves of one whole. And Lady Violet and Lord Arthur might not have known each other long, but I'm confident they're just as in love." He smiled cheekily. "When Lady Violet came to me and Spencer and said she was marrying a Scottish lord she met six weeks earlier at the St. Regis in New York, we weren't surprised. Among her many virtues, Lady Violet is the best judge of character. I wish both couples decades of joy and I know everyone here feels the same. Just being invited to spend Christmas at Braxton Hall seems a guarantee of happiness." He raised his champagne flute. "I've spent the happiest Christmases of my life here and I hope to celebrate many more."

Dinner was over and the party had moved to the ballroom for dancing. Sabrina and Ian stood in the corner with Spencer.

"Doesn't it inspire you to get married when your mother and grandmother get married on the same day?" Ian turned to Spencer.

"On the contrary." Spencer sipped a glass of sherry. "It removes the pressure. No one will be wondering when I'll settle down and start a family when they're busy living their own happily ever afters. And I've never enjoyed life more. I leave on New Year's Day for Sweden to speak at a benefit for the Hunger Project. The woman in charge is named Inge. She was a model before she devoted herself to charity and she's meeting me at the airport. After that I'm off to Australia. The Animal Welfare Institute is holding a gala to protect the platypus." He grinned like a schoolboy. "I heard the beaches in Sydney are packed this time of year."

"It sounds like a full schedule," Ian said. "I've got mountains of paperwork to get through." He touched Sabrina's hand. "Sabrina is only here for a week. I promised I wouldn't touch any of it until after New Year's."

"I certainly hope not," Spencer said before Sabrina could answer. "If my wonderful girlfriend flew all the way from New York, I wouldn't waste a minute of it hunched over a computer."

Spencer drifted off and Sabrina and Ian stood alone together.

"I haven't told you how beautiful you look." Ian took her hand. "That dress suits you perfectly."

Sabrina had been worried the gown would crumple in the

suitcase. It was a silver sheath with a red sash. When she saw it in the Christmas window at Saks, she had to have it. Her book on Braxton Hall had been a success, and since then she'd been asked to write books about other great houses. Coupled with more ghostwriting jobs and some pieces under her own name in *Vogue* and *Esquire,* she was able to treat herself to nice clothes and holidays.

"Thank you." She looked up at him. "And I don't mind if you work while I'm here. I can start research on my next project."

"Actually, I was going to talk to you about that." He fiddled with his glass. "I know we're going to the Tate tomorrow, but I wondered if we could put it off. I have something else in mind."

Lady Braxton and Grayson had donated the portrait of Eloise to the Tate Modern. Lady Braxton believed the Eloise books were for children, and the painting should hang where as many children as possible could see it.

"I was looking forward to seeing the painting," Sabrina said uncertainly.

"We will see it, but there's something I want to show you first," Ian replied. He suddenly seemed nervous. "I want to buy something and need your opinion."

"You want to buy something?" she repeated.

"It's a small house actually," he said hurriedly. "I wasn't going to say anything but I'm afraid someone else will snatch it up. It's not on the market officially; it belongs to a friend of Lady Violet's. It used to be a carriage house but it's been fixed up."

"I see," Sabrina said slowly. They'd been together for almost three years but they still carried on a long-distance romance. Ian spent a few months a year at the foundation in New York and Sabrina made regular visits to England.

"I wanted to discuss it over drinks at Claridge's, but now I've messed it all up," Ian sighed.

"Discuss what?" Sabrina asked. "You can buy any house you like."

"Discuss where we want to live," he went on. "We can't keep picking each other up at JFK and Heathrow forever. I'm happy to move to New York, the foundation there has grown so much—it keeps me busy. But I know you love Braxton Hall, and I thought you might enjoy living in England."

"I don't know." Sabrina took a deep breath. She was in love with Ian but she wouldn't move without being married.

"You don't have to decide right away, I'm sure there will be other houses." He reached into his pocket and took out a velvet box. "But maybe you can decide about this." He snapped it open. "Sabrina Post, I love you and I will spend my life making you happy. Will you marry me?"

Sabrina glanced down at the ring and gasped. It was an oval diamond on a white gold band. Her heart thudded and she turned her face up to Ian's.

"Yes, I'll marry you," she whispered.

Ian slipped the ring on her finger and pulled her close. His kiss was long and sweet. Sabrina stood on tiptoes and kissed him back.

When they parted, Lady Violet was standing near them.

"You were in such deep conversation, I didn't want to disturb you," Lady Violet started.

She looked elegant in a pale pink wedding gown. A diamond necklace glittered around her neck and she wore ruby earrings.

"Arthur went to get more champagne. I wanted to thank you for the silk gloves," Lady Violet said to Sabrina. "Lady Braxton thought they were perfect."

"I'm glad," Sabrina said. Her lips were still warm from the kiss. "We were commenting how Braxton Hall is the ideal setting for a Christmas wedding." Her cheeks flushed and she held up the diamond ring for Lady Violet to see. "We thought about making it a tradition."

Lady Violet studied the ring. She glanced from Sabrina to Ian.

"A wedding next Christmas at Braxton Hall is a wonderful idea." Lady Violet beamed. "I would be honored to help plan it."

Fireworks exploded outside the window and guests gathered to watch them. Ian put his arms around Sabrina and she sighed with happiness. She knew with absolute certainty that her wedding was going to be the most magical night of her life.

Acknowledgments

As always, thank you to my amazing agent, Johanna Castillo, for making me a better writer. Thank you to my wonderful team at St. Martin's Press, especially my editor, Sallie Lotz, and Jennifer Enderlin for making St. Martin's the perfect home for my books.

And the deepest thanks to my family: My children, Alex, Andrew, Heather, Madeleine, and Thomas, and my daughter-in-law, Sarah. And to my granddaughter, Lily. I can't wait to introduce you to the Eloise books and all the magic of reading.

About the Author

ANITA HUGHES is also the author of many novels, including *Christmas at the Chalet, Christmas in London, Christmas in Paris,* and *Christmas in Vermont*. She attended UC Berkeley's Masters in Creative Writing Program, and lives in Dana Point, California, where she is at work on her next novel.